DAUGHTER OF FATE

The Knights of Alana Book I

AARON HODGES

Edited by Genevieve Lerner
Proofread by Sara Houston
Illustration by Joemel Requeza
Map by Michael Hodges

Aaron Hodges was born in 1989 in the small town of Whakatane, New Zealand. He studied for five years at the University of Auckland, completing a Bachelor of Science in Biology and Geography, and a Master of Environmental Engineering. After working as an environmental consultant for two years, he grew tired of the 9 to 5 and decided to quit his job to travel the world. During his travels he picked up the old draft of a novel he once wrote in High School—titled 'The Sword of Light'—and began to rewrite the story. Six months later he published his first novel—Stormwielder.

FOLLOW AARON HODGES:
And receive free books and a short story!
http://www.aaronhodges.co.nz/newsletter-signup/

ALSO BY AARON HODGES

THE THREE NATIONS

The Sword of Light Trilogy
Book 1: Stormwielder

Book 2: Firestorm

Book 3: Soul Blade

Legend of the Gods
Book 1: Oathbreaker

Book 2: Shield of Winter

Book 3: Dawn of War

The Knights of Alana
Book 1: Daughter of Fate

Book 2: Queen of Vengeance

Book 3: Signup for Updates

OTHER WORKS

The Evolution Gene
Book 1: The Genome Project

Book 2: The Pursuit of Truth

Book 3: The Way the World Ends

THE THREE NATIONS

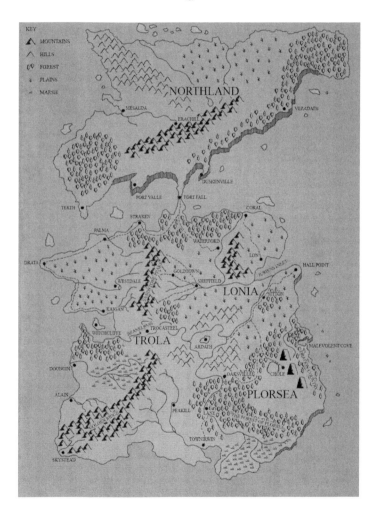

PROLOGUE

I kar's heart quickened as his horse rounded a curve in the mountainside, revealing a town nestled on the edge of the fiord below. The setting sun shone on the crystal blue waters, where several ships bobbed at anchor, shielded from the open ocean by the enclosing arms of Golden Ridge. Barely a cloud could be seen in the sky and the slopes ahead were a parched-brown, strewn with gravel except where the thin line of the trail wound its way down towards the village.

Studying the quiet seaside settlement, Ikar wondered how a place so beautiful could breed such treason.

"We have arrived," he announced, twisting in his saddle.

His armour creaked, confining his movement, and though the heavy steel had long been a part of him, he felt a moment's longing to hurl it from him. The journey through the mountains had taken over a week, and in all that time he had removed his armour only to sleep. It was forbidden for a Knight of Alana to remove his helmet in public, least an unbeliever learn their identity.

But with the summer sun beating down upon them, the faith of even the most devout of Knights had been tested. The Saviour had granted them her strength though, and none had given in to temptation.

Only Merak, an Elder of the Order of Alana, was permitted to go without his helmet. He edged his horse past Ikar to study the landscape.

"The Saviour has blessed us." His voice was soft, for he was far older than the rest of their party. He was one of the first of their Order, born in the days before magic left the world. His days as a Knight were long past, but an Elder had been needed for this quest, and he had volunteered. "We have arrived in time to thwart another of their profane ceremonies."

"You are sure?" Ikar asked, edging his horse alongside the Elder.

The shuffling of hooves on gravel came from behind them as the other Knights pressed forward, eager to see an end to their quest. Word had reached their Castle weeks ago, brought to them by a devout farmer who had stumbled upon the ritual while tending his goats. They'd been fortunate; this was old country and there were few believers in the Saviour. Ikar shuddered to think how long the evil here had been left unchecked.

Ikar tightened his grip on the reins. How anyone could commit such blasphemy was beyond him. For a thousand years, the Three Nations had suffered beneath the yolk of the False Gods. Only thirty years ago had they finally been liberated, when the divine Alana had slain the Gods and purged the world of their magic.

Before that fateful day, Magickers had roamed the Three Nations at will. Granted powers beyond imagining by the False Gods, they had wielded their magic without thought of consequence. Those not cursed with power had been reduced to nothing, slaves to the will of Magickers.

After the death of magic, many had despaired, so accustomed had they been to the rule of the Gods. Thousands had suffered as the rulers of the Three Nations sought to survive without the crutch of magic. Amidst the chaos, the Order of Alana had been born. The first Elders had shown the lost the way, revealing a new path—the *true* path—for humanity, one of independence and freewill.

But there were those who still longed for the past, who wished to restore the power of the False Gods. They gathered in the shadows, joining their minds, seeking out old secrets. Perhaps they even knew the truth, that with the solstice approaching, the old powers were rising.

The thought filled Ikar with rage, but with an effort of will he pressed it down. A Knight must always remain in control, for they were blessed with the strength of the Saviour, and had sworn to wield it only in service to the Order. The Elders had plans for the ones below, designs that would ensure their false Gods would be forever bound in the darkness.

"I am sure," Merak finally answered Ikar's question. He turned and addressed two of their Knights. "There is a ship at the pier. You will go ahead and convince the captain to grant us passage."

"We will not fail you, Elder," the Knights answered, their voices made metallic by their helmets.

Ikar shivered as the Elder's eyes fell on him. "Ikar."

He inclined his head. "Yes, Elder."

"They say you are descended from Alan the Great, who fought the False Gods on the walls of Fort Fall."

"It is true, sir," Ikar replied, his heart pounding hard in his chest.

"Then in the name of your ancestor, I ask you to lead our Knights against the enemy."

Merak pointed down the path towards the town, and Ikar saw now the ruins of a temple rising from the slope of the mountain. The three spires of the False Gods had begun to crumble. Only one now stood. Ikar took it as a sign and smiled.

"May Alana bless our swords."

CHAPTER 1

P ela let out a long breath as she topped the stone stairs and stepped onto the ramparts of Skystead. She had finished her chores early—mopping up the floors of the dining room, hanging out the linens for drying, refilling the stable troughs—and had departed before their guests in the upstairs rooms had awoken. Despite growing up in the town's only inn, Pela preferred her own company, and had little desire to stammer through pleasantries with the strangers.

They were leaving today anyway, heading out on the ship that had come into port the night before. Hearing the shouts of the captain from below, Pela stepped up to the edge of the crenellations. The wall fell sharply into deep water beneath where she stood, but away to her right were the main gates of the town. They opened out onto the stone docks, where sailors carrying wares darted frantically to and fro. With high tide only two hours away, they would need to be quick if they wanted to depart this morning.

Pela thought they would probably make it. The captain

looked like an experienced hand. With no other travellers in sight, the inn would be peaceful tonight—though her mother, Kryssa, would be worried at the lack of business.

Thinking of her mother, Pela sighed. No doubt Kryssa would be searching for her by now, to drag Pela to their weekly meditation at the temple.

As though summoned by her thoughts, a distant voice echoed from the town. "Pela!"

Pela slid off the crenellation and ducked down, hoping her mother had not spotted her. The walls stood some thirty feet high and the two-storey roofs of the town were well below her. Most of the buildings in Skystead were built of stone and stood side by side with no space between them, except where the narrow alleyways crisscrossed the larger avenues. Below the streets were a maze, but for the agile, the flat rooftops often offered faster passage around the town.

But Pela's mother, who turned her nose at such notions, would be in the alleys below. She would not spot Pela on her remote perch.

"Pela, I know you're up there!" Her mother's voice rang from the stone walls, sounding as though she were directly below.

Cursing, Pela stood and looked into the alley behind the wall. Kryssa stood with hands on hips, a furious scowl etched across her face. In many ways, she was Pela's twin, though Kryssa was outspoken where Pela was quiet. Her mother wore the platinum hair that marked them both as outsiders in a tidy braid. The sight made Pela wish she'd at least run a brush over her head that morning. Their sun-kissed skin, narrow noses, and sharp cheekbones proved their relation. Only their eyes were different: her mother's a brilliant silver, while Pela's were a hazel-green she was told had come from her long-deceased father.

"What do you want?" Pela called down.

"You know what, young lady," Kryssa hissed, her voice quieter now.

"I told you, I don't want to go anymore," Pela groaned. "All those people…can't I just meditate up here?"

Kryssa tapped her foot on the tiled road. "You still live under my roof, young lady. Until you turn eighteen, you'll do as I say."

"Or what?"

"Would you like to clean out the barn tonight?"

Pela suppressed a groan. "Fine!" she relented. "I'll meet you there."

Before her mother could call her back, she darted along the ramparts to one of the taller buildings. Here, the drop to the rooftop was only five feet. She leapt before her mind could dwell on the fall, her boots thumping down hard. A voice called up from the alley, but Pela was already gone, leaving her mother behind.

She took the circular route across the town towards the mountain path, her good mood restored. She was in no rush to beat her mother to Temple. If she took enough time, meditation might already be underway when she arrived, and she would not have to bother herself with any clumsy conversations.

Mountain peaks loomed overhead as she wandered the rooftops. Skystead straddled a narrow patch of land where Golden Ridge met the deep fiords of the coast. They were as far south as anywhere in Plorsea, and it was a long boat ride and a longer walk to anything else resembling civilisation. Only once in her seventeen years had Pela made the trip to Townirwin, the nearest settlement, and that had been so long ago she barely remembered it.

Her gaze roamed the skyline as she neared the mountain gate. A winding road led up the steep slope, where a dozen workers could already be seen making their way to work. High above, beyond sight of town, the coffee plantations that were Skystead's lifeblood awaited. Even further up, the road led eventually to the nation of Trola. But no one ventured there now, not since the Trolan King had closed their borders under penalty of death.

But Pela's destination was nowhere near so far. Three hundred feet above the town, a second path branched from the main road, leading along the stark slopes to where a cluster of ruins clung to the mountainside.

Once three spires had risen above the walls of granite and marble, but only the jagged remnants of one remained now. The outer walls were mostly solid, though small sections had begun to crumble, the mortar rotted away. Summer storms had taken their toll, smashing in the roof in several places, leaving the insides exposed to the elements. One day, it was said, the whole thing would be washed away, and all that remained of the Three Gods would vanish from Skystead.

The temple had been abandoned for over thirty years, but only in recent times had the ruins become a source of controversy. There were those who said now that the Three Gods had been evil, that the gift of their magic had been a poisoned chalice, that they had enslaved humanity to some unknown purpose.

For Pela's mother and others who still knew their history, the Three Gods remained the true saviours of the Three Nations.

Coming to the edge of town, Pela found a narrow staircase and returned to ground level. There was no sign of her mother at the gates, but far above she spotted Kryssa at the fork in the road. Despite the distance, Pela could sense the anger radiating from her mother's distant figure. Her cheeks warmed, and feeling slightly abashed, she hurried up the winding path.

Within minutes her calves were burning. The mountainside was steep here, rising sharply from the fiord up to the peaks three thousand feet above. There were exactly 1,555 steps from the town to the temple—Pela had counted them many times before—and in the burning summer sun, her tunic was quickly soaked with sweat. The undulating mountains of Golden Ridge stretched away to the north in an unbroken line, dividing the lands of Plorsea from Trola to the west.

It took half an hour to make the crossroad, and another ten minutes to reach the ruins. The mountainside was quiet as she approached; her mother and the others must have already begun their meditation. Her shame returning, Pela darted through the doorway. Darkness engulfed her and she let out a sigh, relieved to be out of the sun.

Inside, cursory efforts had been made at repairs, though rays of light still filtered through cracks in the ceiling. Whispers carried down the corridor, drawing Pela deeper into the ruin. The temperature dropped as she followed the familiar path towards the central chambers. Rubble lay strewn across the granite tiles hazardous in the dark, but Pela had explored these corridors as a child, and could have negotiated the temple blindfolded.

The whispers grew louder as Pela turned a corner and found herself at the entrance to the main chamber. At least two dozen villagers were already present. Many had taken up positions on the faded emerald and sapphire carpets, their eyes closed, and legs crossed as they sought the inner calm taught by the Gods. Several others still stood near the entrance speaking quietly. An old man, his face wrinkled and hair grey with age, saw her and offered a greeting.

"Welcome, Pela," he murmured, "it is good to see you. How are you?"

Pela's heart beat faster as he held out both hands, palms up. She took them in hers and smiled, though internally she was struggling desperately to recall his name. The awkward silence stretched out as he looked at her with kind eyes.

She opened her mouth, garbled something nonsensical, then blurted out: "*Thank you!*"

Her cheeks grew hot and she darted past him before he could ask anything else. Internally, she cursed her bumbling tongue. Slipping between the seated meditators, she approached the altar and lit a stick of incense to honour the Goddess Antonia, setting it alongside those already left by others.

As she turned away, she caught the scent of rose petals and earth in her nose. Instantly, her mind was whisked away to a forest grove, lit by sun and filled with the chattering of squirrels and the whispers of branches in the breeze. She clung to the image, but inevitably the realm of the Earth Goddess faded, leaving her standing once more before the altar.

Letting out a long sigh, Pela searched for her mother. Finding Kryssa seated cross-legged nearby, she sat beside her. Kryssa cast a sidelong glance in her direction and Pela quickly lowered her eyes. She didn't know why her mother dragged her here every week.

Everyone knew the Three Gods were dead.

Hearing her mother's breathing deepen, Pela looked back up. Her mother had begun to meditate, but Pela's heart was still racing from the climb. Silence had fallen over the room, the last of the meditators taking their places on the carpet. Coffee incense burned on the altar at the front of the room, where candles illuminated a mural that took up the entire wall. It depicted the Three Gods—Jurrien, Antonia, and Darius—united together against the Dark Magicker Archon, who had twice tried to conquer the Three Nations.

In the end, the Three Gods had destroyed him utterly, but in doing so they had retreated from the world. Their temples had been abandoned then, the citizens of the Three Nations turning to other pursuits.

But the gift of their magic had remained, and in the Gods' absence, Magickers had thrived, and many had abused their power. Eventually the Tsar had risen, uniting the Three Nations beneath his tyranny and vowing to sponge all magic from the land.

Some legends claimed the Gods had tried to cast him down, others that they'd supported him. Only one thing was agreed upon—that it had been Alana, the Tsar's daughter, who had destroyed the Three Gods.

And magic with them.

The world had changed in the thirty years since. Now it was the warrior who ruled, the power of the sword worshiped above all else. And a new cult had been born with the death of the Gods—the Order of Alana. They worshipped her as their Saviour, believed her sacrifice had cast off the shackles of the Gods, beckoning in a new era of enlightenment.

Only a few, like Pela's mother and her departed grand-mother, remained faithful to the Three Gods. It was partly in respect for her grandmother that Pela came at all. Selina had been a ferocious woman, well known around the village for her sharp knives and sharper tongue. Even approaching ninety, she had still visited the temple for the weekly meditation. In the end, only death had stopped her.

Pela had asked her once why she bothered. After all, Selina had been alive during the days of magic. She knew better than anyone that the Gods were truly gone. But the old woman had only smiled.

Antonia saved my life once. She and her brothers may be gone, but what they did for us should never be forgotten.

Smiling at the memory, Pela's mind drifted to the days before her grandmother's passing. They had often gone to visit her uncle after temple, who would greet them with honey cakes and ginger ale. The best roof-builder in Skystead, he was a giant of a man and not really her uncle, though that was all Pela had ever known him as. There were those in the village who said he had been a warrior once, but Pela had only ever known him as a kindly man with greying hair and smile lines on his cheeks.

She had not seen him since her grandmother's funeral. Kryssa had insisted that Pela keep away, though she had never offered any explanation. That had been almost five years ago now. It saddened Pela to think of him alone in the big house he had shared with her grandmother. As a child, they had all lived in the inn, running it together, but those days were long ago now. All Pela could recall from those days was the faded image of them all gathered around the fireplace on a cold winter night.

Realising she'd become side-tracked from her meditation, Pela dragged her thoughts back to the present, concentrating instead on her own body. Eyes closed, she centred herself, focusing on the slow in-out of her breath, on the distant thudding of her heart, the pulsing of blood in her ears. Nearby, she heard the faint whisper of another's breath, the rustling of cloth, the faint *tap-tapping* of some rodent hidden in the walls. Her mind examined each of them in turn before releasing them. Slowly, her consciousness sank, and she reached for her inner cal—

Bang.

Pela startled out of her trance as noise erupted from the rear of the chamber. Angered at the intrusion, she swung around in time to witness armed men swarming inside. All wore heavy suits of plate mail armour and full-faced helmets. They spread out around the door, barring the only exit.

Her eyes were drawn to the centre of their breastplates, where each had been adorned with a flaming red sword. A chill slid down Pela's spine as she recognised the symbol.

The Knights of Alana.

"On your feet!" a Knight boomed.

CHAPTER 2

"On your feet!" The Knight's voice echoed strangely from behind his visor, giving it a metallic quality, as though the man within was not entirely human.

Crouched on her knees, Pela found herself frozen, unable to so much as cry out as the Knights advanced. The summer solstice was only a few weeks away and most of the congregation had gathered to begin preparations for the sacred day of the Goddess Antonia. Pela was near the back of the chamber, furthest from the Knights, but those at the front scrambled over one another in their desperation to escape the shining blades. With over forty meditators present, it was chaos.

Pela's heart hammered hard in her chest as her mind raced, struggling to understand where the Knights had come from. The nearest Castle was in Townirwin, a journey of many days by ship, and a week over land. How had they come upon the temple so suddenly? And what were they here for?

Death.

She shuddered. No, those were just rumours. Otherwise, the Plorsean King would have outlawed the Order of Alana, regardless of who they worshipped.

But why then were they here, with naked steel in hand? What other purpose but murder would have brought them?

"*Silence!*" the Knight roared over the screaming, "By order of the Crown!"

The command went unheeded. With a start, Pela realised she was the only one still on her knees. The crowd was pushing towards the altar, putting her at risk of being trampled. She had just scrambled to her feet when a vice-like hand gripped her by the wrist.

"*Pela!*" her mother hissed, suddenly beside her.

Kryssa pulled her towards the rear of the chamber. Stumbling after her mother, Pela glanced back as another scream came from behind them, and tripped over a tear in the carpet.

"Quickly!" her mother snapped, dragging her bodily behind the altar.

"There's no way out," Pela moaned.

"There is," Kryssa replied.

Pela shook her head, knowing her mother was wrong. Behind the altar they were hidden from the Knights, but there was nowhere left to go. The rear wall was made of brick and held up by stone pillars.

Still Pela's mother pulled at her arm, and she relented, allowing Kryssa to pull her into the corner where a pillar had fallen against the wall.

"Quickly, you must find your uncle!" Kryssa gasped, pushing Pela towards the broken pillar. She said something else, but her words were drowned out by the screaming.

"*How?*" Pela yelled, anger lending her strength. Her mother never explained, only told.

A gurgling cry rattled from the walls. Pela looked back and saw an older villager stumbling away from the Knights. Blood spurted from his throat and he went down clutching the wound with both hands.

Pela stared, unable to tear her eyes away. She had never seen someone die before; let alone someone she knew. It was the old man who had greeted her at the temple door. She remembered him now—it was Fervil, the village baker. He had given her a sticky cream bun once, when she was young, as a reward for safely delivering some bread to her grandmother.

Now his lifeblood was soaking into the dusty carpet of the ruined temple, and Pela could not begin to understand why.

"*Pela!*" Kryssa shrieked, shaking her. With an effort of will Pela focused on her mother's face. "Inside!"

"Inside what?" Pela gasped. Nothing made sense anymore.

Her mother pointed at the wall beneath the pillar, and finally she saw. Where the pillar had come to rest, the wall had cracked and crumbled away. Higher up, the break was barely noticeable, but at the base it widened enough that Pela might be able to fit.

"Go!" Kryssa moaned, her eyes flicking toward the Knights. Most of the congregation had already been subdued, and the few remaining villagers were pressed against the altar. They had only seconds before the Knights saw them.

"What about you?" Pela asked.

"Don't worry about me," her mother hissed. "Get out. Take the back trails down the mountain. Find your uncle!"

Pela swallowed, heart suddenly in her throat, but Kryssa didn't give her an opportunity to argue. She gripped Pela by the shoulders and pushed her into the crack. The pressure did not relent until Pela crawled into the darkness beyond the candle-lit hall. Then an angry voice shouted out and her mother's hands vanished.

Blood thundering in her ears, Pela continued forward. She glanced back only once, in time to see a pair of thick leather boots appear alongside her mother's moccasins, then she was through the other side and on her feet, racing through the shadows of the temple.

In her panic, Pela didn't think about where she ran, only that she needed to escape the men who had taken her mother. Then a stray pile of rubble caught her foot and she went crashing to the ground. Pain flared as her elbow struck the ground and she cursed, the sound shockingly loud in the dark corridors.

Reason came rushing back and Pela clamped a hand over her mouth to keep from crying out again. The hackles on the back of her neck rose as a voice called from somewhere ahead, followed by the heavy thump of leather boots.

They're coming!

Struggling to calm her racing heart, Pela scrambled to her feet and went back the way she'd come. Her eyes strained against the dark, trying to place where she was. She needed somewhere to hide, or the Knights would surely find her.

Finally, she recognised a mosaic of the Three Gods. Half of it was gone—only the face of Darius, the God of Light, remained complete—but she now knew where she was. She scanned her memories, thinking back to long ago when she had explored the temple as a youth. There were a thousand hiding places for a child, but few for a girl almost fully grown.

Only one was near, though it would test her courage.

She turned left, then right, and ducked into a narrow door-way. A long rectangular room stretched away from her, a massive fireplace taking up most of the far wall. Once it had been a kitchen, with a stove large enough to feed a hundred meditators, but now all that remained of the stove was a rusted ruin in the empty fireplace.

Stepping over the twisted iron, Pela moved into cavernous space beyond and looked up. The chimney was so long it could have fit two of her lying down, but it was narrow. If she was careful, she could wedge herself in place above the level of the room, out of sight.

If she could climb that high.

Don't think—do!

It was something her grandmother used to say, and Pela drew inspiration from the words now. Taking care to be quiet, she jammed her hands into the cracks left between the bricks by the crumbling mortar and tried to haul herself up.

Pain flared in her hand as it slipped free. Pela gasped as she slammed into the ground. A voiced echoed from the corridor, closer now.

Covered in black ash, Pela scrambled up and tried again. This time a clump of soot fell in her face, but she managed to wedge her feet into a crack and hold herself in place. She sucked in a breath, and soot rushed up her nose.

Her eyes watered as a sneeze built, until she could hold it no longer. Quickly she released a hand hold and pinched her nose. She was just in time, and only the tiniest of squeaks came out.

Even so, she held her breath, listening for the telltale crunch of boots on rubble. Suspended just out of sight of the room below, her arms shook...but she dared not move, lest she give herself away. A minute ticked by, then another, until finally she was convinced the Knight had gone another way.

Letting out a breath, Pela shifted so her feet were beneath her, and started to climb. She did not look down, though in the darkness she could not have told how high she was. The chimney had once extended far above the temple's roof, but age had toppled it along with the three spires. Light streamed through the narrow gap a dozen feet above, showing her the way, and there were no more accidents.

Clambering onto the rooftop, Pela crouched amongst the rubble of the ruined chimney and squinted against the sudden brightness. The roof had been painted white and reflected the sun, though thankfully the fallen spires covered much of it. She searched for sign of the Knights, but there was no one in sight.

A shout carried to her on the ocean breeze, sending a tingle of premonition down her spine. Her heart began to race again. Crouching low, she crept across the broken stone, silent as a cat. She had to skirt several places where fallen rock had caved in the temple roof. Long minutes passed before she reached the front of the temple. Voices carried up from below. Craning her head, she peeked down at the speakers.

Dust billowed up from the two dozen men and horses gathered below, and she quickly ducked back out of sight. Rolling on her back, she gasped, struggling to control her panic. If they had seen her…

Her blood went cold. *Had* they seen her? Even now they might be drawing their swords and scrambling up the lead drainage pipes…

Pela scrunched her eyes closed and sucked in a breath.
Listen.
Slowly she exhaled, focusing on the action and not the

AARON HODGES

fear. The wind whistled through the nooks and crannies of the ruin. She strained her ears, seeking out sounds of pursuit. Voices rose from below, raised in anger but directed elsewhere, not at the hidden watcher on the roof.

Her heartbeat slowed. They had not seen her.

Pela had only caught a glimpse of what was going on, but it was all she'd needed. The villagers had their hands bound behind their backs and were roped together in a line. She'd had no time to count but it looked like everyone inside had been subdued. Now the Knights were mounting up in preparation to depart.

What do I do? Pela shrieked in the silence of her mind.

Her mother must be below, but there was no way to reach her, no way to free her from the armoured Knights and their terrible greatswords. At the thought, she saw again the image of Fervil choking on his own blood, his fingers unable to stem the terrible bleeding…

Stop it.

Pela forced herself to breathe, pushing back the onset of panic. She couldn't afford that luxury. Kryssa was in trouble and she was the only one who knew!

"Ready men?" A voice carried up to her. "Let's ride!"

The sharp *crack* of a dozen whips followed as the Knights set their horses on the narrow trail. Several villagers cried out, but from where Pela lay, she could not see who or why. Angry curses and more *cracks* followed, and a woman wailed. Pela prayed to the Three Gods it was not her mother. Finally, the clip-clop of hooves on stone faded away.

Cautiously, Pela lifted her head and watched the Knights move off, their captives strung out between them. She waited several minutes before pulling herself up, wanting to be sure no one had remained to keep watch. A dust cloud clung to the mountainside where the Knights rode, their captives in tow. They were already a quarter of the way down the mountainside. Beyond, the deep blue waters of the harbour waited.

Her heart fluttered as she thought of the ship waiting there. That must be how they intended to escape, though what they intended for the prisoners...

Pela tore her thoughts away from torture and death. High tide was still an hour away; the ship would not depart until the currents turned. The Knights couldn't move quickly with the prisoners in tow. If Pela ran, she might beat them to Skystead. Balling her hands into fists, she focused on her mother's last words:

Find your uncle!

CHAPTER 3

Rivulets of sweat trickled down Ikar's forehead as the sun beat down on the mountain trail. Outside the refuge of the old temple, there was no escaping it, and the heavy armour made the heat all the worse. He fought the temptation to remove his visor, calling on his ancestors for strength.

He had not lied to Merak, it was well known his family had descended from Alan the Great, who had died over a century ago in the war of the Gods. But of the man's children, Ikar was descended from the lesser line, and his family had done little of note since. Nothing but…

Ikar shook his head, determined to leave the past in the past. His family might have once sinned, but he had been born on the day the Gods fell, and had never known any power but his own strength. He had been raised in Lonia, the poorest of the Three Nations, though their king had designs to change that fate. Ikar had served as the man's bodyguard for a time, and later for his daughter, only departing their household a year ago, when his faith had called for his service.

And so he had joined the Knights of Alana, and been sent as a missionary into Plorsea. The Order was still young here, its growth hindered by antagonism towards Lonia, where the cult had been born. Though few still worshiped the False Gods, they had been equally reluctant to embrace the Saviour. Townirwin, where he had settled, was one of the few towns to boast a Castle—the fortresses of the Order.

Anger stirred in Ikar's chest as he inspected the villagers they had captured. They stumbled along the path, hands bound, barely able to keep upright. His fellow Knights rode alongside them, brandishing their riding crops at those who slowed the progression. The sight made him sick. Such weak, selfish creatures they were, to beg the False Gods to save them.

Did they not realise their prayers endangered all the Three Nations? That their belief fed strength back to the False Gods, so that they might one day threaten the world once more? The Order would not allow it, though the cowardly King of Plorsea had forbidden interference.

Ikar snorted. As far as he was concerned, Braidon was a weak and ineffective king, though the man's tolerance for the False Gods and their followers bordered on outright blasphemy. It still surprised Ikar that Lonia had made a pact with such a man—had even offered him their princess's hand in marriage in order to buy peace.

Sucking in a stifling breath, Ikar forced his thoughts from politics. He tried to judge their progress down the mountainside, but the town was still far below and several of the prisoners were already flagging. He cursed. They needed to be away on the high tide, before the townsfolk might learn of their presence and attempted a rescue. He had no doubt his two dozen Knights could fend them off, but there had already been enough bloodshed.

Ahead, a young boy stumbled on the uneven ground and fell. Ikar cursed and rode closer. The boy struggled to right himself with his hands tied behind his back, but only succeeded in toppling himself face-first into the ground. When he saw the Knight looming overhead, he screamed.

"Stupid boy!" Ikar growled, lifting his crop.

"Stop!" Another prisoner, a woman, darted between Ikar and the boy.

"Get out of my way, woman," Ikar snapped. He flicked the crop at her, but she leaned back, and the blow missed by a hair's breadth.

The woman sneered. "Such a brave man," she said, her voice rich with sarcasm, "that you must beat women and children to show your power."

Angered, Ikar prepared to strike the woman down. She did not shrink away. Her silver eyes flashed in the midday sun as she watched him. There was not an inch of give in those eyes, and Ikar hesitated, then lowered his crop.

"Get him up," he grunted.

With her own hands still bound, the woman could do little to help the boy, but eventually she got him on his feet. Taking him under her wing, she moved off down the track without a backwards glance at Ikar.

He edged his horse after her, equal parts disturbed and fascinated. The other villagers had shown little defiance since the bloodshed in the temple. The baker's death had robbed the rest of their courage, and now the rest marched wilfully to their fate.

"Ikar."

Ikar looked around as Merak called his name and found the Elder riding several horses back. He had removed his helmet once more, but sweat still beaded his forehead, drenching the greying hair that hung in tangles around his face. Dragging on his reins, Ikar waited for Merak to catch him before setting off again.

"What was that, with the woman?" Merak questioned.

Ikar shrugged. "She was right. They might be blasphemers and traitors, but we should not sink to their level. We are Knights of Alana; we must uphold our own honour."

"Ay," Merak mused, "but I do not like how these peasants defy us. It should not have taken a death to subdue such creatures."

"Hard country, the mountains," Ikar replied. "In Lonia, they breed strong warriors."

"Even so, it would serve them well to be reminded of their place. I will take five to the town square and conduct a cleansing. Shall I include the witch who challenged you?"

Ikar looked ahead to where the woman walked alongside the boy, turning over the man's offer in his mind. It would be just, to repay her earlier defiance. Yet their orders were to return with as many prisoners as possible, for the Elders needed candidates for their Great Sacrifice.

He shook his head. "No," he replied. "She is strong, we may need her for the solstice."

Merak laughed. "You are right, brother." He offered a grim smile. "I will take the weak and cowardly. They will not be needed."

Ikar shuddered as the Elder moved away. There was something about Merak that set his teeth on edge, a cruelty that went beyond the bounds of what was needed to preserve the natural order. Watching the man inspect the prisoners, Ikar was reminded of a wolf circling its prey.

As they neared the town, Merak cut five prisoners from the line, all men. "Make for the ship and load the prisoners," the Elder ordered. "I will join you within the hour. If I am postponed, do not wait. The candidates must be brought before the Order without delay."

With that, Merak moved off, taking five Knights along with the prisoners. Ikar waited until they disappeared down the broad avenue through the centre of town before shaking himself into action.

"Let's go!" he bellowed.

The prisoners stood staring after Merak. They had not been told what the Elder intended, but from their defeated looks, several had guessed. Ikar scanned their ranks, catching the eyes of the woman from earlier staring back at him. Her gaze was strangely unnerving, and he quickly looked away.

"I said get moving!" he screamed.

Several of his Knights brandished their crops, and the group moved off, making for the port.

CHAPTER 4

Devon sat back on the slate roof and let out a long breath. Taking a rag from his belt, he wiped the sweat from his face. The familiar ache had begun in the centre of his back, and his knee had been troubling him for close to an hour now. He would need to stop soon, but he was determined to continue for as long as possible. Already the longest day of the year was just weeks away, and he was not yet half finished with the repairs.

He should have started sooner, but as always, he had put the needs of the village first, had dedicated too much time to other projects. Now he would need to rush to get the holes in his own villa fixed before the autumn rains arrived.

Selina would have shaken her head and cursed him for a fool. The thought of his former business partner brought a smile to Devon's face. Her loss still hurt, though Selina had been so old at the end she could barely make it up the steps to the temple.

A shiver went through him at the thought. How long before the same weakness claimed him? He already felt its approach. Once, he would have finished retiling his entire roof in the span of a week; now he would need to enlist help if he was to avoid being bogged down in the winter.

Devon cursed and straightened. He wasn't dead yet, and he'd be damned if he allowed despair to rule him. He might be approaching fifty-five, but he was still the strongest man in the village. Just last month he'd carried the Lifting Stone further than any other challenger, and he was yet to meet the man who could best him in battle.

That thought brought another pang of sadness. Fifteen long years had passed since his last campaign. It had ended in such disaster that even now he regretted accepting the call. At the time, Selina had railed against him, had begged him not to go, but Devon had left anyway, marching to the aid of his old friend, Braidon.

How he wished he could take that decision back. He had lost everything because of it: friends and family and his own honour. But Braidon had been desperate—and if Devon was honest, he had longed to experience the thrill of battle one last time.

But with the wisdom of age, Devon could see now what he had never accepted as a young man. He did not have the courage to live as an ordinary man, to toil day in and day out to add something to the world. Selina had recognised it in him, when they had stood on the plains of Trola and fought the Tsar and his armies. But her advice had helped him little then, and it was too late to admit it now.

Sitting back on the roof, Devon found himself wondering after the king. He had not heard from Braidon for many years now. He supposed with the peace treaty signed between Lonia and Plorsea, Braidon had little need for old warriors.

Devon shook himself from his reverie and reached for

his hammer. If he pressed on for another hour, he might just keep to schedule. If the rains came late…

"*Uncle!*"

Devon started as a scream came from below. Sitting up, he saw a young girl race into his courtyard. Tangled platinum hair bounced around her face as she stumbled to a stop, her hazel-green eyes whipping about in search of somebody. She had not noticed him sitting on the roof.

A broad grin stretched Devon's cheeks as he recognised his niece. Pela had taken to calling him "Uncle" when she was just a child, though they had no direct relation. If anything, he was more like her grandfather. Years ago, when he and Selina had run the Firestone Tavern in Ardath, the old woman had adopted an urchin from the streets. He recalled with a mixture of regret and fondness the night she'd returned with Kryssa, and changed their lives forever.

But Kryssa had not spoken to Devon since Selina's death, nor allowed her daughter, Pela, to visit him. He could hardly blame her, after his failure…but the absence had hurt. Seeing Pela now brought a smile to his face, and sitting up, he waved a hand.

"Morning, missy. Where have you been hiding?" he shouted down.

"Temple…Knights…Mum…Uncle!" Pela gasped, her voice echoing incoherently from the walls of the courtyard.

Devon frowned. Her words made little sense, but there was no mistaking her urgency. A spark of worry lit in his stomach, and he levered himself up. He strode across the roof, taking care to step lightly on the slate tiles, and clambered down the ladder to join her in the courtyard.

"What's that, missy?" he asked when he was on the ground.

Still struggling to catch her breath, Pela straightened.

"They have Mum!"

"What?" Devon asked, his chest tightening. "Who?"

"They have her—the Knights of Alana!"

"Slow down, missy," Devon said, though there was a roaring in his ears now.

Pela's words made no sense. Skystead did not have any of the cult's ridiculous Castles, and was about as remote as a village could get in Plorsea. There was nothing to bring them here. And they wouldn't want anything with Kryssa, not unless…

"It's true!" Pela panted. "We were at Temple—"

"*What?*" Devon boomed, worry giving way to anger. "I told your mother to stop with that nonsense years ago. What was she thinking?"

Pela paled in the face of his rage. Her mouth hung open, but no more words came out. Devon groaned, running a hand through his thinning hair.

"When did this happen?" he asked, trying to keep his voice calm. Pela was…sixteen? A woman grown, but inexperienced in the world and its dangers. He tried to reassure her: "Don't worry, we'll get this sorted."

"*They killed Fervil!*"

Devon knelt and placed a hand on her shoulder. "Listen to me, Pela," he said, face to face with the girl now. "I promise you; we're going to get your mother back. Okay?"

Pela nodded, her head bobbing up and down like it was on a chain. Her eyes were still wild, but at Devon's words she sucked in a great, shuddering breath, and seemed to calm a little.

"Okay," she whispered.

"Good," Devon rumbled. "Now, when did this happen, and where have they taken Kryssa?"

"Half an hour ago," Pela replied. There was still a

quiver to her voice, but the panic was fading. "I think they're heading for a ship at the port. High tide is soon!"

"How did you get away?"

"Mum sent me through a crack in the wall. She said to find you. *We have to help her!*"

"We will," Devon said, rising. "Did you see how many there were?"

The girl hesitated before replying, "A dozen, maybe two dozen."

Devon cursed inwardly. Even in his prime, a dozen would have been too many for him. The ache in his back seemed to redouble, dragging on his confidence. Slowed by age and old injuries, he wouldn't stand a chance against those odds.

But neither could he simply allow them to leave with Kryssa. Whatever they were here for, whatever their intentions for the prisoners, he doubted they were good. He had never liked the Order of Alana, though he had known the woman herself a long time ago. Perhaps that was why, for the Order and its Knights resembled little of what Alana had stood for at the end.

But despite his reservations, the cult had flourished over the last thirty years, finding fertile soil in a world suddenly without magic. The God's sudden absence had left a power void in the Three Nations, and the Order had taken full advantage.

"*Uncle!*" Pela shrieked, dragging him back to the present. There were tears in her eyes and she looked ready to crumble. "What are we going to do?"

Devon forced a smile. Striding across the courtyard, he hefted the sledgehammer he'd been using to break the old roof tiles, then looked at Pela.

"Let's go."

CHAPTER 5

C aledan let out a groan as he lowered himself onto the
tavern bench. The four days at sea had been the
longest of his life, made all the worse by the sudden squall
that had struck yesterday. The pounding rain would have
been a relief after the relentless sun, if not for the surging
waves that had made his already knotted belly convulse until
he was throwing up bile.

Now he could not wait to wash away the taste of salt
and vomit. Sucking down a long draught of his ale, he
wondered again what had possessed him to make such a
trip. By all logic, he should never have accepted the ship
captain's commission. Work might have been scarce for a
sellsword in recent years, but there was always need for men
of Caledan's calibre and he'd had no need for the coin.

But something in the captain's tale had awoken his
curiosity. The man had claimed a ship full of Baronians had
almost set upon his ship on the journey from Lon. Baronians were tribes of nomads who roamed the Three
Nations, preying on whomever was unlucky enough to fall

within their power. But their presence alone had not been enough to pique Caledan's interest. It was the Captain's claim of magic, of a ship with an unnatural ability to sail against the wind, that had captured Caledan's imagination.

He still wasn't sure of the story's truth, but it had been enough to buy Caledan's protection for a few days. Such a power might have advanced his own goals. But the Baronian vessel had never appeared, though with Caledan brought down by seasickness, that might have been for the best.

They had made port in Skystead last night and Caledan had promptly retired his commission, telling the captain he'd rather walk back to Townirwin than set foot on the *Red Seagull* again. The man had been enraged, but Caledan had little sympathy for him.

After all, he knew better than most that life was full of disappointments.

The captain must have been sailing under lucky stars though, for two Knights of Alana had ridden up before Caledan had even left the port and requested passage.

Seated at a table in front of the tavern, Caledan glimpsed another group of Knights riding past. The sight brought a frown to his face, and he wondered whether a new Castle had been opened in the sleepy village. He doubted it; Skystead was a long way from anywhere that mattered.

The tavern opened out onto northern edge of the town square. From his vantage point, Caledan could see the quiet stalls of the bazaar directly opposite. A slate roof protected its occupants from the elements, but with the sun approaching its midday position, most of the stalls were already packing up for the day. On the eastern side of the plaza was the town hall, its front lined with granite pillars.

Gargoyles stretched out from its roof, overhanging the square. The other buildings bordering the plaza were mostly eating houses and taverns, already beginning to fill with noon approaching.

Caledan expected the Knights to turn at the bazaar and head for the docks, but instead they cantered up to the town hall and all but one dismounted. He noticed now that only five of the party were Knights. The rest were plain-clothed men, their hands bound behind their backs. They stumbled to a stop behind the Knights, eyes fixed to the ground.

Sipping his ale, Caledan watched in fascination as a Knight took rope from his saddlebags and flung it over one of the gargoyles. A crowd began to gather as the Knight tied a noose.

"What's going on here?" an onlooker shouted.

The Knights ignored the question, but one of the prisoners looked up. Seeming to notice the crowd for the first time, he came alive. "Help us!" he shouted, tugging at his bindings. "They attacked—"

He broke off as a Knight bounded forward and slammed a mailed fist into his head. The man went down with a *thump*, unable to break his fall with his hands bound. When he tried to recover, the Knight drove a boot into his stomach. The rattle of iron striking flesh whispered through the square, silencing the crowd.

Arms resting against his table, Caledan said nothing. Several of the townsfolk had not lost their courage though, and the whispers soon began again.

"That's *Zenner*…who are you…where…what right…?"

The crowd had recognised the prisoners as their own people. But before they could gather their courage, the Knight who remained mounted edged his horse forward. Unlike the others, he did not wear a helmet, and his cape was dark red, while the rest wore white. He drew his sword and waved it at the crowd.

"Back!" The man's voice boomed across the square. His horse reared, its cry echoing its master's. "Or suffer the wrath of Alana!"

As one, the villagers retreated, though the agitated whispers did not cease.

Sword still in hand, the man turned his horse on the spot. "My name is Merak, Elder of the Townirwin Castle! We come before you today in the name of the Saviour, to cleanse from these lands those who would undo her saintly work."

Amidst the villagers, a man stepped forward in defiance of the Elder. "Why are these men bound? What do they stand accused of?"

"They were found in the ruins above your town, sending their blessings to the False Gods!" Merak bellowed.

"Ay, and what of it?" The villager didn't back down. "Skystead does not belong to your Order. In whose name do you deny these men their freedom?"

"In the name of the Crown!" Merak snapped, his irritation showing. He pointed his blade at the villager. "Now get back, or you will suffer the same fate as these sorry blasphemers."

"Be damned—"

Merak's sword flashed down before the man could finish, severing his throat. Blood sprayed across the dusty cobbles. Caledan watched with detached curiosity as the villager staggered back, clutching his throat in a desperate attempt to stem the bleeding. He'd seen many such wounds in his lifetime; the man was already dead. Within seconds the villager crumpled to the ground and lay still.

The crowd drew back, their anger turning to sudden

fear. Silence fell across the plaza as they stared at the Elder. Blood still dripped from Merak's blade. He sneered down at them.

"Blasphemers must be cleansed from our lands, lest the False Gods return and bind us once more with their magic."

Caledan watched on, bemused by the performance. There were over a hundred villagers in the plaza now, against the Elder and his five Knights, but not one lifted a hand as the killer turned his horse towards the prisoners. He dropped a hand to his sword hilt. He was tempted to interfere, if for no other reason than to irk the Elder's arrogance.

But there was no profit to be made upsetting the Order of Alana. Caledan had learned to trust his instincts long ago; he recognised a rising power when he saw one. Just like Lonia before it, the cult would grow until it touched every aspect of Plorsea's governance. If the Elder was to be believed, they already had the ear of the crown.

Not that corrupting King Braidon would have been difficult.

Caledan waved for a server to bring him another pint of ale. But the man had been distracted by the altercation and had abandoned his post. Swearing, Caledan returned his attention to the Knights. At least there was entertainment, even if his drink was empty.

Merak had dismounted now. He stood before the crowd, arms raised. "Bring the first to be cleansed!"

Two of his men grabbed a prisoner and dragged him forward until he stood before the dangling rope. At a gesture from their leader, the Knights looped the noose around the captive's neck. The man cried out as the fibres tightened around his throat and tried to fight back, but his armoured assailants held him tight. After a moment he slumped in their grip, defeated.

"Please…don't do this…stop!" The villagers were growing restless again.

"Silence!" Merak's voice boomed out. "Darkness has infected your town, but we have come to deliver you! We bring the blessings of Alana."

No one spoke as the Elder approached the prisoner in the noose.

"What is your name, traitor?"

"Ze…Zenner."

"Zenner, you stand accused of blasphemy against the Saviour, and worship of the False Gods. How do you plead?"

The man's mouth opened and closed, but he couldn't seem to find the words. Caledan felt for him. There were no laws outlawing belief in the Three Gods, though Caledan knew that in Lonia their worshipers were now hunted. Such foulness had not reached Plorsea though, certainly not a small town like Skystead. At least, not until now.

"Will you repent, blasphemer, and surrender yourself to the mercy of Alana?"

"I…I…please?"

The man still seemed to think he could reason with his captor, but Caledan recognised the eyes of a fanatic. It was no surprise; Elders were generally zealots of the highest order.

"No?" Merak asked. When the man still did not answer, he nodded to his followers.

The two Knights took hold of the rope. The prisoner's eyes widened and he cried out, "Wait—"

Before he could say more, the noose snapped tight around his throat and he was dragged into the air. He kicked out wildly as the rope swayed, but he could find no purchase in the empty air, no relief from the fiery grasp of the noose. The villagers screamed, but with their comrade lying dead on the ground before them, none were bold enough to intervene.

Caledan watched on, slightly bored by the lack of a fight. He had expected at least a few townsfolk to try and save the man. Instead, they stood and did nothing as the prisoner's eyes rolled back into his skull and his struggles grew feebler.

Finally, the man stilled, and Merak nodded for the Knights to cut him down. As though choosing a chicken at the market, the Elder moved down the line of prisoners and stopped in front of a white-haired man.

"You, what is your name?"

The old man stared calmly back at his accuser. Unlike the others, there was no fear in his eyes. He smiled at the question.

"May the Three Gods bless you, brother."

"Blasphemy!" Merak screamed. Face flushed, he raised his blade.

"I wouldn't do that if I were you, sonny."

The Elder froze as a voice boomed across the square. Frowning, he turned and sought out the speaker. Caledan did the same, scanning the crowd before settling on a figure standing in the shadows of an alley. A whisper went through the plaza as he stepped into the sunlight. Age lined the man's face and his beard was grey, but he strode towards the Knights as though he owned the world. He carried a sledge-hammer in one massive fist.

"Who's this now?" Caledan mused.

"That's Devon," the tavern's server answered, appearing finally with a fresh jug of ale. "They say he fought for the king, back in his day."

"Interesting." Caledan nodded his thanks and handed over a shilling for the drink.

Caledan studied the giant as he advanced on the Knights. Could it be true? Devon was a name carved into the legends of the Three Nations. The Trolans knew him as the "Butcher of Kalgan," the Lonians as the "Consort of Alana," while most Plorseans were divided between "King Killer" and "Liberator." All agreed he'd played a part in the fall of the Empire so many decades ago.

But surely this couldn't be the same man?

CHAPTER 6

Pela stood transfixed as her uncle strode through the crowd, seemingly unconcerned by the armed men awaiting him. Gone was the gentle giant of her childhood; in his place was a man of ice, a face that promised death. The crowd parted before him, swept aside by his rage, leaving the Elder, Merak, standing alone.

Yet Devon too was alone, and armed only with the sledgehammer he'd taken from his home. Merak seemed to realise this too, and with a start he came alive. Lifting his blade, he pointed it at the advancing hammerman.

"This is none of your business, greybeard," he cried. "I suggest you depart, before I have you join your fellows!"

The man's voice rang with power, and many in the square found themselves stepping back from the Elder. But Devon continued as though he hadn't heard the man. Teeth bared, the Elder flourished his blade again, then apparently thought better of it, and turned it on his prisoner.

"Stop!" he snapped.

"Kill him, and your body will be the next to strike the

stones," Devon rumbled, coming to a stop several feet from the Elder.

Merak's lips drew back in a sneer. "Such blasphemy cannot go unpunished. Swanson, Cidar, take him!"

Two Knights advanced, drawing broadswords from their sheaths. Stepping around their leader, they approached Devon with broad grins on their faces, already anticipating an easy victory.

Pela clenched and unclenched her fists, still frozen on the edge of the square, where they had first noticed the commotion on their way to the docks. She longed to go to her uncle's aid, but she had no weapon, not even a rock to throw—and anyway, she knew nothing of the warrior's arts.

Did her uncle even know? Or was this all an act?

"This village is under the king's rule," Devon said, his voice low, though every soul in the plaza heard his words. "You have no authority here. Leave now in peace, or die."

The Knights paused, glancing back at their leader, suddenly uncertain. Though they wore full-faced helmets, from the way they moved Pela guessed they were young, confident in their abilities and used to being feared. In their plate mail armour they seemed to Pela untouchable, and she couldn't begin to think how her uncle could threaten them.

"*I said, take the bastard!*" Merak shrieked.

The Knights jumped, shocked out of their hesitation, and continued. "Put down the hammer, old man," one shouted, his voice rattling from inside his helmet.

"So be it," Devon murmured.

He surged forward, the construction hammer already in motion. One of the Knights had drawn slightly ahead. He cried out, taken unawares by Devon's charge, and raised his broadsword to defend himself, but Devon's hammer swept below his guard. A crash echoed loudly across the square as it struck.

Pela gaped as the Knight staggered back, his breastplate caved in by the blow. The sword slipped from his fingers and he toppled backwards, slamming into the cobblestones with a shriek of twisting metal. His helmet was knocked loose. Seeing his pale face, a scream built in Pela's throat. His eyes were wide open, staring into the sunlit sky, but there was no life there now. Where a second ago there had been a young man in his prime, now there was only death.

And still Devon was moving, stepping past the fallen Knight and charging the second. Shocked by his comrade's death, the man barely had time to lift his blade before Devon was on him. Steel shrieked as hammer struck sword, then again, before Devon's third blow found its mark. There was a sickening *squelch* as it struck the man's helmet, the steel giving way like putty. The man crumpled without a sound and lay still.

This cannot be happening.

Awed and disbelieving, Pela watched as her uncle stepped over the second body and stopped in front of Merak.

"Last chance," Devon said. He did not raise his voice, but a collective shiver went through the crowd at his words. "Leave, or die."

"*Be damned!*" Merak shrieked.

Before Devon could react, Merak plunged his sword through the neck of the prisoner he was holding. The old man's eyes widened as blood gushed from the wound. Pela slapped a hand to her mouth, shocked by the suddenness of Merak's brutality. Dragging back his blade, the Elder kicked the old man in the back, toppling him face-first to the stones.

"You shouldn't have done that," Devon murmured.

"Be damned!" Merak snarled, leaping at Devon.

His blade hissed for Devon's face, but her uncle's hammer leapt to meet it. A great *shriek* tore through the plaza as the weapons met, and Devon leapt back. Pela gaped as a chunk of metal fell from Devon's hammer. The greatsword had carved straight through the dense metal.

Devon flicked a glance at his weapon, but the rest remained intact, and he advanced again. The Elder snarled, but as Devon neared his opponent seemed to stumble, his face paling. With a roar, Devon charged and the Elder turned and fled.

"Kill the blasphemer!" Merak shrieked as he leapt for his horse. His foot jammed in a cobble and he would have fallen if he hadn't caught the reins and dragged himself up.

Devon was almost on him, but before he could drag the Elder from the saddle, the remaining Knights cut him off. They spread out to encircle the hammerman, broadswords at the ready.

Watching the scene unfold from the shadows, Pela's heart sank. Her uncle's speed and skill had taken the other men by surprise, but there would be no such luck with these three. They edged forward slowly with blades extended, eager to avenge their comrades' deaths.

Devon stood fixed in place, hammer clenched in both hands now, his face impassive. Only the slightest flicker of his amber eyes betrayed any emotion. Encircled, Devon could only keep two of his foes in sight at a time, and the third was readying himself for the attack.

Before Pela could call a warning, the Knight leapt forward with blade raised. But the rattle of his armour must have given him away, for Devon spun, hammer already in motion, and batted away the attack. The Knight scrambled back as Devon parried, and the blow struck empty air.

Then the other Knights were charging in, and Pela knew her uncle would be overwhelmed, cut down by sheer weight of numbers…

Before the men could attack again, a man dressed in a leather jerkin and tight-fitting pants leapt into the battle, silver sword in hand. He struck at the hilt of a Knight's weapon, deflecting the attack into the cobbles, and with a screech of tearing metal, the blade shattered. The Knight staggered back and stared at the now useless weapon. The newcomer's sword took him through the visor before he had a chance to recover.

Pela watched as the stranger and Devon faced off against the last two Knights. Though they appeared evenly matched, it was clear the balance had changed, and now it was the Knights who hesitated, confused by the new element posed by the plain-clothed swordsman.

Devon leapt at the Knight still facing him. The man staggered back, his confidence evaporating like water in the summer sun, and Devon barrelled into him. The power behind his blows rendered the Knight's armour worse than useless—even his non-fatal blows warped the steel, twisting it to incapacitate the man within. The Knight fell with a cry, and Devon spun in search of his last foe.

He was already dead. Blood seeped from where the knife had been driven through his gorget to pierce his throat. The swordsman retrieved the blade and wiped it clean, before returning it to a hidden sheath on his person.

Hooves thundered across the cobbles as Merak kicked his horse into a gallop. Devon roared but he could not catch the Elder on foot. He spun, scanning the fallen Knights, then the crowd, but whatever Devon was searching for he did not find it. Cursing again, he swung his hammer at the cobbles.

Stumbling across the square to join her uncle, Pela's eyes were drawn inexorably to the dead Knights. Their blood pooled amongst the stones, already turning black with the dust and the heat. A fly buzzed in her ear before darting towards the bodies. She swallowed and tore her gaze away.

It was soon caught by a fresh horror. The innocent old man lay dead where Merak had left him, his chest torn open, eyes staring blanking up into the cloudless sky. Beside him another villager lay dead. He sported no wounds, but the purple mark around his throat told the story of how he'd died.

A shudder swept through Pela and she fought to keep from throwing up. It was a full minute before she noticed the other prisoners standing nearby, arms still bound behind their backs.

"Where's my mum?" she gasped, racing to where they stood. "Where's Kryssa?"

The prisoners stared blankly back at her, as though not comprehending the words. The fear in their eyes was palpable, but in that moment, Pela didn't care about anything but her mother.

"Here, girl." The strange swordsman stepped around her and drew a dagger.

One of the prisoners cried out, while the other two whimpered, still in shock. But the stranger only cut free their bindings before stepping back. The newly freed men rubbed their wrists, hardly seeming to comprehend the sudden reversal in their fortunes. Their eyes kept darting to where Merak had vanished, as though expecting him to return at any moment to follow through with his threat.

Leather scuffed on stone as Devon approached. "Any of you lads know where they took the others?"

The men exchanged glances. "The docks," one said finally. "There was a ship they were meant to catch."

"Ay." Pela looked around as the strange swordsman spoke. "I arrived on it last night. The *Red Seagull*, it's called. It'll be gone by now."

Devon eyed the man before nodding. "Thank you for your help back there, sonny. Not sure I could have taken all three myself."

The swordsman laughed. "I suppose that depends whose legends you believe. If you're *mortal*, like the followers of the Three Gods claim, surely not. But these lads..." He gestured at the fallen Knights. "Not sure they'd have been so quick to tackle you, if they'd known they were going up against the Consort of Alana."

Devon's face darkened and he stepped towards the swordsman. At six feet tall, the stranger was by no means a small man, but he looked tiny in her uncle's shadow.

"So you know who I am," Devon rumbled. "And who might you be, sonny?"

CHAPTER 7

Devon stared down at the man who'd come to his aid. A dull throbbing came from the centre of his back and the ache behind his left knee had returned with vengeance, but he refused to show any hint of his pain. He drew in a breath, his heart still racing from the brief fight, and cursed again his aging body.

Exhaling, he studied the strange swordsman. His clothing was nondescript and the weapons he carried plain, but he had shown unusual skill earlier. It was no easy feat to defeat a man in armour with only a sword and dagger—let alone two. Yet Devon's unlikely benefactor had made it look easy.

He was sure the man was new in the village—Devon recognised all Skystead's citizens by sight if not by name. So how did this stranger know him? Had he come looking for a legend, or had he been told by someone, his arrival here coincidence?

"So you know who I am," Devon rumbled finally. "And who might you be, sonny?"

"Only a humble sellsword," the man said, spreading his hands in a gesture of peace and offering a half-bow. "I go by Caledan."

The name was familiar, but scanning his memories, Devon could not recall where he'd heard it mentioned. He swore silently; his recollection was not what it had been. So many friends, so many comrades, had been lost to the mists of time. Staring at the stranger though, he was sure they had never met.

"Might be I've heard of you," he said, "but I do not care to be reminded of my past."

It was true. Devon rarely spoke of his service as one of Braidon's King's Guard, and even less about the time before that. The Tsar had taken so much from him, he could hardly bear to think about the friends who had died in that battle. Even thirty years later, the memories still stung.

He knew his silence had allowed the rumours to spread, but so long as he'd been allowed to retreat from the world, he hadn't cared.

Only now the world had come for his family, and he was beginning to regret his absence.

"My apologies, hammerman," Caledan was saying. "I did not know."

Devon scowled. "Never mind that. What were you saying about the ship? Are you sure it's gone?"

The man shrugged. "They might have missed the tide, but I doubt it. Two Knights came last night and booked passage. They would not have allowed a late departure."

"Dammit," Devon muttered.

"They have Mum!" Pela cried, grabbing at his arm. "Devon, what are we going to do?"

Devon could see the girl was on the edge of panic again,

but time was slipping through his fingers, and with every passing second Kryssa got further and further away.

He knelt beside her and placed a hand on her shoulder. "Go to the house and wait."

"But—"

"Pela," Devon said patiently, "I'm going to get her back, I promise you. But I need you safe, okay?"

Eyes wide, she nodded, and Devon released her. As she moved away, Devon faced the crowd. He knew some of those present by name, and liked and respected most. They were farmers and fishermen, solid folk, men and women you could rely on to clear a landslide from the road or work through the night to extinguish a burning building. But what faced them now was a different kind of challenge, and Devon did not know how they would react.

One of the villagers caught his eye and shouted, "Devon, what do we do now?" More voices quickly joined in.

"Where have they taken them?

"The king must be told—"

"Damn the king, the man never cared about us—"

"*Quiet!*" Devon shouted over the chorus, bringing silence.

He drew in a lungful of air. If only it could be so simple as calling the king. But Ardath was many weeks' journey from Skystead and by then it might already be too late for Kryssa and the others. Whatever the Knights of Alana had planned, they would not want to be caught with the evidence of their crime.

"They have our people," he said finally, his voice soft now, but still powerful. "The king is far away; he cannot help us."

The villagers looked back at him, their eyes filling with

49

fear as they realised what he was asking. Devon tried to keep his own worries concealed. He could not go after the Knights alone—even in his prime, the two dozen who had raided the temple would have been too many. If they reached Townirwin, and the protection of their Castle, the odds would be even worse.

"I'm going after them," he said, his eyes travelling over the crowd, and when he spoke, he spoke to all of them. "Who will go with me?"

Devon's heart palpitated as the villagers stared back at him. Not one spoke, not even the three he had freed. Anger took him then, taking light in his fear for Kryssa, in his frustration at his failing body.

"Are you all such cowards?" he bellowed. "Are you sons and daughters of Skystead, or are you field mice, skulking in the grass before the cat? Are you truly such wretches, that you would allow evil to walk unchecked amongst you, to take your neighbours, your friends, your family, and you will do nothing?"

Still no one spoke, though few were those that could meet his eyes. A wave of despair swept over Devon and he turned away. These people weren't soldiers, used to the violence that had just played out in the plaza. Few would have seen a man die by the blade before today.

"I will."

The voice was so soft, so trembling, he almost missed it. Devon turned to find Pela still standing behind him. Her face was pale, but she met his eyes resolutely.

"I'll come with you, Devon," she continued. "I'll help you bring them home."

Devon stared at her, too stunned to reply. He had thought she'd left, gone home to wait for him. For a moment he was reminded of her father, on that fateful day…

"I'll come too," another voice piped from the crowd. A man stepped forward, wearing the plain-spun cloth of a coffee farmer. He looked nervous, his eyes flickering from Pela to Devon, before he nodded and drew himself up. "They won't get far."

"Me too."

This time it was a woman who spoke. She carried an axe slung over one shoulder and wore a knife on her belt. Sweat shone from her brow and she looked like she'd arrived in a rush. Devon recognised her as one of the trappers who made their living harvesting the pelts of mountain hares and marmots, though he had never spoken with her before.

The rest of the crowd shifted nervously, exchanging glances, but no one else volunteered. Pela had shamed them all, but not enough to move them to action. Devon let out a sigh, disappointed, but at least two was better than none.

"Very well," he murmured. "Begone then, the rest of you, if you will not help. But at least send word to the king, about what happened here."

Muttering to each other, the crowd departed, leaving Devon and Pela alone with their two volunteers. Devon recognised the man now as one of the captives—the one who had screamed when Caledan drew his knife to cut them free.

"My ship will carry you as far as Townirwin, Devon," a man announced, extricating himself from the departing crowd, "but I won't fight."

Devon's heart lifted as he recognised Tallow, a captain from Skystead's fishing fleet. His ship, the *Seadragon*, was small, but had a reputation for being well-kept, not that

Devon knew anything about boats. Smiling, he offered his hand in thanks, then noticed the sellsword still lurking nearby.

"What about you, sonny?" Devon asked, eyeing the man.

He still had no idea why the man had intervened in the fight with the Knights. Sellswords were notoriously obsessed with self-preservation. Involving himself in a conflict with the Order of Alana seemed out of character for such a character.

Caledan shrugged. "What's in it for me?"

"I don't have the gold to pay for a sellsword."

"I wasn't thinking of coin," Caledan answered quickly.

"What then?" Devon pressed. "Unless you're suggesting you'll work for free."

Caledan chuckled. "If even a fraction of the legends about you are true, then you have a friend I'd like to meet."

"Who?"

"The king."

Devon stared at the man, weighing his options. Remembering the speed with which Caledan had dispatched the Knights, he knew the man was no ordinary sellsword. With such skill, he might have commanded a small fortune in the service of a noble. An introduction with the king should not be hard to arrange, despite the years it had been since they had last spoken. But what did Caledan want with Braidon? He sensed the man would not say, but even so...

"Very well," Devon said.

He had no choice; he could not rescue Kryssa alone. Turning to the two who had volunteered, he ran a professional eye over them. Both were well-muscled, toned by the toils of their professions, but he doubted they'd ever killed before. Then he saw the look in the woman's eyes, and reappraised his initial thoughts. There was steel there, that much was sure.

"If you join us, are you ready to fight?" he asked the two finally.

They nodded, though the man had a nervous look about him. Even so, he stepped forward, as though eager to convince himself he could in fact do what Devon asked. "Whatever it takes," he said, then hesitated. "If…you really think we can bring them back?"

Devon realised that the man must have had someone taken by the Knights. It was as strong a motivation as any. He offered a grim smile and nodded.

"We'll get them back, sonny, don't you worry," he rumbled. "Now, let's get moving."

CHAPTER 8

Sitting on the railings of the *Seadragon*, Pela watched as the light faded from the world. Patterns of blue and white and grey swirled on the smooth waters of the southern sea, but there was no sign of the sun itself in the cloud-streaked sky. The ship rolled with every swell, though the waves were gentle, unbroken. Sea spray obscured the mountains of Skystead, and she strained her eyes for a last glimpse of home.

She could hardly bring herself to believe that the last twelve hours had been real. Any minute, Pela expected to wake and find herself warm and safe in her bed, her mother calling for her help with the daily chores.

But as darkness claimed the world, and Tallow's sailors scuttled across the deck lighting lanterns, she knew this was no dream. It was too real, too stark and unrelenting. Images flashed through Pela's mind as she recalled the baker dying on the temple floor, her mother's terrified face as she told Pela to run; then Devon in the plaza, standing in defiance against the Knights with their armour and their swords.

Another shock. She had always dismissed the rumours about her uncle, but now that she had seen him fight, she found herself wondering what else might be true. Had he truly served with the king, or fought the Tsar, or spoken with the Gods? Had he known Alana? Surely not, or the Knights of Alana would not have stood against him.

She shook her head, trying to clear the clutter from her mind. Her thoughts turned to Kryssa. Where did the setting sun find her mother tonight? How fast had the merchant's ship carried her away from Skystead?

By the time Pela and the others had gathered their supplies, high tide had long passed, and they'd been forced to wait out the day, only setting sail an hour before sunset. Unfortunately, the *Seadragon* was built for fishing and short voyages, not speed, and there was little chance they could catch the Knights before they reached Townirwin.

Stuck in the twenty-foot skiff without so much as a cabin or bathroom, it was going to be a long three days. Still, at least Pela did not suffer from seasickness. Her uncle and the swordsman who had come to his aid back in the plaza had already been laid low.

She could see Devon in the bow of the ship, his eyes on the distant shoreline, the lines on his forehead knitted in concentration. Or so it would have appeared to the casual observer. Pela knew he was only trying to keep the remnants of his supper in their rightful place. At the stern, Caledan crouched with head in hands, looking as pale as a ghost. He had already lost that fight.

Chuckling to herself, Pela wondered at how such fear-some warriors could be brought low by the power of the ocean. Tallow and his two crewmembers certainly didn't seem affected, nor did the quiet trapper, Genevieve. She sat on a barrel leaning against the single mast, running a whetstone down the blade of her hatchet. With every stroke, a shrill grinding carried across the deck, joining the gentle lapping of water on the bow and the creaking of the sails.

The woman had said little since coming aboard, other than offering her name. Pela already knew Genevieve as a regular at their inn, though they'd rarely spoken in the past. She thought the huntswoman might have been a friend of her mother. Perhaps that was why she'd volunteered.

Tobias the farmer, on the other hand, was difficult to avoid. Since boarding the *Seadragon*, he had darted from Devon to Caledan to Tallow, offering his assistance wherever he thought it needed. He carried a nervous energy about him, an eagerness to help that might have come from fear, or simply a need to be busy. He stood beside Tallow now, pointing at the emerging stars and discussing navigation with the sea captain.

Along with herself and Tallow's crew, there were eight of them aboard the *Seadragon*. Suddenly, Pela found herself wondering what she was doing there. She was sixteen years old. This morning, her biggest worry had been avoiding awkward conversations at Temple. Now she was winging her way across the southern sea on a rescue mission, upon which she could only be a burden.

Devon had his hammer, Caledan his sword. The others were at least adults, experienced in the hardships of life, ready for what awaited them at the end of this voyage.

But what could Pela offer? What had possessed her to volunteer back in the plaza? She had no place here, no skill with weapons that might save the day. She was terrified of confrontation, and pain, and the unknown, all of which she was likely to face in the coming days. If only she hadn't been so stubborn, she might have listened to Devon when he'd told her to go home, and remained safe in Skystead.

Pela shuddered as goosebumps ran down her neck. There was no going back now. And anyway, she was a woman grown. If there was danger to be faced, she would not run from it. Her mother needed her to be brave. She would not fail Kryssa now.

Leather scuffed on wood as Caledan staggered from the stern and drew his sword. Pela started as lantern light caught on the blade, but Caledan only held the weapon over his head. Standing on one foot, he closed his eyes. His breathing deepened and he stilled, perfectly balanced, in harmony with his weapon.

When he moved, the act was so sudden that Pela almost fell backwards over the railing in surprise. The silver blade flashed as Caledan lunged, skewering empty air. Then he was leaping and slashing, sword arcing sideways as though to deflect an invisible foe, his footsteps so soft they made no sound on the wooden deck.

A stillness fell over the *Seadragon* as all eyes turned on the swordsman. There was a pattern to his movements, a rhythmic beat that only he seemed able to hear. Caledan continued through the deadly dance, every twist and turn coupled with another jab or thrust. His sword flashed up, then down and back, spearing an invisible opponent. Spinning, he blocked high, then kicked out to his right, before turning to bring his sword down in a double-handed attack.

By now even Devon in his sickness had taken note of the impromptu performance. Silence hung over the ship as Caledan continued his deadly dance, sword rising and falling, his movements growing faster, until the silver blade was little more than a blur.

Suddenly the weapon slipped from Caledan's fingers. Pela cried out as it spun through the air, arcing to half the height of the mast before plunging down. Others echoed

Pela's fright, but Caledan was already diving, rolling across the deck and coming to his knees. His hand snapped out, plucking the blade from the air.

Releasing a long breath, Caledan rose to his feet. Surprise showed in his eyes as he saw the others watching. His jaw hardened, and spinning on his heel, he started back towards the stern.

"Wait!" Pela was on her feet before she could stop herself. Her cheeks warmed as everyone looked at her, but she knew what she needed to do. "Can you teach me that?" she asked in a rush.

Her mother had never let Pela learn the warrior's arts, never let her hold anything larger than a steak knife, for that matter. What use were such skills in a town like Skystead? Yet with her mother gone, Pela was now confronted by the world beyond their sleepy village. She no longer had the luxury of running from her fears.

"No!" Pela jumped as Devon's voice came from the bow. Swinging around, she watched the big man approach, his bulk emerging from the gloom. "Your mother forbade it."

Despite her nerves, Pela bristled. "Well she's not here now, is she?"

"I should never have let you come," Devon said, shaking his head. "I don't know what I was thinking. First thing when we make port, I'll find a ship to take you back."

A lump lodged in Pela's throat as she looked into her uncle's amber eyes. This was the opportunity she had wanted, a chance to take back her words in the plaza, to return to Skystead, and hide from the dangers of the world outside.

An image flickered into her mind, and she saw again the baker dying on the Temple floor, the Knight standing over him. The world had brought its evil to them. There could be no safety in Skystead now. The evil would return with renewed strength.

If she allowed it.

"*No!*" The word left her in a rush, carrying across the deck for all to hear.

Silence answered her cry. Devon stared down at her, the flickering light of the lanterns seeming to age him. In that moment, Pela realised his fear, that he would not be able to protect her, that he might fail, that she would die. Cold touched her then, the weight of what she was committing herself too pressing down on her shoulders. Yet still she refused to relent.

"Please, Uncle," she said. "There's nothing for me in Skystead, not without Mum."

Devon's shoulders slumped, and Pela knew she'd won. He waved a hand, already turning away. "Very well," he murmured, his words whispering in the night. "Though your mother will kill me for it."

Letting out a long breath, Pela closed her eyes, relieved she'd won the battle.

"You ever used a sword, girl?" Caledan asked.

Jumping at the swordsman's question, Pela spun to face him. In the heat of the moment, she'd forgotten what had started the argument with her uncle. Her mouth opened and closed, words abandoning her. Caledan raised an eyebrow, his eyes showing his disdain, and Pela cursed herself for a fool.

"Ummm…" she managed finally.

The man snorted and made to turn away. Gathering herself, Pela leapt into his path.

"Please!" she gasped. "They have my mother; I need to be able to help."

Caledan scowled. "I don't have time to teach a brat how

to hold a blade." He sidestepped her and started for the stern again.

"What are you afraid of?" Pela shouted at his departing back, anger giving her courage. "That you'll fail?"

The swordsman paused. Sword still in hand, he stood looking away from her. But there was a rage in the way he stood, in the rigidity of his stance, and Pela felt a sudden fear of the deadly man. She swallowed as he turned to face her.

"You may as well give in, sonny," Devon rumbled from the shadows. "If she has half her mother's will, she'll wear you down eventually."

Caledan's eyes flickered, but after a moment, the anger vanished from his eyes. "Very well, Devon," he said. "I'll teach your niece a few things." He flicked his sword into the air and caught it by the blade, then offered it to Pela, hilt first.

Taken aback by his sudden change in manner, Pela hesitated before tentatively accepting the blade. The sword itself was a plain thing, its leather hilt unadorned, the blade thick at the base and some thirty inches long, ending in a razor-sharp point. Testing its weight, she gave a practice swing—and cried out as the leather slipped from her grasp.

The blade *clanged* loudly as it struck the deck point first and lodged there. Laughter burst across the *Seadragon* as her so-called companions doubled over in mirth. Even the farmer Tobias wore a broad grin on his bearded cheeks.

Her face aglow, Pela stood frozen to the spot, horrified by her own clumsiness. She wanted to race home and bury her head beneath the sheets, but on the ship, there was nowhere to go, no place to hide from the shame.

Footsteps thumped on the wooden planks as her uncle

returned from the bow. His eyes swept the faces of their companions, silencing them with a glance. Gingerly, he reached down a massive hand and plucked the sword free, before offering it back to Pela. Cheeks still burning, she shook her head, but Devon was insistent, and finally she accepted the blade with a trembling hand.

"Your mother really is going to murder me, you know," he murmured. She frowned, but he was already turning. "Who are you to laugh?" he bellowed at the others. "Who of you would have done any better, at sixteen? Which of you could do better now?"

In the darkness, Pela could not see the faces of her fellows, but the silence was palpable. In other circumstances, it might have bolstered her confidence. Instead, her heart sank at the reminder that her mother's life now rested in the hands of untrained villagers. Pela's grip on the sword tightened as she realised her fellows were just as unprepared for this mission as herself.

"I thought as much," Devon continued, his tone turning gentle. "Well, we have three days before we reach Townirwin. I suggest you take heed of my niece, and ready yourselves. The Knights will not surrender their prize without a fight."

"Will you teach us, Devon?" Tobias asked.

Devon eyed the farmer for a long moment, then shook his head. "Not tonight," he said softly, his voice sad. Before anyone could press him, he returned to his spot at the bow, and sat staring out at the dark shore.

Swallowing, Pela looked from Devon to Caledan. Movement came from around them as Tobias and Genevieve stepped closer. Tallow and one of his sailors also approached, arms crossed.

"So, where do we begin?" the captain asked.

This time when Caledan smiled, it was genuine. He gestured to Pela, then waited until everyone was paying attention, before pointing at the ground. "With your feet."

CHAPTER 9

Devon's spirits were low as he sat listening to the clashing of swords. Twice already he'd heard Caledan cursing his new students. Plagued by doubt, Devon wondered whether he'd been wrong not to come alone. What difference could a few inexperienced villagers make, courageous though they might be?

And how could he hope to protect his niece where they were going? He should have refused her back in the plaza, rather than entertain this fantasy of a rescue mission. Timid as she was, he hadn't expected her to come this far. But Pela had surprised him. Perhaps there was more of her parents in the girl than even she realised.

His hammer lay beside him and he picked it up. Gripping the haft tight in one hand, Devon swore to himself he would not allow anything to happen to her. He owed Kryssa that, after everything they'd been through.

Holding the old hammer, Devon's gaze was drawn to the chunk Merak's blade had torn from the steel head. He shivered; that too gave him pause. It should not have been possible. Perhaps there had been an imperfection in the metal, though he knew the hammer well. An old friend had made it for him back in Ardath, after his ancestor's hammer had been destroyed by the Tsar. But then it *had* been made for construction, more than war.

He spent another few minutes inspecting the weapon, but he could see no other damage. Finally, he set it aside and returned his eyes to the night's sky.

After an hour, Caledan ended his impromptu training session with an explosion of curses, and silence returned to the *Seadragon*. Silhouettes flickered in the lantern light as the others made themselves comfortable for the night.

Devon was about to do the same when Pela appeared at the railing.

"What are you still doing awake, missy?" he asked gently.

"You don't want me here." She said the words matter-of-factly, a sad smile on her lips.

He sighed. "No, but then I rarely get what I want."

"I never knew you were a warrior," she murmured, taking a seat beside him. "Mum never wanted me to learn how to use a sword."

"No," Devon replied, "she…didn't believe in violence."

Pela snorted. "Could have fooled me…" She trailed off, looking to Devon for a response, but he said nothing, and she went on. "It isn't just her though. *You* don't want me to learn. Why?"

"I don't want to see you hurt," he replied, obfuscating. "Where we're going…I can't protect you."

"Who asked you to?"

"I can't fail your mother, not again."

"Again?" Pela's voice rose an octave.

Devon cursed his loose tongue. The girl was astute. "I only meant…I failed to rescue her."

"No…" Pela gripped the cuff of his shirt, her hand dwarfed by his own. "You know something, Devon…what is it? Why don't you or Mum want me to learn how to fight? Why did she push you away after my grandmother passed?"

"Pela…" Devon trailed off, struggling for the words. "I can't, I promised your mother…"

"I might not even *have* a mother anymore," his niece snapped, struggling to her feet. "What are you keeping from me?"

Devon lowered his eyes. "Your mother…she's…Selina and I raised her," he said, remembering the scrawny ten-year-old who had first shown up on the doorstep of the Firestone.

It had been Selina who had invited her in. Devon had been reluctant to be dragged into the role of a caregiver, but eventually the fiery youth had wormed her way into his heart. How she had grown, these last thirty years. Tears stung his eyes as the years flashed by, and he recalled her marriage to Derryn, the arrival of Pela. They had all moved to Skystead not long before the birth, in search of a safe place to raise a child.

They should have found peace there.

Would have, if not for Devon's weakness.

"I wanted to protect her from the world, but I failed. I couldn't save him," he whispered.

"Save who?"

"Your father," Devon grunted. He rubbed his cheek, trying to conceal his tears, trying to decide how much to tell her. "He fought alongside me many times…your father."

"*What?*" Pela gasped.

"This was before you were born, before we moved to Skystead, when we lived in Ardath."

Pela was on her feet. "Mum...how...she never!"

"Breath, Pela," Devon murmured, placing a hand on her shoulder. She nodded, her eyes as wide as saucepans, and he swallowed. Guilt weighed heavily on his chest as he went on, "We...he and I were both members of the King's Guard, the most elite of his soldiers. But when your mother became pregnant...we retired and moved to Skystead. Except, not long before your birth, the king sent for me, begged for my help with the war. I could have refused him, *should* have refused him, but...that was ever my weakness."

He hung his head, no longer bothering to conceal his tears, as the memories of that time rushed through his mind. Pela sat beside him, silent now, and he dared not meet her gaze.

"I would have gone alone," Devon whispered, "but... your mother wouldn't hear of it. She asked your father to go with me, though he didn't want to leave the two of you." He balled his hands into fists and squeezed his eyes closed. "I should have protected him. I failed."

"My father..." Pela croaked. "You saw him die?"

"Ay." His voice barely rose above a whisper. "In the foothills north of Lake Ardath, the enemy came upon us. No one knew they were so close. The army was far ahead of us; the king was unprotected but for twenty of his guard. Derryn and I stood at the centre and defied the Lonians until reinforcements could reach us. But when the last enemy was slain and I looked for him, he...he was already gone."

He hung his head, unable to even look at his niece. If not for him, she would have grown up knowing her father.

If not for him, Kryssa would have enjoyed many more years with her love…

"How could you keep this from me?" Pela hissed. He looked up at the anger in her voice. "I thought he was killed by Baronians!"

"Your mother wanted to protect you—"

Pela laughed harshly. "Well the two of you have done a great job of that, haven't you?" Her shoulders slumped suddenly. A shudder swept through her and the tears returned. "If you'd taught me to be a warrior like my father, I might have saved her. I might have done *something*, anything but run away."

Devon realised then what had driven his niece to join this ill-fated quest—she was ashamed. Ashamed that she'd frozen, ashamed she hadn't fought back when the Knights came, that she'd run away. Gingerly, he placed a hand on her head.

"To run when there is no hope of victory is not cowardice, Pela."

"*You* would not have run."

"Perhaps not, but even I could not have won that fight. Not even in my youth could I have defeated so many alone. If you'd fought, even if I'd taught you to use a blade, you would have only thrown away your life. That was why your mother never wanted you to learn in the first place."

Pela frowned. "What do you mean?"

"She was afraid of losing you, that you might follow in your…father's footsteps, and become a soldier."

"I…" Pela swallowed, averting her eyes. "Why would she think that? I never wanted anything like that…"

"Ay, but would it have been different if you'd known the truth? Maybe you wanted more than what Skystead can offer."

"Even so…" she murmured. "She should have told me, should have given me the choice."

Devon eyed his niece closely. She had always been a timid child, when Kryssa had brought her on their weekly visits after Temple. There had been little of her parents' fire in Pela then; now he wondered if she possessed that flame after all. Back in Skystead, while Pela had been packing for the journey, he'd retrieved some things from Kryssa's basement. With weapons in short supply in Skystead, he'd intended to arm the villagers. Now though…

"She didn't want you to die young, never knowing your family," he said, his voice little more than a whisper. The blood drained from Pela's face at his words, and he went on, "She wanted more for you than to lose your life fighting someone else's war. But…maybe you're right. Maybe it should have been your choice."

Reaching into the worn canvas sack he had brought, Devon rummaged around until he found what he was looking for. He drew it out and unwrapped the silk cloth Kryssa had bound it in all those years ago. The light of the nearby lantern revealed a polished leather sheath and a hilt inlaid with gold wire.

"This was your father's," he said, offering it to Pela. "If you intend to fight, he would have wanted you to have the best."

CHAPTER 10

I kar stood at the railings of the *Red Seagull* and breathed in the fresh ocean breeze, savouring its coolness in the humid air. The prisoners were all locked in the hold, but with the sailors scuttering about the deck, the Knights were still forced to wear their suffocating helmets. Along with the heavy plate mail and the thick woollen padding beneath, it would make for a long journey.

The sun remained low on the horizon, but already he could feel the sweat beading his forehead. Cursing, Ikar checked if anyone was watching, but the crew were occupied and most of his fellow Knights still slept. Quickly, he ducked into the shadows alongside the captain's cabin and removed his helmet. He wiped his face with a cloth from his belt, before replacing it on his head.

"Uncomfortable, Ikar?"

Ikar spun around at Merak's voice. The Elder leaned against the railing where just moments before Ikar had stood. With the prisoners secure, Merak had removed the rest of his armour and now wore the swathing red robes of the Elders. At first glance the man seemed relaxed, but as Ikar approached, he glimpsed a hint of irritation in the man's eye.

"It is nothing," Ikar replied, thinking of the Elder's return in Skystead. The ship had been preparing to depart when Merak had come galloping into the port and leapt aboard. The fear in the Elder's eyes had been palpable, but Ikar was tactful enough not to mention it. "I persevere in the name of our saviour."

Merak smiled grimly. "As do we all." His sapphire eyes flickered in Ikar's direction. "Tell me, Knight, would you give your life for our cause?"

"Of course," Ikar answered without hesitation, before adding, "as my brothers in Skystead did before me."

He watched the Elder for his reaction. Merak claimed his party had been set upon by a mob in the town square. His fellow Knights had been slaughtered and the blasphemers freed, the Elder himself barely escaping with his life.

Yet when Ikar had volunteered to lead the rest of their company back into Skystead, Merak had refused, instead ordering the *Red Seagull* to set sail.

The memory burned at Ikar. It shamed him that they had fled, allowing their brothers to go unavenged. Worse, they had given the followers of the False Gods a victory. It would make the blasphemers bold. Skystead must be purged, its infection scourged before it could spread to other settlements, lest all the Order's work come to naught.

"Ay," Merak smirked. "Perhaps one day Alana will call on you to make that sacrifice."

Ikar bowed his head. "I can only pray."

"For now though, our preparations must continue, despite the loss of our brothers. Thirty years have passed since Alana made her sacrifice, and the solstice approaches.

The power of the False Gods grows stronger with each passing day; candidates to renew her sacrifice must be found."

The Elder's words sent an icy fear racing through Ikar, raising the hackles on his neck. The False Gods could not be allowed to return. His people had fought too hard to free themselves from the yolk of magic, to be returned to the shackles of the past.

"What do you require of me?" he asked.

"Take the blasphemers their supper," Merak replied. He gestured at a pair of pails. "The ship's cook prepared them some food. Speak with them, discover if any might be worthy of our needs."

Ikar's shoulders fell at the menial nature of the assignment, but nodding, he turned his back on the Elder and retrieved the pails. Within, a murky liquid resemblant of stagnant water slopped back and forth and split over the edge of one bucket. He cursed as the muck stained his leggings. Thinking he heard laughter, he glanced back at Merak, but the Elder had already moved on to other tasks.

Muttering under his breath, Ikar staggered to the ladder leading into the hold. The stench of vomit and rotting fish swamped him as he carried the first bucket down, and it was a relief when he returned above-deck for the second. Cursing Merak, he gulped down several mouthfuls of fresh air before stumbling down the ladder a second time.

The prisoners had been relegated to a section in the bow, where the rocking of the ship was worst. It was a pitiful act of retribution for their fallen brothers, though Ikar had to admit it was effective. He doubted many of their prisoners would be interested in the food he'd brought. Placing the buckets on the shifting boards, he folded his arms and waited for them to take notice.

"What do you want, Knight?"

Ikar scowled as the woman who had defied him on the mountainside rose to her feet. She seemed to be one of the few who had not succumbed to seasickness, though her face was pale and he guessed she was not far from joining the others. The boy she had helped earlier crouched at her feet, but she stepped forward, as though to separate her fate from his.

"To feed you," Ikar snapped, sliding a bucket forward with the toe of his boot.

The woman fixed him with a glare. "Are we to eat like dogs then?" she asked, one eyebrow arched.

It took Ikar a moment to realise what she meant. With their hands still bound behind their backs, the prisoners wouldn't even be able to lift the buckets, never mind spoon the broth into their mouths. He was about to reach for his knife to cut them loose, when he caught the defiance in the woman's eyes. Scowling, he released the hilt of his knife.

"Do as you please, witch," he snapped. "If it were up to me, you would all have been cleansed with your fellows in the town square."

The woman paled. "I have a name," she said. "As did those your Elder took."

Ikar's retort died on his lips as he heard the woman's sorrow. He hesitated, his anger quenched as though plunged into ice water. Swallowing, he stepped towards her and placed a hand on her shoulder.

"I am sorry," he said, though he could not have said why, "I should not have spoken so harshly. What is your name?"

"Kryssa," the woman murmured.

"Fear not, Kryssa, you shall all have the chance to repent before the end," Ikar reassured her.

Her eyes flashed silver as she looked up at him. "Repent?" she asked. "And for what do any of us have to repent?"

A long sigh whispered between Ikar's lips and he took a step back. "You were caught worshipping in a temple of the False Gods, committing blasphemy against the apostle Alana."

"Do our beliefs threaten you so much, oh Knight?"

"Your Gods would threaten us all!" Ikar snapped.

"And yet we lived peacefully beneath their rule for centuries," Kryssa replied.

"Peace?" Ikar asked, disbelieving. "Were you not taught of the scourge of Archon? Or the devastation wrought by the Tsar? Or the countless other atrocities committed by their Magickers, down through the centuries?"

"The Gods gave us power, and the free will to use it," the woman replied. "It is not upon them what we chose to do with it. And what of the good that was done? The Magickers who healed the sick? And those who stood against the dark? Do they count for naught?"

"We never had free will, only servitude," he retorted. "Against the forces of magic, what power did we mortals have? What hope, when a single Magicker could slay hundreds? No, the only freedom your Gods offered was for the powerful, to those they deemed worthy of their gift. The rest of us were doomed, enslaved by their power."

"Us?" the woman asked. "You speak as though you were there—yet you sound no older than me, sir Knight. How do you know what the Gods desired?"

"It is there for any with open eyes to see."

"Ay, the truth is there," Kryssa whispered. "Who is it that enslaves us now? Who has hunted us down, who seeks to take our freedom from us?"

"Your beliefs endanger us all!"

"How?" Kryssa asked, her eyes aglow in the darkness.

Ikar swallowed. "You would restore the Gods to life." Somehow, his words suddenly seemed hollow, as though he were a fool to speak them.

Kryssa laughed, the sound harsh and mocking. "The Gods are dead, you fool," she replied. "We all know that, and do not seek to change it, however much some might wish it. We go to Temple in honour of their memory. And to meditate, to find our own harmony, and seek the true paths for our lives."

"Lies," Ikar whispered, backing away from the woman.

Her eyes followed him, accusing. "Look around, oh Knight," she replied, gesturing behind her. Huddled on the ground, the other prisoners watched him, terror written across their faces. "Where is the danger here? The threat? Do you not see? We are just a scapegoat, a false evil for your Order to strike down."

"Stop!" Ikar roared. Steel hissed on leather as he drew his sword and pointed it at her. "No more of your falsehoods, witch!"

Kryssa's face wilted at the sight of the blade. Shaking her head, she took a step back, a pall of fear coming over her. Ikar scowled and stepped after her, unsure whether the change was an act. Her mouth opened, but he darted forward, resting the tip of his blade against her breast.

"Not another word from you."

She nodded, the fear no act now. A sense of power surged through Ikar then. Savouring in her acquiescence, he looked around, ensuring the others saw his strength, knew the Knights of Alana were not to be defied.

"You are all worse than the sorriest wretch," he said vehemently. "Less than the lowest beggar on the streets of

Lon. You asked if you are animals to us, woman? I say you are worse! Vermin who would drown us all in your filth."

As he spoke, he kicked at her legs. Kryssa cried out as his heavy boot connected with her shins, and crumpled to her knees. With one foot, he pushed the bucket of slop closer. She looked up at him with horror written across her face.

"Please," she whispered.

"Eat," he growled. When she did not move, he drove his boot down into the woman's back, forcing her head down into the bucket. She cried out, but her shrieks were cut off by gurgling. Ikar's eyes swept the other prisoners, so that when he spoke, they knew his words were for all of them, "Like the vermin you are."

CHAPTER 11

Caledan was already awake when the first hints of sunlight touched the horizon. The gentle rocking of the ship had kept his stomach roiling all night, and no amount of practice with his blade had helped to settle it. Whatever food he'd eaten before embarking on the *Seadragon* was long gone, and he was beginning to wonder if joining Devon had been the right choice.

"Of course it is," he muttered to himself, though the words meant little for his nausea. Only the fact his stomach was empty kept him from vomiting again.

"What is?"

He jumped as Devon appeared at the railing beside him. For such a big man, he moved with an unnatural quiet, even on the tiny ship. The rest of the crew were just beginning to stir, and Caledan let out a long sigh at the thought of spending another day trapped with the foolish villagers.

"Nothing," he murmured.

The hammerman leaned his arms against the railing and fixed his amber eyes on the distant coast. Overnight, the shoreline had changed. They had left behind the towering cliffs and peaks of Golden Ridge, and now the land had given way to marshland, its myriad of twisting streams and dense mangroves all but impassable by foot. The tide was out, exposing close to a mile of mudflats upon which great crocodiles basked.

Caledan's gaze drifted from the mud to the waters around the ship, as he considered what might happen should they capsize. The crocodiles were larger than any man, with massive jaws lined with dagger-like teeth. He had seen a man caught by the arm once. The witless fool had been dragged into the water before he could do anything more than scream. Caledan and the other bystanders could do nothing but watch as the man was torn apart.

A great splash drew his eyes back to the shore, where a trail of mud now led into the ocean. There was no sign of the croc though, and shuddering, Caledan turned his attention back to Devon.

"I was only wondering, what is our plan once we arrive in Townirwin?"

The big man shrugged. "Find wherever the Knights are keeping our people, and take them back." Devon grinned. "Kill whoever gets in my way."

"Sounds promising, if a little light on the details," Caledan commented.

Devon chuckled. "I never was one for planning," he replied. "Although…at this time of year, the tax collectors should be making their rounds. Bound to be a few of the King's Guard in town for their protection. I'll see if we can't enlist them to our noble cause."

"When was the last time you visited Townirwin?"

"Five…no, it must be closer to ten years now. How the years fly." Devon sighed, running a hand through his thinning hair. "There will be those in the Guard that remember me, though."

"Of that I have no doubt," Caledan replied, then hesitated. Much had changed since the war with Lonia had ended. "However, you may…find the people of Townirwin less than receptive to your cause."

"Oh?" Devon asked, raising an eyebrow.

"The Knights of Alana are well-liked there. It would be foolish to denounce them, without proof of their crime."

"What more proof could we need than catching them red-handed with our people?" Devon snapped, his brow hardening.

Caledan held up his hands. "Easy, man. I only meant we would be wise to keep our heads low, until your daughter and the others are safe."

"She's not my daughter…" the old hammerman said, though his thoughts were obviously elsewhere. "At least… you might be right though. We cannot risk the Knights… disposing of the evidence before we can free our people." He glanced at Caledan. "But we can trust the King's Guard."

Trying not to roll his eyes, Caledan nodded. Devon was a fool if he believed he could trust anyone associated with Braidon. Though of course, the two had fought alongside each other, early in the civil war. Last night, lying awake in the darkness, Caledan had heard the story about Pela's father.

"Whatever you say," Caledan replied, keeping the doubt from his voice. He nodded at the hammer lying at Devon's feet. "Were you planning on finding a new weapon?"

Devon chuckled. Hefting the hammer, he turned it in his hands. Light shone from the corner that had been carved away by Merak's sword. "This will do, whatever its flaws. Truth be told, no weapon has ever been able to replace *kanker*, the warhammer I inherited from my ancestor."

"They say it was cursed?" Caledan asked, recalling the legends.

"Cursed? No, only spelled by a Magicker named Alastair. It protected me from magic, so long as I was holding it. Allowed me to stand against all manner of Magickers and demons. Now…"

"Now a man, and women, must stand behind their own strength," Caledan muttered. "The strong rule, and the weak make do with the scraps that we leave."

The lines in Devon's face deepened as he looked down at Caledan. "Ay, sonny," he replied sadly, "and we are all the lesser for it." Letting out a long breath, he looked out over the ocean. "So, what were you doing in Skystead in the first place? The town is no place for a sellsword."

"Perhaps it was fate that brought me there, to help with your cause."

Or to bring me closer to my goal, he thought silently, careful to keep the excitement from his face.

Devon chuckled. "I've seen Gods and demons and dragons, but I've never believed in fate, sonny. A man, or indeed a woman, forges their own path in this world."

"Then perhaps it was intuition," Caledan replied with a grin. There was at least truth in that. He had learned long ago to trust his instincts. They had rarely led him astray, though he'd had his doubts when he set foot in the backwaters of Skystead. "I was following a story. The captain who hired me claimed there were Baronians in these waters, that they possessed some new magic that allowed them to sail against the winds."

"And how did that turn out?"

"After three days of misery, I decided the story wasn't worth pursuing."

"Lucky for us, I guess," Devon grunted. He flicked a glance at Caledan, his eyes hardening. "Though your story seems a little too convenient. You'd best not cross me, sonny. It won't end well."

Unable to help himself, Caledan smirked at the hammerman. "You think you could take me, old man?"

Devon's face darkened and he straightened. Caledan's hand dropped to his sword hilt, but when he looked into the hammerman's amber eyes, the blood froze in his veins. In that instant, it seemed as though death itself stared back at him, and Caledan knew the old warrior would not hesitate. The second he tried to draw the blade, his life would end. It took an effort of will for Caledan to release his sword hilt.

"Good decision, sonny," Devon said, his voice barely rising above a whisper.

With that, he turned and wandered away. Caledan stood staring after him, the hairs on his neck still standing on end. Slowly the coils that had wrapped themselves around his stomach loosened, though the ice in his veins took longer to melt. Finally he let out a breath he had not realised he'd been holding.

"We'll see," he muttered to himself, trying and failing to draw strength from the words.

Out on the mudflats, one of the crocodiles slid down the bank into the ocean, without so much as a splash.

CHAPTER 12

Pela rolled her shoulders, trying to loosen the ache that had taken root in the muscles of her neck. For two days now, Caledan had pushed her and the others hard, drilling them in the basic attacks, stances, and parries of sword fighting. It was hard work, and the poorly-weighted blades they'd managed to scavenge from Skystead's decrepit dungeon made the work all the harder.

She hadn't touched the blade Devon had given her yet. She could hardly even bring herself to believe it had truly been her father's at all. All her life, she had grown up believing he'd been killed on the road by Baronians. To suddenly learn that had been a lie, that he had died defending their king from enemy soldiers…

Pain flared in her arm as Tobias's sword slipped beneath her guard and struck her wrist. Cursing, she leapt backwards out of range. The clumsy farmer tripped over his own legs chasing after her, and she struck back, her sheathed sword tapping him lightly on the side of the head.

"Enough!" Caledan shouted at them.

Breathing hard, Pela lowered her sword and spun around. Caledan sat on a barrel leaning against the mast, equal measures of anger and frustration writ across his face. Since accepting them as students, his expression had hardly changed, and Pela wondered whether he regretted taking her on. So far, neither herself nor anyone else had shown much sign of improvement, though at least Genevieve had started with some basic knowledge of how to wield a blade.

But Caledan was not a man to accept defeat. He would either turn them all into something resembling warriors, or toss them overboard to hide his failure. His hard attitude had turned them all against him, even the unfathomably cheerful Tobias, and if it came to it, they might be the ones to throw him overboard.

Not that it seemed to matter to Caledan. With a weapon in hand, the man was cold, bordering on cruel, and when they took turns sparring with him, he did not pull his blows. Wielding an old fire poker one-handed, he'd given Pela more than bruises when she'd been careless enough to lower her guard. None of them had even managed to touch him yet.

The heavy footsteps of her uncle approached from the bow where he had been napping all afternoon. Tomorrow they would finally reach Townirwin, but she could see the worry in his eyes, the fear that they would be too late. For herself, Pela had tried not to think about what would happen when they got there.

Rubbing his eyes, Devon yawned and gestured her to join him. She glanced at Caledan for permission, and the swordsman waved a hand, dismissing them for a break. Pela retrieved a jug of water and wandered over to Devon.

"I haven't seen you with your father's sword yet," he said without preamble.

Pela quickly looked away. "No…" She trailed off, her throat contracting. She glanced at her bag where she had stashed the blade. It remained out of sight, but she could sense it there, a presence in her mind. "I…what if I'm not worthy?"

"Worthy?" her uncle pressed.

Lowering her eyes, Pela fought back tears. "I'm no good, Uncle!" The words went from her in a rush. "I keep dropping my sword, tripping over my own feet, flinching when someone swings at me. How can I use my father's sword when I'm so *useless?*" She kicked the side of the ship to emphasise her last words.

To her surprise, Devon chuckled. Pela swung on him, shame giving way to anger. "What are you laughing at?" she snapped.

Devon smiled. "Do you think your father, or myself, were any different when we first began?"

Pela blinked. "I…what are you talking about? I'm *terrible!*"

"A man my size, you wouldn't believe the trouble I had keeping my feet under me in my first year as a recruit," Devon said. "I didn't know your father when he was younger, but I have no doubt he was the same. The warrior's arts require skill, and *practice*—you cannot become a master like Caledan overnight."

"Oh." Pela blinked, feeling suddenly foolish for her worries. She glanced at her pack again, and the sword within. "Still, though…I should wait, until I get better."

"Or you could use it now," Devon replied. "If you want to be a good swordswoman, you need a better blade than that thing you're currently calling a sword."

Pela sighed. "Fine." She strode across the deck, dragged the blade from her bag and carried it back to Devon.

"Why don't you draw it for me?" Devon asked.

There was the slightest of sheens to Devon's eyes when she looked at him. Pela remembered then that the last time this sword had gone to battle, her father had been carrying it, marching at Devon's side. Swallowing, she did as her uncle bid.

Light caught on the blade as it emerged, so that for a moment it seemed to be sheathed in flames. Then she turned it in her hand, and the fire died, and there was only the silver sword of her father. She sucked in a breath, struggling with a sudden wave of emotion.

My father.

He had carried this weapon into battle, had saved the *king* with it, had died with it in hand...

She didn't want you to die young, never knowing your family.

Pela lowered the blade quickly as Devon's warning came back to her. She let out a breath, the pride dying in her throat, replaced by a sudden terror. Was that to be her fate, now that she had embraced Derryn's legacy?

No, this is not my life. I only want my mother back.

But then she remembered Devon, back in the plaza, as he had carved through the Knights like death itself. She remembered the screams of the young men as they had fallen. They hadn't expected to die either—how could they? The villagers had removed their armour to bury them, revealing their youthful faces, barely older than herself.

A trembling began in her knees as she stared at the blade. What was she doing? Who did she think she was, holding the sword of a King's Guard, believing she could be a hero?

"How did you do it?" she asked suddenly, her voice several pitches above normal.

Devon frowned, one silver-streaked eyebrow lifting above the other. "Do what?"

"Win!" she gasped. "Defeat all those Knights! There were so many of them, but you won and they died or ran. How?"

Letting out a long sigh, Devon leaned one elbow against the railing. "You've been training with Caledan for three days now, little one. How do you think I did it?"

"How should I know?" Pela snapped.

"Think."

Pela tried to quell her racing heart. They were nearing Townirwin now, and still she knew nothing. How could she help her uncle, her mother, when she couldn't even beat the coffee farmer? It wasn't possible. But then, Devon had been able to do the impossible. Despite his age, despite being outnumbered, he'd crushed the Knights and caused their Elder to flee in…

"Fear?" Pela asked, the blood still pounding in her ears.

"Fear." Devon nodded in agreement. "It is a warrior's greatest weapon—and greatest weakness."

"What do you mean?"

"In small doses, it gives us caution, keeps us alive," Devon replied. "But when left unchecked…"

"Like that Elder…" Pela finished for him.

"Ay. He saw me kill two of his men in as many seconds. Never mind that they were taken by surprise—he panicked. His fear spread to the others, and they hesitated. If they had gone for the kill then, I could not have beaten them all. They might have won before Caledan intervened."

"But how did you know that would happen?" Pela pressed. "What if he'd sent all of them against you from the start?"

Devon shrugged. "Then I would be dead."

A cold hand gripped Pela's belly. "Then why were *you* not afraid?"

A sad smile touched Devon's lips. "I have lived for a long time, little one, far longer than I ever expected. Most of my friends are waiting for me on the other side. What do I have to fear from death?"

Pela shivered, but before she could respond, a call came from Caledan.

"Back to it!"

Swallowing, Pela looked from her uncle to the swordsman. Devon's explanation had done little to quell her own concerns. He might not fear death, but she did, and she had little doubt it would find her if she continued down this path. Even so, she nodded her thanks and returned to stand beside Tobias and Genevieve.

"A new sword, Pela?" Caledan commented, nodding to the blade in her hand.

Pela blinked. She'd forgotten she still carried her father's blade. After a moment she nodded, and Caledan smiled grimly.

"Very well then," he said. "Let's see whether it helps, shall we?"

He gestured her forward. After a moment's hesitation, Pela nodded and looked around for the scabbard to sheath the blade while they fought.

"Leave it," Caledan ordered. "Ready?"

Pela lifted her father's sword and nodded, sliding one foot behind her in an attempt at a fighting stance. Caledan strode forward, eyes hard, and hefted his iron poker.

"Defend yourse—"

"Sails to starboard!" a voice called down, interrupting Caledan before he could launch his first attack.

Pela had bunched herself up in preparation to spring,

and almost tripped over her own legs trying to spin around in search of the new ship. She had assumed her mother's captors would have already made port, but what if they had been delayed?

Squinting at the horizon, she couldn't see any sign of another ship. She tried to recall which direction was starboard, but wherever she looked there was nothing but empty ocean. The ship, if it existed, hadn't come into view for the rest of them yet, only for the man in the rigging.

"There's nothing out there," Caledan murmured, moving to the right-hand railing of the ship. "Who would be mad enough to sail out of sight of land?"

"No one with good intentions on their mind," the captain replied. He rushed past the villagers and grabbed the tiller. "Hope your people are ready for a fight, Devon!"

"Fight?" Tobias asked, the colour fleeing his face.

Pela's heart started to race as a black dot appeared on the horizon. Beside her, Caledan cursed, then glanced at the sails.

"The breeze is coming from the north," he muttered. "They'll never catch us sailing from the south."

"It's flying a black flag!" the man in the crow's nest called down.

"You'd better pray to whatever Gods you worship you're right," Tallow replied, before turning to his men. "Sails at full tilt, lads! Let's outrun those Baronian bastards!"

CHAPTER 13

Caledan watched in silence as the black dot grew larger. The Baronian ship had changed direction to cut off the *Seadragon's* escape and was no longer sailing directly against the wind, but it was still moving far too quickly for his liking. Already it had halved the distance between them.

So the captain was right, Caledan thought, and cursed out loud.

Tallow's shouts were becoming more desperate. As the gap between the two vessels narrowed, the Baronian crew came into view. Most stood waiting at the railings, swords and axes in hand and grins on their faces. Behind them, several crew members scurried around the deck, but it appeared there was little that needed doing. Only one of the ship's three masts had a sail up, and that hung loose in the wind, seeming to only be for show. Sunlight reflected from the other two empty masts, and Caledan realised with a start that they were made of steel.

His frown deepened as a puff of black smoke bellowed from the top of one of the masts.

They're not masts at all, he realised, *they're smokestacks.*

Though what they were for, he could not have guessed.

"What in the damn *hell?*" the captain muttered beside him.

Wood creaked as Devon appeared alongside them. "We're not going to escape them."

"Impossible," Tallow snapped, then shouted another string of orders to his men.

The *Seadragon* surged forward as another span was added to the sails, though Caledan could see by now it would not matter. Whatever magic the Baronians were working, they were faster, with or without the wind. Clad in their black-leather armour, their fighters packed the deck, waiting in grim silence for their prey to come within reach. They outnumbered Caledan and the others ten to one.

"Well, folks, I hope you've been paying attention to Caledan!" Devon bellowed, turning to address the villagers and Tallow's crew. "Ready those weapons, you're going to need them. Pela, to me."

The girl rushed forward, still gripping her father's blade. Caledan watched as Devon kneeled in front of her, wondering what he would do. Despite his best efforts, neither Pela nor the others were ready to go up against battle-hardened warriors like the Baronians. They would be cut down in moments.

Then again, against so many, Caledan doubted even he would last much longer. Studying the oncoming ship, he searched for another way to strike.

"Your mother wanted a better life for you than this," Devon was saying to Pela, his voice barely audible over the shouts of the sailors. "So did I, once upon a time. But such is fate. Are you ready to use that sword?"

There was open fear on the girl's face, but to her credit, she lifted her jaw and nodded.

"Good," Devon replied. "Your father would be proud to see you carry it."

Tears formed in the girl's eyes, quickly wiped away.

"You'd best stick close to us, girl," Caledan said, still watching the Baronian ship. "You're quick; use that. And remember, the Baronians are born killers."

"They're not all bad," Devon murmured. A grin crossed his bearded face. "I led one of their tribes once—albeit, only for a few weeks."

"Whoever was calling themselves Baronian back then, they're a different people now," Caledan snapped, irked by the old man's seemingly cheerful mood. "These ones will show you no mercy. If you see an opening, take it!"

Devon hefted his hammer. "Never said I wouldn't, sonny," he growled, and Caledan was reminded of their earlier disagreement. Then the hammerman turned back to his niece. "Caledan is right though, they're experienced warriors. Keep a tight hold of that sword, but stay back unless the fight comes to you. Caledan and I will lead the charge, see if we can't scare them off."

Pale-faced, Pela nodded and took her place alongside Genevieve and Tobias. The other sailors had retrieved long knives and were gathering around their captain. It seemed they'd given up trying to escape the oncoming ship.

Studying his companions, Caledan wondered whether they would hold. He'd been impressed with their resolve these last few days. He'd pressed them to breaking point, but they'd risen to every challenge he'd set, even timid Pela and nervous Tobias. He would not blame any one of them for fleeing at the first clash of battle, but he sensed they would stand strong.

Caledan loosened his sword in its scabbard, then transferred the poker he still carried to his left hand. He did not have a shield, and he would need every advantage he could get in the coming fight.

"Damnit, how is this possible?" the captain growled as he came to stand alongside them. A big man himself, he had armed himself with an axe. "They barely have any sail out."

"We can worry about that if we survive," Caledan snapped. "Are your men ready?"

Tallow answered with a string of vulgarities that would have made even the hardest veteran blush.

"If we keep on this heading, they're going to take us side-on," Devon observed.

"Did you have a better idea?" Tallow asked.

"Ram them," Devon replied.

"What?!" the captain exploded. "This is a *fishing* ship, we have no ram, we'd be torn apart."

Devon shrugged. "Do they know that?"

"You want to play chicken with the Baronians?"

"They want your ship and whatever goods we have on board. We're no good to them on the bottom of the ocean. They'll turn away. Trust me."

"Trust you?" Tallow asked with a scowl.

He stood staring at Devon, expecting an answer, but the big man just grinned. Letting out another string of curses, the captain gave in and leapt to the tiller. The ship turned slowly as he swung them away from the coast.

Caledan's stomach roiled, reminding him uncomfortably of his seasickness. It had improved over the last few days and he'd managed to eat a little, but he was still weaker than he would have liked.

"There's too many!" one of the sailors shouted.

"They've got to board us first!" Devon bellowed back. "So long as they're over there, we're safe. If they throw hooks, cut the ropes. If they jump aboard, kill 'em!"

Silence settled over the ship as they watched the gap narrow. The two vessels were rushing headlong at one another now. Running with the wind, the *Seadragon* had picked up speed. Overhead, the mast and rigging creaked and the sails went *crack*, and Caledan wondered for a moment whether they might tear themselves apart before they ever reached the Baronian ship.

The gap was hardly a hundred feet wide when the enemy ship swung violently to the left, its speed slowing abruptly. Onboard, the Baronians stumbled over one another, thrown off-balance by their sudden change in the direction. The *Seadragon* surged onwards. For a moment it looked as though they might sweep past into open sea, that the Baronians would be swamped. They were close to Townirwin now, if they kept going at this pace, they might reach port before…

Sunlight glinted on metal as a hook shot from the Baronian ship, a black line trailing out behind it. They must have fired it from a bow, for it flew far further than Caledan would have believed, clunking down onto the deck of the *Seadragon*. Before anyone could react, it snapped backwards, and the steel hook sank deep into the wood of the railings. The deck lurched beneath their feet as the line went taut, throwing half of them from their feet.

"Up!" Devon bellowed as the *Seadragon* pitched wildly. Overhead, the sails went slack as the line dragged them around so that they sat headlong into the wind. "At 'em!"

Caledan rushed to join the old man. On the other ship, the Baronians jeered as another line grabbed hold of the

Seadragon, dragging them closer. Caledan hacked at the first cord, but his blade sprang back, the line untouched. He stared at it in shock, realising the rope was made of steel. There would be no cutting themselves free.

Grimly, he turned to face the Baronians, sword and iron poker in hand. Only a few feet separated the two ships now, and roaring, a giant of a man sprang over the railings and leapt at them. His shoulder slammed into Devon, staggering him. An axe shone in the sunlight as the Baronian lifted it above his head.

Surging forwards, Caledan drove his blade low, catching the man unawares. The Baronian staggered as Caledan's sword pierced his chest, but as he fell, two more jumped to take his place. This time they came at Caledan, giving Devon a chance to recover.

Caledan caught the tip of a spear with his sword, then spun, reversing his blade and driving it into the stomach of his attacker. The man staggered back, and Caledan roared, his blade rising to block the second's sword—but he was already dead, his skull crushed by a blow from Devon's hammer.

Nodding his thanks, Devon bellowed a war cry and vaulted onto the railing of the *Seadragon*. A horde of Baronians awaited on the other ship, but most had not yet been able to cross to the wallowing fishing ship. Devon's laughter washed over them.

"Come on then, cowards!" he roared. "Come and get me!"

Angry screams answered his challenge as the Baronians surged forward, each desperate for a chance against the grey-haired warrior. Caledan joined Devon on the railing. A Baronian spear shot right by his shoulder. Caledan's blade flashed out and the Baronian on the opposite railing fell back into the crowd of black-garbed enemy.

An axe flew at Caledan's face, but he wrenched himself back. Balanced precariously on the edge, he felt the breath of the weapon sweep past, then straightened and skewered the wielder. Beside him, Devon's silver beard was drenched with sweat and his face seemed a shade paler, but his hammer still rose and fell with devastating power.

Aboard the Baronian vessel, three faced them now across the narrow gap. More could have come, boarding the *Seadragon* from other vantage points, but the enemy was focused now on destroying the old man who had dared to call them cowards.

Caledan readied himself to face his next foe, but the ship pitched wildly beneath him as a rogue wave struck. His arms windmilled as he struggled to keep upright, while alongside him Devon dropped to his knees and gripped the railing tight. On the other vessel, the Baronians weren't so quick, and two toppled forward into the sea. Their screams were silenced as the ships slammed back together.

Regaining his feet, Devon's hammer claimed the third. Before others could take their place, Devon leapt across the gap to the other ship. Caledan stared in shock, unable to believe the old hammerman had just boarded the Baronian vessel.

"Back!" Devon boomed, his voice ringing out over the black-garbed men.

The Baronians were as shocked as Caledan, for they obeyed, taking a collective step away from the madman and his hammer. It gave Devon the space he needed to speak.

"My name is Devon, great-grandson of Alan!" he roared. "Are you not Baronians, that you do not know me?"

Caledan gaped at the man. He'd thought Devon was

joking earlier. Had the man actually lived amongst the Baronians? He seemed to recall some obscure legend from around the time of the fall of the Tsar, but so much folk law and legend was attached to that time, one could never know truth from fiction.

Aboard the Baronian ship, the black-garbed warriors wavered.

Then a man at the front raised an axe and shouted. "To hell with history!" he shrieked. "We are Baronian, and we take what we want!"

A roar of agreement came from the others, and Caledan tensed, preparing to join the old man, but another voice rose to silence the enemy cheers.

"Hold!"

It was more of a croak than a bellow, but the speaker must have held great authority over the enemy, for every soul aboard the Baronian ship froze in their tracks. Movement came from the rear of their ship as a man appeared on the upper deck. Leaning on the railings, he squinted down at them.

"Is that truly you, Devon?" he called.

Devon stared back. "Ay, Julian, though I had not expected to find you in such company."

The old Baronian chuckled. "Times change. After your escape in Lon all those years ago, the blame eventually found its way back to me. The Tsar confiscated everything I ever owned."

"I'm surprised he didn't kill you," Devon retorted.

"In his mercy, he spared me. I *did* betray you to him, after all."

"Ay, you did," Devon rumbled. "Do you intend to finish the job this time?"

The Baronian named as Julian stared at them for a long

while. "No," he said finally. "I did you a great wrong, Devon. I have regretted that day for a long time. Let today be my penance."

He made a gesture with his hands, and the Baronians retreated, giving Caledan enough breathing room to appreciate their discipline. The black-garbed fighters were renowned for their ferocity, but this was something different.

"Thank you, Julian, though I forgave you a long time ago."

"Go in peace, Devon," Julian said, "though should we ever meet again, I cannot promise the same mercy."

"Fair enough." Devon started to turn away, then paused. "What are you doing all the way out here, anyway? I thought the Baronian hunting grounds were to the north"

Julian chuckled. "I might ask the same thing of you, old man."

"I'm looking for a friend. She was taken by the Knights of Alana."

"They're a day ahead of you," Julian replied. "We saw their ship, though they were too heavily armed for my people."

"So that's all you're up to, pirating the southern seas?"

A chuckle came from the old Baronian. "Don't press your luck, hammerman," he replied. "My purpose is my own. Now get off my ship and out of my waters, before I change my mind."

Devon nodded and returned to the *Seadragon*. Hammers were retrieved and the hooks torn from the railings. The Baronians wound them in with great wheels, then smoke erupted from the ships chimneys and they were powering away, leaving Caledan and the others standing aboard the *Seadragon* wondering what exactly had just happened.

CHAPTER 14

The wailing rose above the clanging of bells as Braidon followed the procession down the streets of Lon. Mourners filled every alleyway, spilling out into the broad avenue and hampering those at the front who carried the body of the Lonian King.

It seemed as though the whole country had come to farewell their fallen leader. And no wonder; for over a century, Lonia had been ruled by council. But upon the fall of the Empire and the death of the Gods, the Lonians had called for a new kind of leader. Elections had been held, and Ashoka had become king. He had quickly set about rebuilding the impoverished nation, endearing himself to the people.

That had been twenty-five years ago, when Braidon himself had just been coming into his own as King of Plorsea. Seeking to take advantage of Braidon's youth, Ashoka had marched on the southern nation, provoking a ten-year-long war that had left thousands on either side dead.

97

It had taken a marriage pact between Braidon and the young Lonian princess, Marianne, to bring an end to the conflict. She walked hand in hand with him now, and he gave her fingers a reassuring squeeze as they continued after her father's coffin. Her blue eyes shone with unspilt tears and the ocean breeze blowing up the street whipped her auburn hair about her face, but she smiled and nodded her thanks.

Plorsean soldiers marched to either side of them, King's Guard to his left, the Queen's Guard on her right, their ranks marked by gold or silver streaks on their scarlet cloaks. Catching the eye of his captain of the guard, Rylle, Braidon offered the slightest of nods. The Plorsean crown weighed heavily on his head, and Braidon was glad of the man's presence. While there was now uneasy peace between the two nations, an undercurrent of hate still tainted the relationship, leftover from the Tsar's tyranny.

Braidon might have helped end the Tsar's reign, but he was also the man's son, an unforgivable fact for many here. There would be those in the crowd who still wished for Braidon's death, despite his marriage to their beloved princess—or perhaps because of it.

The crowds, if anything, grew thicker as the procession left the cobbled streets and entered the port. The mourners wore all style of colours: red and white and blue and yellow, and a dozen others, creating a jumbled rainbow that covered the wooden docks as far as Braidon could see. They pressed forward, each desperate for a glimpse of the fallen king. A group of Knights, their Order more populous here than in Plorsea, spread out to form a barrier between the procession and the crowd.

Braidon felt a touch of admiration for his former rival. Though he had loathed Ashoka during the war, it was apparent his people had loved and respected him above all others. He was the man who had raised them up, lifting them from the darkness left by Braidon's father.

Though of course, there was only so much one man could do, even a king. Looking out over the crowd was a study in inequality. The royal family and their retainers were richly garbed in expensive silks and jewellery—even the king's body had been adorned with enough gold to feed a small town. Many of the onlookers, though, were lucky to have even thread-worn tunics to protect their fair skin from the harsh sun. More still sported sunken cheeks and withered limbs, as though food were a privilege they rarely enjoyed.

Such starvation was a strange sight in the capital of a farming nation, and Braidon wondered briefly where the food from their crops and livestock had gone. His eyes roamed, spotting child beggars amongst the crowd, some even clutching babies of their own. There were amputees as well, men and women with limbs cut short below the joint, their gaunt frames looking as though they lacked the muscle to even stand.

Yet the eyes of all were filled with tears, and as the procession reached the edge of the docks, a great silence fell over the crowd. Braidon returned his gaze to the body of Ashoka. The Lonian soldiers were carrying him aboard an old ship. Sunlight had warped the wooden boards of the deck and everything of worth had been stripped clean. Even the masts had been taken, cut short to be used for other designs.

The soldiers lowered the Lonian king onto a bed of thatch in the centre of the vessel, then retreated to the docks.

Braidon tightened his hand around Marianne's. "Are

you okay?" he whispered as the crowd began to sing, a mournful tune that was little better than the wailing of earlier.

Marianne nodded, a smile crossing her face. Two soldiers cut free the lines tying the ship in place, and with the soft creaking of timber, it drifted out into the harbour. No other vessel sailed the waters of Jurrien's Inlet today, and the king's ship encountered no obstacles. Soon it was a hundred yards offshore, and the eyes of the crowd turned to Marianne.

Releasing Braidon's hand, she stepped up to the edge of the docks. A longbow was pressed into her hands, its steel arms shining in the noonday sun. Despite the sombre atmosphere, Braidon's curiosity was piqued by the weapon. He edged sideways for a better view. His own men used bows of yew or oak, but the Lonian weapon had somehow been crafted entirely from steel.

An attendant passed an arrow to the queen and a burning brazier was already set in place. Braidon wondered how anyone could be expected to draw a bow of steel, let alone his wife. While she wore a slim rapier on her waist and had practiced archery as a child, she'd shown no interest in such activities since moving to Ardath. Petite as she was…

Marianne dipped the arrow into a brazier until it caught light, then nocked it to her bow. Her stance shifted slightly, turning side-on. Braidon thought he glimpsed a smirk on her lips as she glanced back at him. Then she drew smoothly, tiny wheels on the arms of the bow turning to assist the movement, and released.

A hush fell over the crowd as the arrow rose, arcing out over the waters of the harbour. Not a single man or woman breathed as they waited to see where it would fall. For a moment it seemed the wind might catch it and hurl it away…then gravity took hold and it fell smoothly to land amongst her father's pyre.

The wood caught with a great *whoosh*. Flames spread with unnatural speed across the wooden deck, as though some accelerant had been used, until the entire ship was ablaze. Thick black smoke spewed from the doomed vessel, filling the harbour. A gust of wind carried it over the crowd, making Braidon's eyes water and his throat burn.

He looked away, and several ships docked at the end of the wharf caught his attention. They were unmistakably war galleys. That in itself was of little interest, for the Lonian coastline was often plagued by pirating Baronians. But there was something different about the galleys. Each sported two large masts, but there were also several smaller masts at the stern and bow. Braidon realised with a start they were made of steel.

Braidon was tempted to take a closer look, but Marianne reappeared beside him before he had a chance. He made a note to ask his emissaries to investigate later, and forced his attention back to his duties.

"You did well," he said, putting an arm around his wife's waist.

She raised an eyebrow at him. "Did you expect anything else?"

A smile crossed Braidon's lips at the fire in her eyes. "My love, you could conquer the world if you desired it."

With that, he turned his gaze back to the harbour. Sadness touched his heart as he watched his rival burn. Ashoka had been a bitter enemy, but he had been a known quality. Who would the Lonians raise as their next king?

Marianne might have taken the title once, but she was Plorsean now, and would never be accepted.

Whoever it was, Braidon prayed they would honour the pact between the two nations.

CHAPTER 15

D evon groaned as the sharp light of day dragged him
from his sleep. There was a pounding in his temples
and an ache in his spine that reminded him of the months
he'd spent on the march as a youth. Only now, he was
suffering from what amounted to little more than a
skirmish.

He hadn't felt it in the heat of the moment. Facing the
Baronians with hammer in hand, it had been as though the
clock had been wound back, as though he were a young
man again, able to overcome whatever his enemies hurled
at him.

It hadn't taken long for that sensation to fade. Even
amidst the rush of battle, he had noticed the dulling of his
reactions, the diminishing of his strength. If not for
Caledan, he might have been killed in the first seconds,
when the charging Baronian had knocked him from his feet.

No, you are Devon. You would have beaten him.

He shivered. Those were the words of a younger man,
one convinced of his own immortality. Devon no longer had

any such disillusions. Whatever Pela and the villagers and even the Baronians might think of him, he was just a man—an old man, at that. And today he was paying for his defiance.

At least he'd had a proper bed in which to sleep. They'd reached Townirwin before sunset and Devon had settled them all in an inn for the night. He'd slipped a few extra shillings to the innkeeper to keep their presence quiet. There was no point forewarning the Knights of their presence.

The clashing of steel came from outside. Devon rose from his bed and crossed to the window. Down in the courtyard, Pela was already up and running through a drill with Caledan. Their swords rang with each blow as they worked their way back and forwards across the smooth tiles.

Devon sighed, saddened by the sight. Once, he'd held hopes the world might move on from such pursuits, that a new generation might grow up in a world without war. For a while it had seemed his dream might come true, after the fall of the Tsar and the liberation of the Three Nations. Then Lonia had marched south, forcing Plorsean farmers from their lands, and the wars had begun again.

An awful fatigue touched him in a moment of premonition. The world had come full circle. All his long life he'd been a warrior, fighting to keep the darkness in check. But it had all been for naught. Evil had returned to the land, and now his niece would pick up the sword and continue the charade.

The thought left a bitter taste on Devon's tongue, and silently he cursed the king he had served so faithfully. He had trusted Braidon to bring peace to the land; instead, his friend had allowed the Knights of Alana to spread like a disease, infecting Plorsea with their hatred.

He let out a heavy sigh, then threw off his melancholy and dressed himself. Heading downstairs to the tavern, he was greeted by the sweet aroma of honeyed oats and roasting coffee. He smiled. At least the seaside port was near enough to Skystead to stock the bitter drink; it was rare elsewhere. The plant preferred high altitudes and did not fare well in the harsh winters further north. Only the plateaus above Skystead were suitable for the coffee plantations. Devon had disliked its taste when he first arrived in the small town, but he had become accustomed to it through the years.

After ordering himself a mug and a bowl of oats, he sat down for his meal. It wasn't long before Pela and Caledan joined him. The double doors to the courtyard squealed as they pushed their way inside—Pela still red-faced and puffing, Caledan with just a hint of perspiration on his forehead. There was no sign yet of Tobias or Genevieve, while Tallow and his crew had opted to sleep on the *Seadragon*.

Devon waved to the innkeeper for a round of food as they sat down opposite him. Pela grinned when a mug of coffee was placed before her, but Caledan wrinkled his nose.

"How can you drink that mud-water?" he asked.

Devon chuckled. "It grows on you."

Caledan snorted. There was silence as they broke their fast, before the swordsman leaned back in his chair and raised his eyebrows at Devon.

"So, what's the plan?" he asked. "Ready to storm the Castle?"

"Not quite," Devon replied, keeping the irritation from his voice. The swordsman's confidence irked him, and while the aching in his bones had settled slightly, he was in no mood for jokes.

"Oh yes, you wanted to speak with the King's Guard

first," Caledan replied, eyeing him across the table. "I'm still not sure that's such a great idea."

"We'll find out soon enough," Devon retorted. "I'm heading to the barracks after we finish up here."

Caledan sighed. "Very well. In that case, I'll make some inquiries around town. If we're going to go up against the Knights, we'd better at least be sure the prisoners are in the Castle."

"Thank you," Devon said with genuine gratitude. He had never been a subtle man and if he started asking questions in Townirwin, it wouldn't take long for word to get back to the Knights. "And thank you for your aid on the *Seadragon*," he added as an afterthought.

A smile crossed the sellsword's face. "A good thing you didn't die, or the lot of us would have ended up as croc food. Don't think the old Baronian would have spared us over your dead body."

Devon's melancholy deepened. "He was a good man once," he murmured. "A coward, but then who could blame him, the way the Tsar waged his wars?"

"He betrayed you, man," Caledan replied. "If he'd done the same to me, I'd have gutted the pig."

"And then yesterday you would have died," Devon commented, drawing himself to his feet. "Better to forgive, if you want the opinion of an old man. Dead men can't help you."

"They also can't stick a sword through your back," Caledan snapped, his eyes flashing.

Devon waved a hand. "I'll see you later," he said, then turned to Pela. "You coming, missy?"

Pela jumped, looking around in confusion before realising he was talking to her. Nodding, she quickly spooned down the last of her gruel, gulped a mouthful of coffee, and raced out the door after him.

"Where did you say we were going?" she gasped as they started through the muddy streets.

Devon smiled. "The guard barracks. The King's Guards occupy a dorm there—during tax collection, at least."

As far as he knew, Pela had only been to Townirwin once, and then she'd been little more than a child. Swampy backwater as it was, the town was four times the size of Skystead and all the more exciting for it. It was well past sunup now and the streets were already crowded. Wagons rumbled up the main avenue from the port, winding their way over the narrow bridges that spanned the multitude of canals upon which the settlement had been built. Townirwin was the only port on the western coast of Plorsea that connected with the Gods Road, and most would be bringing their goods farther inland.

The town grew busier as they left the main avenue and continued through a network of unsavoury canals and narrow alleyways. Unlike in Skystead, there was no dedicated marketplace here, and merchant stalls appeared at regular intervals through the settlement, the sellers shouting their wares at the tops of their lungs. Pela spent the entire journey looking around with wide eyes, an equal measure of amazement and fear written across her face.

"Relax, missy," Devon rumbled, "we're almost there."

Pela shook herself. "What was it like, fighting for the King's Guard?"

Devon smiled. "Tough. Long days on the march, longer nights without sleep. Especially during the war with Lonia."

"Then why did you keep going back?"

His smile faltered. "I…" He sighed, glancing at his

niece. "It was all that and worse, but...there is nothing so thrilling as marching to battle."

"You fight because you enjoy it?" Pela twisted her lips, and Devon knew what she was thinking.

"Yes, and no," he sighed. "It is difficult to explain. It was always awful, in the moment. But afterwards, when I returned home and resumed real life...You miss the excitement, miss the comradery. When at war, you know you're alive, that every moment must be cherished. Later..." He shrugged. "Later...everything else seems ordinary."

"I'm not sure I understand," his niece replied, frown still in place.

Devon thumped her on the shoulder and laughed. "I hope you never do."

"What about my father, was it the same for him?"

A smile touched Devon's lips. "Derryn was a good man and a canny fighter. But he wasn't like the rest of us. A King's Guard is usually ice or fire—cold-blooded killers or berserkers that nothing but death will stop. Derryn though, he was like water, cool in the heat of battle, yet razor quick as well, adaptable. And no, he never enjoyed it. He was there because his king needed him, and afterwards, when he retired, he had no desire to return..." Devon trailed off at that, words abandoning him.

"But he went back anyway."

"Ay," Devon croaked. "If ever there was a time I should have spurned the call, it was that day."

"But you didn't," Pela murmured.

"No, and that decision will haunt me to my dying day."

He drew to a stop in front of an old stone building. They were beyond the canals now and the air was fresher, the stench of stagnant water behind them. Solid and nondescript, the only sign the building was anything different from its neighbours was the king's emblem carved into the stone above the door. Townirwin was hardly large enough to require a full contingent of guards, but its position between the Gods Road and the coast afforded the settlement certain privileges.

It had not always been so—a century ago, the lower reaches of the Lane River had been deep enough to allow ships passage. But over the decades, sand bars had formed throughout the delta, making the way impassable to all but the most experienced captains. Most now made port in Townirwin and sent their goods overland the rest of the way, to Ardath and beyond.

The change had enriched Townirwin fortunes, and Devon wondered if that was what had brought his old friend so far south. Could the Baronians be planning a raid on the town?

"This is it?" Pela asked.

Devon shook himself, drawing himself back to the present. "This is it," he confirmed, and thumped a massive fist against the heavy wooden door.

A few minutes passed before a *clang* came from inside the building. With a squeal of hinges, it opened towards them, forcing them back a step. Beyond, a man in the gold and scarlet tunic and polished chainmail of the King's Guard stood watching them. His eyebrows lifted in surprise as he looked them up and down.

"Well met, Aldyn," Devon rumbled, a grin splitting his bearded cheeks.

"Devon?" the Guard said, blinking. "What in the Three Nations are you doing here?"

CHAPTER 16

"So this is the daughter of Derryn and Kryssa?" asked Aldyn as they sat in the courtyard of the barracks. "She must be quite the prodigy with a sword!"

Pela's cheeks grew hot and lowering her eyes, she fiddled with the hilt of her father's sword. Anger and embarrassment warred within her, but she said nothing. How had she not have known about her father? How could her mother have kept it from her? It was galling to hear such admiration in a stranger's voice, and know next to nothing about how her father had earned it.

And worse still to know she had none of his talent.

"Her name is Pela," Devon answered for her, "and Kryssa chose not to teach her the warrior's arts."

"You can't be serious?" Aldryn cried. Pela's uncle shot him a dark look, and he quickly masked his shock. "A wise choice." He nodded solemnly, then blinked. "Err, then… why is she wearing Derryn's sword?"

Devon sighed. "My fault, though it couldn't be helped. Kryssa's been taken. We're here to get her back."

"What?!" Aldyn leapt to his feet and spun around, as though her mother's kidnappers might be hiding somewhere in the courtyard. "By who?"

"The Knights of Alana," Devon rumbled. "They came to Skystead and attacked the old temple, took everyone they found there. One of their Elders, Merak I think his name was, took five of their captives to the town square where he planned to execute them. I stopped him. But the rest were brought here, including Kryssa. I don't know why."

"Oh." While Devon spoke, Aldyn had sunk back into his chair. There was now a wan look to his face. "That's...bad."

"Agreed," Devon grunted, then paused, eyeing his former comrade. "Though I sense you know more about this than we do."

Aldyn shook his head. "You've been away in that backwater awhile, haven't you?"

Pela would have bristled at the casual way he dismissed Skystead as a backwater...if it hadn't been true. As it was, the man's tone sent a chill down her spine.

"The war almost bankrupted Plorsea," Aldyn was saying. "Braidon had to raise taxes just to keep the Gods Roads in order, but even that wasn't enough to keep every town and village properly armed against thieves and the resurgent Baronian tribes."

"You mean there aren't enough guards here to protect the town?" Devon asked.

"Not exactly..." Aldyn murmured. "The queen had an idea, a few years back. She believes in the Saviour, you see, like many Lonians. Goes to Castle every week. And she saw all these armed Knights, this force that wasn't being used. She suggested they could take some of the responsibilities from the city guards..."

"*What?*" Pela shrieked, leaping to her feet.

Aldyn held up his hands in entreaty. "Myself and many others argued against it, but Townirwin was one of the first places they were trialled. We've had a lot of trade with Lonia over the years, so the people here were already more comfortable with the Order and their Knights. And for all appearances, they've done a good job, kept the peace, so to speak."

"They murdered our baker!" Taking a step closer to the King's Guard, Pela pointed a trembling finger at his chest. "They kidnapped my mother!" She slumped back to her chair, suddenly lost, the hope slipping from her in a rush.

"How could Braidon let this happen?" Devon groaned.

"Like I said, Devon, you've been gone a long time. But you were there when magic died. You know how it was, the hopelessness, the fear. People have been looking for something to believe in for a long time. If it hadn't been for the civil war, the Order might have appeared here sooner. As it is, their talk of free will and power for all, it's proven popular."

"I refuse to believe cold-blooded murder has become popular with our people," Devon snapped. He rose and began to pace.

"There have been rumours of a more sinister faction within the Order. There are some who believe Alana's 'sacrifice' must be repeated every year—"

"*Nonsense!*" Devon bellowed. "I was there. Alana died because…"

Fists clenched, he trailed off, and Pela remembered that other rumour about her uncle. What had Caledan called him, back in Skystead? *The Consort of Alana…*

"Regardless, they're only rumours. Nothing ever came of them."

"Until now!" Pela interrupted.

"Until now," Aldyn agreed, though there was a hesitant note to his voice.

"What?" Devon growled.

"We'll need proof," the King's Guard replied. "If you want the king to believe…"

"Surely Braidon must see the truth about these Knights."

"Braidon does not see half as much as he should," Aldyn replied.

"Then we'll bring him his evidence," Pela growled, enraged that the king who professed to protect them would ignore such evil amongst his people.

"Ay," Devon agreed. "Let's search their damned Castle and find the prisoners. They might control the streets, but surely they don't have the authority to refuse the King's Guard."

"They don't," Aldyn replied, "only…"

Devon gave the man a despairing look, as though to say "what now?" while Pela's heart sank.

"Yesterday a Raptor sighting was reported on the Gods Road. A group of Knights came calling for our help. It's… been a while since the men and women here saw any action. Most of our contingent went with them."

Raptors were a ferocious creature leftover from the time of Archon. They had been driven almost to extinction during the Tsar's reign, but with the death of magic, they had become…hazardous to hunt, let alone kill.

"*Dammit!*" Devon slammed his fist into the table. It creaked beneath the blow, and Pela scrambled back in case it collapsed. "When are they back?"

"A week, if they find its tracks. Sooner if it left no sign, but who knows?"

"That's too long," Pela whispered. "My mum…"

"No, we can't afford to wait," Devon agreed.

"How many Knights were in the group that took Kryssa?" Aldyn asked.

"Two dozen, minus a few we killed."

Aldyn swore bitterly. "Twenty Knights went with the King's Guard, but the Castle barracks have forty. We'd still be badly outnumbered."

Devon let off a string of profanity that made Pela blush. "How did Braidon let things come to this?"

"The treasury vaults are almost empty," Aldyn said, shrugging. "Even the King's Guard have missed our pay a few times. Maybe if the border opens with Trola one day, things will get better. Or maybe relations will improve with Lonia, now they're to have a new king. Either way, Braidon has larger concerns than a few religious zealots in the far south."

"Damnit, the girl's father once saved his life. He *cannot* let this continue. Can you get him a message to the capital?"

Aldyn sighed. "I could, but he's not even in the country. He went to Lon for Ashoka's funeral. You won't want to wait that long."

"No," Devon rumbled. "So we're going to rescue them tonight."

"That's more like the Devon I remember," Aldyn laughed, a grin crossing his face. "Mind if I join you? I wouldn't mind putting a few of those bastards back in their place!"

CHAPTER 17

E xhaustion weighed heavily on Ikar as he made his way
along the corridors of the Townirwin Castle. The *Red
Seagull* had arrived late at the docks, and they had unloaded
the prisoners under cover of darkness, ensuring there were
no witnesses. There was no need to add to the rumours
already swirling about the Order.

By the time the prisoners were secure, the night had
been old and Ikar had barely snatched a few hours sleep
before being called to the pantheon. Now he would have to
hurry if he was not to keep them waiting. At least now he
could forgo his armour in favour of a tunic and breeches—
only the devout were allowed within the Castle walls, so
there was no risk of an outsider learning his face.

The hallways narrowed as Ikar neared his destination,
an old design from darker days when the keep had been the
last bastion of safety for Townirwin.

But those times were long since passed. The fortifications had been a dilapidated ruin when the Knights of
Alana had taken possession. The first brothers to occupy the

Castle had reinforced the crumbling mortar and repaired much of the damage, but even after five years, it could not compare to the glorious citadels held by the Order in Lonia.

Turning the final corner, Ikar slowed as he approached the towering double doors leading to the inner chambers. Beyond the iron-studded wood, Merak and his counterparts awaited Ikar's report on the undertaking in Skystead. Ikar had not yet decided how much to say. He was still angered by Merak's refusal to avenge their fallen brothers, but it was a dangerous course to criticise an Elder.

The doors had been left unguarded—none in the Order would dare invade the inner sanctum without permission—and Ikar pressed a shoulder to the heavy oak, pushing them open. The hinges moved with barely a whisper and Ikar stepped inside.

Within was the pantheon—the holy centre of each Castle. Only the most loyal followers of the Order were allowed entrance here—Knights and parishioners who had spent at least five years with the Order. It was here the Elders conducted their cleansings, though Ikar had never witnessed one in the year since his arrival in Townirwin. It was said by many that the Plorseans would not accept such rituals. They would soon find out, for there could be only one fate for the foul blasphemers they had taken from Skystead.

To either side of Ikar, the pantheon opened out into a circular chamber, its high roof held up by thick arches of wood. In Lon, they would have been stone, but here in the south such material was scarce—it had cost a small fortune just to repair the crumbling walls. Thirty feet above, the arches converged in a dome, its cheap plaster concealed by a great painting of the genesis of their Order: Alana towering over the world, three shadows knelt at her feet, begging for their lives. The artist had captured the righteous fury in Alana's eyes as Ikar had always imagined it, and there could be no doubt what fate awaited the fallen Gods.

The whisper of voices drew Ikar's gaze down. Pews lined the pantheon, except where a fine woollen rug let up to a raised dais at the end of the chamber. The three Elders awaited him there, seated on three golden thrones that would have made the Plorsean King weep with jealousy.

Ikar's cheeks grew hot as he found their eyes on him and he quickly strode the length of the chamber and stopped before the dais.

Placing a fist to his chest, Ikar bowed. "Your Excellencies."

"Welcome, Ikar," Merak said, his voice echoing through the hall. "Thank you for joining us. We know your duties kept you late last night. We will not keep you long."

Ikar struggled to conceal a grimace. No sooner had they made port than Merak had bid them farewell, leaving Ikar and the other Knights to oversee the disembarking of the prisoners. No doubt the Elder had enjoyed a full night's sleep while the rest of them laboured.

"It is nothing, Your Excellency," Ikar said, keeping the irritation from his voice. "It was my honour to ensure the blasphemous were safely locked away."

"I'm sure," the second Elder, Servo, murmured. He wore dark blue robes and was the youngest of the three, barely thirty. It was said he had performed some great task on behalf of the Order as a young man, and been honoured in return, though none could say what it had been. His hazel eyes were soft as he looked down at Ikar. "Though no doubt sleep would also have been welcome after such a journey. Merak tells us you captured the peasants in the midst of worshiping the False Gods?"

"Ay, that is what it appeared, though…one claims they were simply meditating," Ikar replied, remembering Kryssa's words.

"They were in the temple of the False Gods?" Servo asked.

"Yes."

"Then the blasphemers lie!" the third and oldest Elder, Putar, bellowed. His hair and beard were long and greying, and his stomach strained against emerald robes as he rose from his throne. Halfway to his feet, he seemed to think better of it and sat once more. He continued in a calmer voice. "And afterwards, it was you who led the prisoners to the port?"

"Yes." Ikar's flicked in Merak's direction. "The esteemed Elder placed me in charge until his return."

"So you did not witness the events in the town square?" Servo asked, his voice low, eyes narrowed.

"No." Ikar bowed his head. "Though I wish I could have stood alongside my brothers."

"You would not have made a difference," Merak snapped, anger in his voice.

"Is that why *you* did not fight with your fellows, brother Merak?" Servo asked pointedly, a smirk on his lips.

Merak scowled. "There were too many. Had I not carried warning to the ship, they might have freed the prisoners. Then we would have had nothing to offer for the Great Sacrifice."

Ikar raised an eyebrow. His orders had been to depart should Merak not return. The ship had been about to depart when Merak had finally appeared—the Elder had not *saved* anything. But he kept his lips tight shut, unwilling to brave the Elder's wrath.

A dry, rasping laughter came from Putar. "You assume

any of your prisoners are worthy of such an honour, Merak," he said. "You stained our Order with your cowardice."

"Ha!" Merak snapped. "Easy to claim for one as old as you. When did you last go questing beyond the dining hall, Putar?"

"Enough, brothers," Servo interrupted as the two Elders started to their feet. "This is unseemly."

Tension hung in the air, before Merak and Putar both sank back into their thrones. Ikar swallowed, aware that disagreements between the Elders were rarely witnessed, and did his best to go unnoticed.

"My apologies, Ikar," Servo continued. "I trust you shall not repeat any of what you have seen here."

Ikar bowed his head. "Never."

"Ikar has shown great loyalty," Merak proclaimed. "Is that all you have to report from our journey?"

Catching the Elder's eyes on him, Ikar knew he'd been right to keep quiet earlier. "It is, Elders, and thank you for your praise," he said, then hesitated. "Though I would ask one favour of you?"

"What would you have of us, young Knight?" Putar asked, his eyes shining as he glanced at Merak.

"Grant me permission to gather my brothers and return to Skystead," Ikar said, looking each of them in the eye. "Allow me to avenge our fallen comrades."

The smile fell from Putar's lips. Merak's face darkened, while Servo only sighed. "Alas, we cannot act so openly. The king still will not condone violence against the blasphemers, though they threaten all our existence."

"They murdered our brothers!" Ikar exclaimed. "How can you let them go unpunished?"

"Patience, sir Knight," Servo replied. "Their penance

may be deferred, but their crimes are not forgotten. Justice will find them, sooner than you might think."

"How?" Ikar pressed, still angered by their dismissal.

"You forget yourself, Ikar," Servo admonished.

Ikar swallowed, aware he had pushed them further than was wise. "My apologies, Your Excellencies," he murmured. "I only wish to see justice."

"And you will, brother," Putar replied. "For now though, we must bide our time, and honour the king's wishes." The Elder's tone was bitter.

"Yes," Servo continued. "To that end, a cleansing must be held with all haste. While the blasphemers still breathe, their lifeforce feeds strength to the False Gods. We will take that strength for ourselves, before the king discovers their presence. Though we have time, I would act tonight, before Braidon returns from Ashoka's funeral in Lon."

"*What?*" Ikar gasped, his heart suddenly racing.

"You had not heard?" Servo frowned. "My apologies, Ikar. The Lonian king is dead."

"How?"

"His heart failed him. His shadow council rules until a new ruler can be elected, since his only daughter is no longer eligible."

Grief washed through Ikar. He and Asoka had been close, when Ikar had served as his guard. And his daughter…His anger flared as he recalled her marriage to the Plorsean king.

"Marianne would have made a great queen. There is no way to free her from the marriage pact?"

The Elders exchanged glances. "You ask ideas above your station, Ikar," Servo said finally. "Though we understand your grief for Ashoka, the leadership of Lonia is none of your concern—nor ours. Though it should be enough for you that Marianne's marriage has brought peace, and allowed our Order to expand into Plorsea."

"Very well," Ikar grated, struggling to keep his anger in check.

Even as a youth, Marianne had sat in on Ashoka's councils, and as a young woman had often spent afternoons debating with her father. Intelligent beyond her years and skilled with bow and rapier, she had been born to rule. It galled Ikar to hear her birth right could be stripped away so easily, all because her father had pawned her off to buy peace. It was the one decision Ashoka had made that Ikar could never understand.

"Now, we must continue preparations for the Great Sacrifice," Servo was saying. "Half our Order has already gone ahead to make our preparations. We must decide if any of these prisoners of yours are worthy. There must be three, strong of will and soul, to aid the Saviour in her eternal battle with the False Gods. Are there any you would deem suitable?"

Shaking his head, Ikar tore his mind from memories of Marianne and faced the Elders. Quickly he cast his thoughts over the prisoners. They had taken eighteen in total, though only a few were memorable. The rest were timid, unworthy creatures by any manner of definition.

Then Kryssa's face appeared in his mind, standing strong. Recalling the anger she had elicited from him, he felt a pang of shame. Rarely had he been so cruel, had he so misused his power. Something about her insolence had worn away his self-control. But even after, hair drenched and half-drowned, there had been a glint of defiance in the woman's eye. He swallowed, and looked up at the Elders.

"There is one…"

CHAPTER 18

The hammer weighed heavily on Devon's back as he stood in the shadows across from the gates of the Castle. It was nearing midnight, and overhead, dark clouds covered the moon and stars. The streets were pitch-black except where the occasional lantern cast back the darkness. The Castle itself stood in the centre of Townirwin, its stone walls rising from a raised mound of earth and encircled by a canal. Shadows flickered atop the ramparts—Knights completing their patrol.

The hoot of an owl sounded from overhead, but otherwise the night was still—until the faintest whisper of footsteps carried to Devon's ears. He tensed, lifting a hand to silence his companions, and peered out into the darkness.

A figure appeared on the street, walking with purpose towards the Castle. The light of a nearby lantern cast his shadow far across the cobbles, but the figure showed no sign he'd noticed Devon and the others. The shadows on the ramparts flickered, darting towards the tower atop the gates.

"Hoy!" a Knight called as the newcomer came to a stop before the gates. "Who goes there?"

"Open up!" the figure replied. A torch was held up atop the walls, revealing Aldyn standing beneath the gates. A scowl wrinkling his forehead, he called again, "I need to speak with the Elders!"

"They're busy! Come back in the morning, scoundrel." The Knight's irritation was obvious.

"I don't care if they're fast asleep!" Aldyn snapped. "I am a lieutenant of the King's Guard, and the Elders will see me, *now*, or the king will hear of it!"

Muttering came from atop the wall, but the gates remained closed.

Aldyn wasn't having any of it. "If you don't open these gates right now, I'll have you hung for insubordination, and to hell with your Elders!" he bellowed.

There was still a moment's hesitation, before the Knight disappeared from sight. Devon held his breath, praying the Knight had bought his friend's act. Then a great groan came from the timbers of the gate and they swung open.

"You stay there," the Knight started, but Aldyn darted forward before he could finish. The Knight's voice rose: "Hey, what are you doing!"

"*Go!*" Devon hissed.

A string of curses erupted from within the Castle walls as Devon raced out into the open. The patter of boots on stone came from behind him as Caledan, Pela and the others followed. They sprinted across the cobbled plaza to where the drawbridge and gates still stood open. At any second, Devon expected a shout to come from the walls, as some unseen Knight spotted their approach. But the only sound was the cursing coming from beyond the gates.

Devon held his breath as the walls loomed. If they were spotted, the Knights would have plenty of time to sound the alarm. With some twenty Knights inside, plus whatever followers had attached themselves to the Order, Devon and the others would quickly be overwhelmed if they were discovered. The rescue attempt would be over before it started.

"Hey what—?" a man was shouting as Devon slipped through the open gates.

Glimpsing Aldyn standing nearby with sword in hand, Devon started towards him, before he noticed the blood on his friend's blade. He slowed, then saw the bodies of the two Knights slumped on the cobbles at Aldyn's feet.

"Quick," the King's Guard whispered, sheathing his sword, "help me with them!"

Devon swore and laid his hammer against the wall and grabbed the feet of the nearest Knight. Together with Aldyn, they dragged him into the garden that ran the length of the small courtyard. Tossing him behind the bushes, they returned for the second.

Only then did Devon take the time to examine their surroundings.

They were in a circular courtyard situated directly between the gates and the castle keep. Solid stone surrounded them, but for the oaken double doors that led into the keep. The gardens in which they'd dumped the bodies lined the walls, twisted trees and vines climbing upwards to the guard tower above the gates.

Aldyn crept to the doors of the keep and pushed them open. Light spilled from within, illuminating the six of them in the courtyard. Devon took a moment to check on his companions. Caledan was his usual composed self, as was Aldyn. Tobias's eyes darted around in his face and he looked like he might bolt at any moment, though so far, he had remained resolute. Genevieve caught his eye and flashed him a quick grin.

Turning his gaze on his niece, Devon wondered whether or not he should ask her to guard the gates. After all, they would need a way out, if they succeeded in rescuing the prisoners. Pela's face was pale and her eyes stared straight ahead, no doubt lost in some terrified imagining of what was to come. She shouldn't be here, wasn't ready for something like this. And yet…he knew she wouldn't listen if he told her to hide.

"The place looks pretty awake for this late at night," Caledan was saying.

Devon shook himself free of his reservations and nodded. A dozen lanterns were burning within the entrance hall and he could hear the distant humming of voices. What were the Knights up to?

"Many of their rituals take place at night," Aldyn murmured.

"That would have been useful to know earlier," Devon muttered, raising an eyebrow, but Aldyn only shrugged.

"It didn't cross my mind until now. It's not like you would have waited," he replied.

"We'd best get moving then, before someone notices the missing men," Devon snapped.

"Where will they be keeping my mum and the others?" Pela asked.

There was a tremor in her voice, but when Devon glanced at her, she met his gaze and gave the slightest of nods. Devon's heart swelled. Her father would have been proud, though he'd never wanted this life for his daughter. Her mother, though…

He shook himself free of the thought. Kryssa could

curse him to the end of her days for endangering her daughter...so long as she lived.

"Close to the pantheon," Aldyn answered. "I've been inside a few times. The cells are there."

"Lead the way, Aldyn," Devon said.

They fell in behind the King's Guard. Devon brought up the rear, swinging the doors closed behind them. They had an hour before the next change of watch—Aldyn knew their schedules well—but that did not guarantee they would remain undiscovered.

"The Knights like to throw banquets for us common soldiers sometimes," Aldyn was saying. "They even make allowances for us to see them without their helmets." He chuckled. "I suppose it would be difficult for them to eat otherwise."

Devon nodded but said nothing, concentrating on the way ahead. The corridor was lit by lanterns and after the dark outside, the brightness hurt his eyes. Fortunately, the hallways remained empty, though voices still drifted on the air. They moved quickly, aware that a group of armed men and women could not go undetected for long, while Aldyn continued his story.

"I think the banquets were thrown to recruit new Knights. Certainly a few of the King's Guard have changed colours over the last few years. Can't say I liked 'em. They were the sort who fight because they enjoy death. Guess it fits well with the Order's whole freewill thing."

"I don't see how," Pela muttered.

"You don't?" Aldyn asked. "Imagine it: a world where everyone did whatever they liked. No laws or rules. The strong would take whatever they wanted. Say what you will about the king, his laws protect those who cannot defend themselves, prevent chaos."

Caledan snorted. "Some job he's doing."

Aldyn flashed him a grimace. "You should walk a mile in a man's shoes before you judge, sellsword," he replied. "If not for Braidon, the Lonian King would have taken half our land and put the rest of us to the sword."

"And he set out new trade routes with Northland," Tobias cut in. "Our farm would have gone broke when the Trolans closed their borders, if not for that."

"Is this really the time to be talking about politics?" Devon growled, gesturing ahead.

Just then, the whispers lifted a notch in pitch. The company slowed.

"We're close," Aldyn hissed, "just around this corner, I think. The voices must be coming from the pantheon."

Devon looked at the others. "It looks like this is going to come to a fight," he said, looking from Tobias to Genevieve to Pela. "If anyone still wants to back out…"

Tobias swallowed and shook his head, while his niece only gripped the hilt of her sword tighter. Genevieve smiled. "We go on."

Devon nodded, and prayed to the memory of Antonia that they weren't too late. "Keep close," he said softly. "Whatever's waiting for us, we get in and get out as quickly as possible."

The others nodded, their faces a mixture of fear and determination, and Devon's chest swelled. The villagers had no business being here, no experience with war and death, but in that instant he knew they would not break. Gathering himself, he turned the corner to the pantheon.

He'd expected guards to be posted outside the Order's innermost sanctuary, but the corridor was empty. Devon started towards the massive oaken doors. Blood thudded in his ears as he glimpsed the murals on the walls, depicting scenes of heroism and war, of evil magic-doers and dark creatures from the north. Amidst them all, a single woman stood tall with sword in hand.

There was no doubt she was a representation of Alana. But while Devon's memory had blurred through the years, even now he knew the image bared little resemblance to reality. The woman in the mural was tall and blonde, her skin unblemished and eyes cold, almost a Goddess herself in her perfection. Alana, for all that he had loved her, had been far from perfect.

"Ready for this, big man?" Caledan whispered as they approached the doors.

The mural stretched up over the entrance to the pantheon, where a final depiction of Alana stood with flaming sword in hand. Devon shuddered, tearing his thoughts from the past. Beyond the wooden panels, the whispers of prayer had risen to a fever pitch.

For a moment, Devon couldn't help but compare their quest to the Knight's attack on the temple above Skystead. How different were they now, to have come to this place of worship with weapons in hand? Yet it was not hatred that had drawn them here, but love. They had not come for blood, only to bring their people home. He nodded to the sellsword and pressed a hand to the door.

"Go quietly," Aldyn said. "They might not realise we're intruders."

Devon checked one last time that the others were ready, then gave the door a push. It swung open with barely a squeak, and together they slipped inside. The roar of voices struck as the door swung closed behind them. Bewildered, Devon reached for his hammer, shocked at the madness within the pantheon.

Towering columns lined the room and rows of pews cluttered the chamber, but few of the congregation were using them. Aldyn had told them only twenty Knights remained in the Castle. There were far more people than that present. They packed the pantheon, standing and sitting and on their knees with hands raised to the sky, as though calling upon some divine power.

A man stood on the raised platform opposite where they had entered. He wore robes of fine green silk and a crown of silver wire, while a heavy gold necklace hung around his neck. Raising a jewelled sceptre skywards, his voice boomed out across the chamber, though Devon could make no sense of his words. The worshipers seemed to understand though, for their voices joined with his, until it seemed the noise might shake the very walls.

Two men sat in silence behind the speaker in the wings of the dais. One was a young man, unknown to Devon, but it was clear from his robes and throne that he was an Elder. The other man was Merak. He wore a broad grin as he watched the proceedings, though in the heat of the thousand candles lighting the pantheon, his face glistened with sweat.

A great *boom* came from a door to the side of the dais, and a Knight in full plate mail appeared, leading a prisoner. Her arms were tied behind her back and a hood had been pulled. She staggered as the Knight shoved her, and her scream rang out over the cries of the audience. The Knight grabbed her by the scruff of the neck before she could fall and dragged her in front of the speaker.

"The solstice approaches!" the man holding the sceptre boomed, returning to a language Devon understood. He was the oldest of the three Elders on the stage, and his voice cracked before he managed to continue, "Thirty years have passed since the Saviour freed our lands, but the power of the False Gods is rising. The profane cannot be allowed to proliferate, lest the tyranny of magic be restored. Today we cleanse their blasphemy from our shores."

He raised the sceptre above his head as the Knight forced the prisoner to her knees. A hundred voices roared their agreement. Devon winced and glanced around, but amidst the madness, the zealots had not taken note of the intruders. He started down the centre of the pantheon towards the speaker.

A sick feeling touched Devon's stomach as he looked out over the crowd and finally noticed the second prisoner. Her crumpled figure lay at the foot of the dais where she had fallen, arms still bound, feet sprawled at odd angles against the stone. The silken hood covering her face was stained red.

Rage touched Devon as he looked at the Elder standing atop the stage. His eyes were drawn to the sceptre, and this time he saw the blood dripping from the heavy gold. The jewels studding the awful instrument shone in the candle-light, almost seeming to take on a life of their own. Devon picked up his pace.

Around him the voices rose higher. Those present wore the fine silks of the rich, and he was surprised to see many sporting knives or even swords on their belts. He had spotted five Knights in their plate mail up on the dais behind the Elders. Others stood lookout at the edges of the chamber, though they had become engrossed by the exhibition on the stage.

The first worshipers finally took note of Devon as he passed beneath the centre of the dome. They fell silent, turning to one another in question, unsure of these new arrivals or their purpose.

Atop the dais, the Elder was speaking again, but his voice died when his eyes fell on Devon. The sceptre in his hand lowered half an inch as a frown creased his forehead.

"Who dares interrupt our sacred ceremony?" he shouted.

Devon grimaced and drew his hammer from its sheath. "My name is Devon of Skystead!" he bellowed. "And we have come to restore our people to their homes!"

The Elder scowled. "What madness is this?"

Behind the man, his fellows rose from their thrones. Fear showed on Merak's face as he pointed a finger at Devon. "He led the mob in Skystead!" he screamed. "Kill him!"

Pela and the others grew close around Devon. They had come to a stop at the foot of the dais, though the Elders and their protectors stood several feet from the edge. Whispers came from the pews as some of the worshipers stood and drew swords.

Locking eyes with Merak, Devon let his laughter boom out over the pantheon. "What mob?" he called. "Is that what you told them? There was only one of me, coward."

"He lies!" Merak screamed. His face a mottled red, Merak grabbed the arm of a Knight and shoved him in the direction of the intruders. "*I said, kill them!*"

Finally the Knight obeyed, drawing a broadsword and advancing. Blood pounded in Devon's temples as he leapt the three feet to the dais. He deflected a wild swing of the Knight's blade as the others followed him, then charged. He slammed into the man's plate mail armour, and pain lanced through his shoulder, but the Knight staggered backwards, off-balance. Surging forward, Devon drove his hammer into the man's chest.

A great *crash* echoed through the hall as the Knight tumbled from the dais. Devon spun, seeking out Merak, but the other Knights on the stage were already advancing. A curse slipped from his lips, before Caledan surged past.

"The prisoner!" a voice bellowed from somewhere, while behind them the worshipers screamed.

Devon risked a glance back. Chaos had erupted across the pantheon, as some tried to flee the melee on the dais, while others charged forward with weapons drawn. They lashed about them in their desperation to reach the stage, showing little concern for their fellow believers. Several fell bleeding or dead to the floor. Horror touched Devon, until he recalled that just moments before these people had been cheering for the deaths of innocent women.

A man reached the edge of the dais and tried to climb up, but Genevieve darted forward and speared him through the throat. He fell back with a cry, and she looked back, catching Devon's eye.

"Go!" she cried. "We'll hold them."

As though to emphasis her point, Tobias swung his sword at a second attacker, almost decapitating the man. He glanced back, his face more sombre than Devon had ever seen it, and offered a nod before returning to the battle.

Devon's heart lurched as he realised he'd lost sight of Pela, but before he could look for her, a voice called him back.

"Drop your weapon, hammerman!"

He spun, finding Merak standing nearby. Two more Knights had fallen to Caledan's blade. A third was battling furiously with the sellsword, but he seemed to have more skill than his fellows, and neither was giving an inch. The other Elders had vanished, leaving Merak alone on the stage, but he had claimed the sceptre and now held it high above his head.

"Why?" Devon growled, starting forward.

"Or she dies," Merak hissed, pointing the golden sceptre at the prisoner lying crouched at his feet.

CHAPTER 19

The breath *whooshed* from Pela's lungs as she slammed into the ground. She groaned and curled into a ball as her blade went skittering between a Knight's legs. Shouts erupted overhead as Caledan leapt past and engaged the Knights.

Gasping for breath, Pela dragged herself to her knees and swore beneath her breath. What had happened? One moment she'd been facing the charging Knights, her throat clogged with terror and blood pounding in her ears, the next, a heavy blow had struck her in the legs, sending her tumbling. But only Caledan had been…

"Bastard!" Pela hissed as she realised he'd tripped her.

The sellsword spun, driving his blade through a Knight's gorget, but he still managed to flash her a smile. Teeth bared, Pela reached for her scabbard, before remembering she'd dropped her father's sword yet again.

Swearing, she darted past Caledan, who was battling furiously with the remaining two Knights. Her eyes swept the dais, finding her blade lying near one of the golden thrones. Heart racing, she scanned the shadows beyond, searching for the other Elders. The dais was empty; it appeared they had fled, leaving Merak to stand alone against the intruders.

Pela recovered her sword and turned back towards the fight. She scanned the chamber. Caledan was still battling with the two Knights. They appeared to be getting the better of him, until he ducked a blow and darted forward suddenly, his blade stabbing low. His opponent staggered back clutching his groin. Blood pumped between his fingers and within moments, he collapsed to the ground.

A roaring sounded in Pela's ears as Caledan launched himself at the last Knight. She couldn't tear her eyes away from the dying man. Even in his armour she could feel his pain, sense his terror as his life's blood fled from him. It had happened so quickly, the shift between life and death.

Her legs began to shake as she turned away, and she saw Genevieve, Aldyn, and Tobias battling furiously with the congregation. In the chaos, the pews had been shoved up against the dais, blocking the worshiper's passage everywhere but the centre of the chamber. Her friends stood there with swords in hand, defying those below. From their vantage point atop the dais, they had managed to keep the zealots from gaining a foothold. But the horde below were too many; they couldn't possibly hope to hold them off forever.

As she watched, Aldyn went down, a gash opening on his calf. Her heart lurched, but he was up again in a second, his blade flashing down to skewer the swordsman that had struck him.

The trembling spread until Pela's entire body was shaking. Fists clenched, she shrank backwards until she struck one of the thrones. Before she could stop herself, she darted behind it. Her father's blade slipped from her fingers as she leaned against the cold steel and slid to the ground. Screams came from behind her and she drew her legs up to her chest.

"No, no, no," she whispered, scrunching her eyes closed in an effort to deny the death creeping towards her.

"Drop your weapon, hammerman!" Merak boomed suddenly.

Pela flinched. It sounded as though the Elder was almost directly behind her. She sat frozen as her uncle's angry retort rumbled through the hall.

"*Why?*"

"Or she dies," came Merak's hiss.

The roaring in Pela's ears rose to a thunder as she leaned out from behind the throne and saw the Elder poised over his prisoner. He held the golden sceptre in one hand, ready to strike the helpless woman dead. Several feet away, Devon stared him down, teeth bared and hammer clutched tightly in both hands. The rest of the room had stilled with the priest's words.

Pela swallowed as she met her uncle's eyes. There was a flicker of recognition, before they returned to Merak. Ever so slowly, he relaxed, lowering the hammer to his side. He held up one hand.

"Easy there, sonny," he murmured.

"*I said put it down!*"

The *thud* as Devon's hammer struck the ground echoed loudly in the chamber.

No, no, no!

His eyes flickered to her again. Pela shook her head. She couldn't do it. If she tried, she would die. There was no doubt in her mind anymore; she had no business being here.

Unable to face her uncle's disappointment, she lowered her gaze.

Her eyes caught on her father's sword. It lay at her feet, its silver blade glistening in the candlelight. A lump lodged in her throat. What would her father think if he could see her now? Her uncle, her friends, they were all relying on her, needed her. All sound drained away as she realised that if she failed, they would all die. The zealots below would tear them apart.

"Very good." The Elder's voice dripped malice now.

A sob came from the woman at his feet. Pela's heart lurched. Had that...been her mother's voice? She craned her head, trying for a better view, but there was nothing she could see to identify the woman. Then she saw Devon, still watching her. His amber eyes shone with a quiet confidence.

Unconsciously, Pela gripped her father's sword tight in one hand. Before she could think about what she was doing, she was on her feet. The throne still hid her from the crowd below, but as soon as she stepped from its shadow, she would be revealed. She could not hesitate, not even for a second. Releasing a shuddering breath, she leapt.

The sword slid into the Elder's back with surprising ease, as though it were not flesh and bone she had stabbed, but soft mud or a melon. Even after all her time practicing with Caledan, she was not prepared for the reality.

A terrible scream erupted from Merak and he staggered away, tearing the blade from his back. The sceptre struck the ground with a sharp *crack*, followed by a flash of light as it split in half.

Pela hardly noticed. She stood frozen, staring down at the bloody sword clutched in her hand. The Elder made it two steps before he collapsed to the floor of the dais. His cries echoed pitifully around the room, growing weaker as he pawed at the floor. Then Devon was beside Pela, drawing her into a hug.

"Well done, missy," he whispered in her ear, and then released her.

A roar came from the worshipers as they charged. Aldyn and Tobias were there to meet them, but they could not hold them back this time. Enraged, the men and women below hurled themselves at the swordsmen.

"Where do we go?" Pela choked.

"Here!" Genevieve's voice called from the side of the stage.

Pela spun, finding her in the shadows from where the prisoner had been led. A door stood open beside her. Caledan had already dispatched the last Knight and was racing towards her. No longer able to think rationally, Pela sprinted after him, bloody sword still clasped in her hand. Behind her, Devon scooped the prisoner up over his shoulder and followed.

Another roar came from the crowd at the sight of their prey escaping. Pela glanced back as they surged forward. A man hurled himself at Tobias and was run through, but the farmer's blade lodged in his ribcage and was torn away. Tobias stumbled back as two more followed the dead man over the edge of the dais. Seeing them in the wings, he ran towards them. Blade still in hand, Aldyn fought on with a cold ferocity Pela would not have expected from the light-hearted soldier.

"Come on!" Devon bellowed as he reached the door and glanced back.

Aldyn started towards them, but as he lowered his sword, a zealot scrambled onto the stage. Throwing himself forward, his hand whipped out and caught Aldyn by the ankle. The King's Guard cried out and went down.

Cursing, Devon handed the prisoner to Genevieve and stepped towards his friend, but now that there was no one to stand against them, the crowd swarmed up onto the dais. Scrambling to his knees, Aldyn looked from the horde to Devon.

"*Go!*" he screamed, launching himself to his feet.

His sword speared down, killing the man that had toppled him, then skewered a second. But the worshipers were all around him now, and a sword flashed out, catching him in the side.

Aldyn screamed and tore himself away. Dragging free his blade, he brought it down in a double handed blow on another zealot. The man's skull split with a horrifying *crack*.

Then a woman leapt on him, driving a dagger deep into Aldyn's chest, and he went down. The crowd swept forward and Aldyn disappeared from view.

"*No!*" Pela shrieked. She leapt at the door, but Caledan caught her by the waist and hauled her back. "Bastard!"

Turning, she tried to attack him with her blade, but he slapped her hand down and the sword clattered to the ground. Pela screamed again, slamming a fist into his cheek. Curses erupted through the room as Caledan tossed her aside. Scrambling across the floor, Pela swept up her blade and swung on Caledan.

Boom.

Darkness engulfed the room as Devon swung the door closed. "Enough!" he bellowed. "Tobias, you have the lantern."

Something heavy struck the door as the farmer scrambled in his bag, then a moment later a spark appeared in the pitch-black. Pela strained her eyes as it brightened, revealing first Tobias, then Devon and Genevieve and the woman they had rescued, then finally Caledan. She bared her teeth and was about to launch herself at him again, when Tobias gave a cry and fell to his knees beside the prisoner.

"Marce!" he cried, engulfing her in his arms. "You're alive!"

Pela lowered her sword as the two hugged. Someone had freed the woman of her bonds in the chaos of their flight. The two held each other now as though nothing else existed. Then another *thud* came from the door to the pantheon. They all spun to face it, and watched a large crack spread through the wood. It was made of heavy oak and secured by a locking bar, but even that would not last long beneath the weight of the crowd beyond.

Pela's sorrow for Aldyn turned to sudden fear as she realised they'd lost their guide. Without Aldyn, how would they find their way out again? Was there even another way out of this room?

"What's happening out there?"

Pela spun as another voice came from the darkness behind them. They'd forgotten the Elders! They must have fled this way, and yet...straining her eyes, Pela approached the shadows at the rear of the chamber. The darkness resolved itself, revealing the bars of a cell. Her heart began to race as she realised they'd found the cells Aldyn had mentioned. This must be the rest of the prisoners from Skystead.

"Mum!" She darted to the cell door.

Movement came from beyond the bars as the occupants exchanged glances. Tobias approached with the torch, illuminating their faces. Pela's heart pounded in her chest as she searched for her mother...and did not find her.

No, no, no...

She checked again, eyes sweeping the gathered faces, but none of them were Kryssa.

Pela scrunched her eyes closed. A scream built in her throat as she realised the truth. She wanted desperately to run back out into the pantheon, to the prisoner who had been murdered before they arrived, to tear the bag from her head and hold her close.

But she could do none of those things. They were too late. They had failed. Sobbing, she sank to her knees and ground her fists into the stone.

A rhythmic thumping was coming from the door. It echoed the pounding of her heart, of some song she could not quite remember.

"Get up, girl." It was Caledan. He placed a hand on her shoulder. "We have to go."

Tears streamed down Pela's face as she looked up at him, her rage from a moment earlier forgotten. "They killed her."

"They'll kill us too, if you don't get up," he growled, dragging her to her feet.

Pela staggered as he released her. Her sword hung loosely in her hand and she looked at it, wondering what was the point. Blood stained its tip, reminding her of the man she'd killed. She hadn't even stopped to process that yet. Hands shaking, she tried to sheathe the blade. It took two attempts before she succeeded. By then Devon had the prison cell open, its lock smashed to pieces by his hammer.

"This way," Caledan was saying, gesturing to a passageway leading into darkness, though without their guide they had no way of knowing the way out.

"Come on." Devon was beside her now. He squeezed her shoulder. "You did a good job back there. If not for you we'd all be dead. Now we need to keep it together until we can get these people to safety."

Looking at him, Pela wanted to throw herself into his

arms. She could see Devon was close to tears himself. But he was right; these people needed them. They had no one else. Straightening her shoulders, Pela swallowed back her grief and nodded, not trusting herself to speak.

There was an open gate of iron in the passageway leading away from the cell. They stumbled through, single-file, and then Genevieve gripped it in both hands and swung it shut behind her with so much force the locking bar jumped back out. She gave it another shove to click it in properly, then checked the lock was secure, before joining them.

They went slowly after that, Caledan and Pela taking the lead. They must have been in a disused section of the Castle, for the passageways were unlit. Every so often they would come to an intersection, and Pela and Caledan would creep forward to check for anyone coming. Shouts echoed from distant passageways, but there was no sign of pursuit.

"The front gates are no good," Devon said at one point. "Aldyn mentioned a canal gate. It'll have to do—if we can find it."

But no one knew which direction to take, and they continued to stumble blindly through the Castle, lost. The sounds of the chase grew steadily closer. Pela's fear came rushing back, growing with every scrape and echo in the dark corridors.

They were approaching their fourth intersection, when a sudden cough whispered from the corridors ahead. Pela froze, glancing sidelong at Caledan. Several feet behind her, he held up a hand to wait. Then the whisper of footsteps came to them, and Caledan nodded. He was too far away, she would have to do it.

Don't think, do!

As quietly as she could, Pela drew her sword. The blade

shook in her hands as she stepped up to the intersection. Afraid her ragged breathing would give her away, Pela settled into the familiar rhythm of her meditation.

In, out, in, out.

The footsteps approached. Drawing on her calm centre, she gathered her courage into a ball and then leapt from her hiding place, her sword coming up to find her foe.

The beady-eyed Elder from the pantheon squawked and jumped in the air, his robes fluttering as he tried to turn away. For a moment, Pela was so shocked she just stood there, but the man tripped over his own feet and crashed to the floor. Then a wave of rage swept through her. This was the man who had first held the sceptre, the one who had wielded it to kill…

Grief choked her and she raised her father's blade to strike.

"Please!" the Elder wailed, raising his hands in front of his face. "Don't kill me. I'll give you whatever you want!"

Pela's rage was all but suffocating now. "*You killed my mother,*" she hissed.

"Pleeeease," the man cried again. "I have coin, I can make you richer than you ever dreamed!"

"Pela, wait!" Caledan hissed, catching her by the arm. "He might be useful."

"Yes, I—"

"Never!" Teeth bared, Pela strained against Caledan until Devon stepped between them.

"He's not worth it, niece," Devon murmured. "Look at him, he's a grub."

The anger went from Pela as quickly as it had come, and she slumped in Caledan's grip. She stared down at the pathetic excuse for a man, who had so bravely slain her helpless mother. "Take him," she choked.

AARON HODGES

Caledan released her and dragged the man up. "Which way to the canal gate?" he growled, drawing a dagger. "And do not lie to me, for your life depends on it."

The Elder blubbered and stammered, but eventually he managed to get out the words. "That way!"

"Show us."

They continued, Pela walking with the prisoners now, her eyes fixed on the Elder's back. Again and again she saw the body on the ground in the pantheon, her grief turning to rage, then regret.

If only they'd been a little bit sooner, if only they hadn't delayed...

"Here!" the priest announced suddenly.

Pela's head snapped up, surprised to find herself outside. Like the front entrance, there was a courtyard before the gates, but here it was tiny—and for the moment unguarded. Used to bring goods by gondola from the port, she hoped no one would have thought to look for them here yet.

"Get them open," Caledan snapped.

Two of the villagers started working on the locking bar while the others edged forward, casting furtive glances back the way they'd come. Thunder boomed overhead and Pela glanced up. The sky was black, the moon and stars concealed, but the rain had not yet reached them. A shout echoed from the keep, but Pela could see no one in the corridor behind them.

The gates swung open with a sharp creak. She stepped towards them, then hesitated. Blood pounded in Pela's ears as she set her sights on the Elder. She tightened her grip on her sword.

"Don't," Devon murmured, blocking her path.

Tears blurred Pela's vision as she looked at her uncle. "Why?" she croaked. "He killed my mother."

"Ay," Devon rumbled, the lines of his face deepening, "but this isn't what she would have wanted, nor your father."

"He deserves it!" A brilliant light flashed across the sky, followed by the *crack* of thunder. As though the heavens had opened up, rain began to bucket down around them.

"He is unarmed!" Devon shouted through the downpour. "Did your parents raise you to kill a man in cold blood?"

"No—"

"Kill him, and you become no better than the evil you seek to destroy, Pela," Devon said, his face haggard as water ran in rivulets down his face. "Trust me. There are many things I regret in my life. Do not follow in my footsteps. Be better. Be the woman your parents would have wanted you to become."

The fight went from Pela in a rush, her anger racing away like water over a cascade. She lowered her sword.

"Mum's gone," Pela croaked.

Devon nodded, and she threw herself into his arms and buried her head in his chest.

CHAPTER 20

The mood was sombre amongst the rescuers as they returned to the inn. They had succeeded beyond anything Caledan had expected, but the sense of loss Devon and Pela carried about themselves was palpable. Not only had the kindly Aldyn been butchered where he stood, but they had failed to achieve the one thing they'd set out to do: rescue the girl's mother.

Only Tobias seemed to have thrown off the melancholy. He had walked the whole way back arm-in-arm with a young woman that could only be his wife. Caledan had to admit, the farmer had surprised him back in the pantheon. He might have been jovial during training, but when it had come to the battle, Tobias had been all business. The man might never have Caledan's skill, but he'd shown his worth.

His thoughts turned then to the huntress. Genevieve too had shown her worth. He searched the crowded inn and found her seated alone in the corner with a jug of ale. Taking his mug, he strolled across to join her.

"Not in the mood to celebrate?" he asked as he sat down.

"Not really." Her eyes flickered but she did not look up. Reaching for the jug, she gulped down a mouthful of the amber liquid.

Caledan raised an eyebrow. "Wha—"

"Not in the mood for conversation either," she snapped, and this time she did look at him. Tears spilt down her cheeks. "*If* you don't mind."

A strained silence stretched out between them, before Caledan nodded.

"Fine," he said, raising the glass. "Mind if I keep you company?"

"You're not my type."

Caledan snorted, drink still extended. He was surprised at her sudden show of emotion—after seeing little of the sort during their voyage from Skystead. But she was still better company than Devon. The hammerman had hardly spoken on the way back, and now sat alone in the middle of the inn, quietly nursing his drink. Caledan's attempts at conversation had been met with a cold stare, and he had quickly stopped trying.

Genevieve eyed him for a long moment, before taking up her jug and clinking it against his glass. They drank deeply and then sat there in silence, watching as the other villagers exchanged stories.

"What will you do now?" Caledan asked finally.

Nose in her jug, Genevieve glanced at him. "I will go wherever Devon does," she answered, as though that explained everything. "What about you?"

Caledan's stomach contracted at the thought and a grin crossed his cheeks. She was right: the rescue mission was over, whether they had lost the woman or not. He had hardly given a thought to his request. To finally come before the king...though now that the time was finally here, he wondered if the hammerman would honour his word.

He considered approaching Devon for reassurance, but one look at the man banished the idea. Stoney-eyed and rigid, now was not the time to pick a fight with the giant warrior.

Cursing into his mug, Caledan waved for another jug. "Tomorrow I'll ask Devon to honour our agreement," he replied finally.

"If there is a tomorrow," Genevieve muttered.

"What's that?" Caledan asked, his head coming up.

Genevieve raised an eyebrow. "You don't think this is going to get back to the Order?" She gestured at the general revelry taking place in the dining hall. "How long before those Knights come looking for revenge?"

A curse burst from Caledan. Why hadn't he thought of that? There'd been a dozen Knights left alive in the Castle, and plenty more of their followers. He started to rise when a tap came on his shoulder. Caledan spun and was reaching for his sword, when he realised it was only Tobias.

"May we sit?" the farmer asked.

His wife was with him, and they pulled up chairs before either could respond. Cursing, Caledan sank back into his seat. His heartbeat eased. Outside, rain still lashed at the windows and the occasional boom of thunder shook the walls. Few would dare venture out in such weather. Word was unlikely to reach the Knights until morning. By then the villagers would be long gone on the *Seadragon*.

"Marce," Tobias said, introducing his wife.

Despite her recent travails, the woman had a cheerful look, though the smile lines on her cheeks suggested this was her usual state of mind. Idly, Caledan found himself wondering why. How much joy could exist in the life of a farmer? To toil day in and day out on the land with never an ounce of excitement—just the thought of it made him shudder.

"I can't thank you enough," Marce was saying. "I know you suffered greatly to save us. He must have been a brave man, Aldyn. Did you know him long?"

Caledan snorted. "A few hours."

Her smile faltered and she exchanged a glance with Tobias. The farmer gave the slightest shake of his head. Caledan almost rolled his eyes. Was he meant to grieve every ally who fell in battle? What he'd said was true—he'd barely known Aldyn long enough to learn his name, let alone *know* him. Why should he grieve a stranger, when there was so much to celebrate?

Like his coming meeting with King Braidon…

"I'm just so sorry about Kryssa and Ariane," Marce was saying, her eyes traveling across the table to Devon. "I knew Selina quite well. We often had coffee together, though the hammerman—I mean Devon—never joined us. He must be devastated to have lost his daughter."

Caledan grunted, but Genevieve came to her feet so suddenly her chair toppled to the ground. Marce's mouth fell open and Tobias rose, but before anything could be said, a crash came from the entrance to the inn. The doors swung open and the winds carried the swirling rain inside, drawing curses from the nearest patrons. They fell silent as an armoured Knight stepped into the room.

The silence spread as others noticed the newcomer. Cursing, Caledan leapt to his feet and reached for his sword.

"Where is the hammerman?" the Knight bellowed.

"Here, sonny," Devon growled, striding past Caledan with hammer in hand.

There was a dangerous look in the man's eyes, and Caledan realised with a start he'd been waiting for this. The floorboards creaked as Devon came to a stop several feet from the Knight.

Two more Knights shouldered their way inside. Caledan wondered how many more were waiting without, but three were more than enough of a concern for the moment. Loosening his blade in its scabbard, Caledan edged forward. Genevieve and Tobias followed just a step behind him. The rest of the villagers from Skystead watched on, fear written across their faces.

"Can I help you lads?" the innkeeper asked in a hard voice. He stepped out from behind the bar, a club gripped tightly in one hand. But the weapon was for dealing with unruly drunks, not armoured men, and the Knights took no notice.

"No," Devon growled, hefting his hammer, "but I can—"

"Easy!" Caledan interrupted, darting forward before the hammerman dragged them all into a fight they could not win. Stepping in front of Devon, he flashed the man a glance before facing the Knights. "I think you'd best be going, lads."

The first of the Knights stepped forward. "He desecrated our sacred pantheon!" he snapped, his voice echoing strangely from the helmet. "He killed our Elder! We won't be going anywhere without the old man's head on a pike."

Under different circumstances, Caledan might have been offended the Knights had not recognised him back in the Castle. Just now though, he would take every advantage he could to defuse the situation.

"But how can that be?" He spread his hands. "The man

has been in this tavern all night, with myself and these good folk from Skystead."

"Lies!" the Knight screamed, though he did not draw his sword. "He was seen with the traitor from the King's Guard. Him and all these others—"

"—came from Skystead," Caledan interrupted. His voice took on a hard edge. "Now, let us be reasonable. We've all lost people this night. No doubt we could keep fighting until there's no one left standing." A yelp came from the innkeeper at his words. "But we all know the truth about what happened in Skystead, and here. Should that truth get out…"

"We are the authority in Townirwin," the Knight hissed. Then his eyes flickered around the room, taking in Devon, Genevieve and Tobias. Several of the former prisoners had also armed themselves. The sight seemed to give him pause.

"The others can stay," he growled at last. "We already took what we needed for the Great Sacrifice."

"You're monsters!" Pela shrieked.

Caledan cursed inwardly as the girl came marching forward, sword in hand.

"You murdered my mother in your foul pantheon. How can you believe your Great Sacrifice is anything but evil?"

The Knight seemed taken aback. "Because it is *necessary*," he said, then smiled. "But…that was only a cleansing! Fear not child, for your mother died free of her evil." He laughed. "The Great Sacrifice is to burn away the tendrils of the False Gods, to keep them from this world. It does not take place until the solstice. The Saviour has blessed the woman Kryssa as one of the three."

Silence answered the Knight's words as every eye in the tavern turned on him. Caledan felt as though he'd been struck a great blow. Was the man speaking the truth? Could Pela's mother truly be alive?

"What did you say?" Devon whispered.

"Do you know her, hammerman?" the Knight sneered.

"If you lay a hand on her—" Devon bellowed, starting forward, but Caledan leapt between them.

"Easy, Devon!" Caledan hissed. The hammerman's eyes were wild, but he stopped when Caledan placed a hand on his chest. Letting out a sigh, Caledan looked at the Knight. "What do you mean, she was 'blessed'?"

"That is none of your concern," the Knight snapped. "She is beyond your reach now. Now hand over the old man, it is time he paid for his crimes this night."

"No." Caledan released Devon and stepped towards the Knights. "Believe me, lads, I'm the only thing keeping you alive right now."

The Knights laughed. "You think we're afraid of a greybeard?"

"Do you know his name?" Caledan asked mildly.

"What do we care for the bastard's name?" the leader snapped.

Caledan smiled. "It might interest you," he murmured, "to know that this is Devon. I believe he has a place in your legends."

A stillness came over the Knights. They stood staring at Devon, and while the helmets hid their faces, Caledan knew he'd struck a nerve. It was said that Devon had known Alana, had been there at the end even, when she had sacrificed herself to banish the Gods. And he was not known as the Consort of Alana for nothing…

"It's not possible," the leader replied.

"I'd be more than happy to resolve any doubts you have, sonny," Devon growled.

Caledan raised a hand. "It's true," he replied. "Look at him. How else could an old man have carved through your Knights?" He adapted a reverent tone. "You should be honoured, that the Consort of Alana deigned visit your Castle." He might have laughed, if not for the seriousness of the situation.

"Then where is *kanker*?" the Knight argued, gesturing at the construction hammer in Devon's hand. "You can't expect us to believe *that* is the hammer of heroes?"

"It was destroyed," Devon rumbled. "Or do you not know your own history?"

"What are you playing at, swordsman?" the Knight asked. "What part do you play in this?"

Caledan smiled. "My ambitions are my own," he said, "but if you think to go against us, you should know my name as well: *Caledan.*" Armour rattled as the three retreated a step. Caledan followed them, his eyes hard now, glad that his reputation still preceded him. "I take it you have heard of me?"

"What is a man of your standing doing with such rogues!" the leader gasped.

"I think we're done here," Caledan said.

The Knights were standing in the doorway by now. It was obvious they were young men, despite their armour and greatswords—their inexperience betrayed them. They believed in the legends, though the tales of his exploits had grown greatly with time. Caledan sneered as they shrank before him.

"Go back to your Elders—what's left of them—and tell them what happened here. Tell them Skystead is under the protection of Devon and Caledan. If they seek retribution for what happened tonight, there will be a reckoning, whether they come alone or with an army."

He stood staring at the three of them. Still, they hesitated. Caledan dropped a hand to his sword hilt. With a rattle of metal, they turned tail and fled into the darkness. Shouts came from outside, made nearly inaudible by the swirling rain, but after a long moment they heard the tramping of departing boots.

Shaking his head, Caledan walked back to his table and took a seat. Silence hung over the room as he reached for his drink. The mug was almost empty, and he poured himself another drink before taking a swig. He shivered as a cold breeze blew through the open doors, damp with rain, and cursed.

"For the Gods' sake," he snapped, "someone close the door!"

CHAPTER 21

S itting in the saddle with the rain pouring down around him, Ikar had rarely been so miserable. They had ridden through the afternoon and late into the night, and the storm had not relented in all that time. Eventually it had forced them to make camp in a grove of trees, but the sparse shelter hardly spared them from the wet, and as the rains continued Ikar had found himself cursing Merak for choosing him.

Even when the morning broke, the rain had continued unabated. Ikar had saddled their horses in silence and they'd set off once more.

His only consolation was that he did not suffer alone. On the packhorse, Kryssa sat with her hands bound to the saddle. Despite the miserable conditions, the woman had not complained, had not said a word so far in fact. He wondered if she knew what they had chosen her for, where they were headed.

The light grew around them as they continued down the Gods Road, and finally it seemed the rain might ease. The thunder faded away and the fog clinging to the damp ground dissipated, revealing the way ahead. Ikar breathed a sigh of relief. The road to Lane was well-travelled, but it could still be treacherous in such conditions.

As the last of the fog lifted, he glanced at his companion. He was surprised that the Elders had agreed with his suggestion, even more so that they'd granted him the honour of escorting her to Lane. Though looking at her now, Ikar couldn't help but wonder if his assessment of her had been wrong. Her head bobbed with each trod of her horse and her eyes were closed, as though asleep in the saddle.

Ikar's frown deepened as he noticed her blue lips, and the pallid colour of her skin. Edging his horse closer, he called out to her: "Kryssa, are you okay?"

The woman gave no answer. His heart began to race, and he leapt from his saddle and rushed across the road to the packhorse. Tugging at the knots of her bindings, he shivered at the icy touch of her skin.

"Damnit, witch" he muttered beneath his breath, cursing his stupidity. He had given her an oilskin jacket to fend off the rain, but she was freezing without anything thicker to protect her. "Don't you dare die!"

"Okay."

The last knot had just come free when Kryssa sat up straight in the saddle and kicked out with her boot. The blow caught Ikar square in the chest and sent him staggering back. In the heavy armour, he almost lost his balance, but some quick footwork kept him from falling. The thunder of hooves sounded in his ears as he swung around.

Swearing loudly, he leapt for his horse and hauled himself up. He was barely in the saddle before the horse set off at a gallop. The beast had been bred for war, a monster to a man of lesser size than Ikar, and they quickly ate up the distance.

Weighed down by their supplies and not built for speed, Kryssa's mount could not outrun him. He almost smiled, before anger at her defiance burned away his mirth. Crouching lower in the saddle, he watched as Kryssa glanced back at him, expecting to see fear in the woman's eyes. She smiled.

"Witch," he muttered.

A moment later he pulled alongside her. He snatched at the reins, dragging the horse to the side of the road. Unable to continue its headlong flight, the packhorse slowed. When they were almost at a stop, Ikar reached for Kryssa, but the woman was faster still. She leapt between the horses with a snarl and smashed into his chest. Entangled, the two of them toppled from the saddle and struck the ground with a *crash*.

Kryssa was up in an instant, but she hesitated for half a second, her eyes darting from Ikar's sword to the open fields. Before she could flee, he caught her by the ankle and hauled. Screaming, she slammed to the ground. Her fist smashed at his visor and she cried out again, but unarmed, there was nothing she could do to hurt him in his armour. Within a few minutes, Ikar had her hands bound behind her back once more.

Stumbling to his feet, he looked around for their horses, and discovered they'd vanished.

"*Damnit!*" He drew back an iron boot and slammed it into Kryssa's side.

She cried out as the blow sent her rolling through the mud. Enraged, he readied himself for another blow, then noticed her silver eyes watching him. There was no fear there—only unbridled rage. In a rush, he recalled his mission, and let out a long breath.

"You're a pain in the ass, you know," he growled.

Sitting up in the mud, she blew a strand of hair from her face and cackled. "My mother used to say the same." Her eyes shone. "So why don't you free me, and save yourself the trouble?"

Ignoring her words, Ikar pulled the woman to her feet. "That way," he said, pointing down the Gods Road. No doubt the horses had continued the way they'd been heading.

"I've been wondering," Kryssa said conversationally as they started off. "Did my...friend catch up with your Knights in Skystead?"

"Your friend?" Ikar asked. He searched the trees alongside the road for signs of their mounts while they walked. "What are you talking about?"

"Devon; he was a friend of my mother's. He would have been...irritated when he discovered you took me. I thought he might have caught up with that Elder and his Knights when they went into town."

Ikar blinked. "You can't mean *the* Devon, the Consort of Alana?"

Kryssa chuckled. "The way my mother told it, they barely exchanged more than a few steamy looks," she replied. "But yes, that Devon."

"I..." Ikar struggled to find the words to reply.

Devon was also a descendant of Alan the Great, though of a different line from Ikar—a line of warriors. While Ikar's parents and grandparents had been tarnished by magic, Devon's family had wielded *kanker*, the hammer of heroes. That is, until it had been destroyed in the final battle against the Tsar.

Ikar could hardly believe his distant cousin still lived. As a child, Devon had been a legend, but by the time Ikar had grown to manhood, the man had vanished from the world.

"I thought so," Kryssa surmised, Ikar unable to keep the truth from his face. "You should *really* let me go."

For a moment, Ikar felt fear. Then excitement touched him as he realised what this meant. Devon's line had always carried the glory of their shared ancestor, but now it was Devon who stood on the wrong side of history. If he fought the Knights now, his legend would forever be stained. He would become the Traitor.

And if Ikar was the one to slay him…

"Finally, I know what the Saviour intends for me," he said, a grim smile touching his cheeks. "I too am descended from Alan the Great. I look forward to meeting my long-lost cousin. But if he stands against the Order, I shall meet him with weapon in hand."

As though summoned by his words, the pounding of hooves came from the road behind them. Spinning around, Ikar grabbed Kryssa by the arm and pulled her close as a horseman came into view. But after a second he relaxed, recognising the amour of the Order, though the rider wore no helmet.

A few minutes later Putar rode up, pale-faced and sweating. His horse gasped and coughed, its eyes rolling in its skull, as though it had galloped all the way from Townirwin. Ikar frowned as the Elder practically tumbled from the saddle.

"Thank the Saviour!" he gasped, grasping at Ikar's chest. "We feared they might have already caught you."

"Who?" Ikar frowned, struggling to hold Putar upright. The man's blubbering was unbecoming of an Elder at any time, let alone in front of a non-believer.

Putar seemed to realise this as well, and straightened. A frown touched his brow as he looked around. "Where are your horses."

"Lost," Ikar said. "The woman…is devious."

"Yes, and her family is hateful. Merak is dead, the Castle in chaos. The Consort wants his daughter back."

Kryssa threw back her head and laughed. "Told you," she smirked, before continuing in a wistful tone, "Though… I am not his daughter."

"And what is the will of the Elders?" Ikar growled, flashing a scowl at the woman.

"This news changes everything." Ikar shuddered, but after a moment, he drew himself up. "The Great Sacrifice cannot be disrupted, there is too much at stake. The power is needed. The woman has been chosen, and must be brought with all haste before her destiny."

"And where in the Three Nations would *that* be?" Kryssa asked, her voice like acid.

CHAPTER 22

Devon sat at the bar, fist clenched around the iron tankard, and stared into the amber ale. His vision swirled, made fuzzy by the strong drink the bartender had served him through the night. The others had retired long ago, but Devon remained, sitting through the night in silent vigil. Now, finally, sunlight had begun to seep through the shutters, burning at his swollen eyes.

All of him ached, his bones, his joints, his every muscle. Death had been a constant presence for most of his life, always close—but now he felt as though he had one foot in the grave. The prodigious strength he'd once relied on was failing, now, when he needed it the most.

He closed his eyes and his head swam. Devon cursed himself for a fool. If not for Caledan's quick thinking, he and everyone else in the tavern would have been killed. Drowned by loss and caught in the grips of an awesome rage, he hadn't cared, but now he saw the futility.

She's still alive.

A groan rattled up from his chest and he slammed a fist into the bar top.

"Enough of that, my friend," the bartender remarked, appearing from the kitchen. "You're lucky I didn't throw the lot of you out last night after that hubbub with the Knights."

"Fortunate my gold speaks louder than your conscience," Devon snapped.

The man had wanted them gone, though the storm had been raging outside and many of the former prisoners were in poor conditions. Another gold libra from Devon's purse had bought them peace for the night, though it was an exorbitant price for such accommodations.

"True that," the innkeeper replied easily. He obviously had no qualms about the deal. "Speaking of which, you want to break your fast?"

Devon's stomach swirled, but he knew the food would do him good. "One minute."

Rising from the stool, he staggered outside to the water trough where the horses drank. He fell to his knees beside it and plunged his head into the icy water. Gasping and spluttering, he stood and returned to his seat. The icy wakeup cleared his head somewhat, but it did nothing for the despair.

"I'll take some sausage and eggs," he rumbled, still dripping water.

The innkeeper nodded and vanished into the kitchen. Devon laid his hands on the bar top and rested his head in his arms. There was a pounding in his forehead and he still wasn't sure he'd be able to stomach food, but at least it might help with the hangover.

"Devon?"

Devon lifted his head as a tentative voice came from

behind him. He was surprised to find Tobias and his wife Marce standing across from him with sheepish looks on their faces.

"What is it, Tobias?" Devon asked.

Tobias cleared his throat, glancing at Marce as though for reassurance, before the words tumbled from him in a rush. "I'm going back to Skystead," he said quickly. "We… ah, I'm sorry about Kryssa, Devon. I'll never forget what you did for us, but…I'm only a farmer. I can't go on with you. I'm taking Marce back to the *Seadragon*. She's setting sail in an hour for Skystead. I'm sorry."

An awful weariness rose within Devon as he stared at the farmer. Finally he nodded. Without saying a word he turned away and reached for his mug. Realising it was empty, he cursed and bellowed for the innkeeper.

"Sorry, Devon." Tobias repeated, sadness in his voice. Footsteps followed as the couple departed.

Scrunching his eyes closed, Devon fought back the urge to scream at the man, to name him a coward. Tobias was right; he was out of his depth here. Devon could not expect him, or anyone else from Skystead, to continue. After suffering so much loss, they deserved to hold their loved ones tight, to return to their homes in peace.

How he longed to do the same, to return to Skystead and live out the last of his days in the quiet of the fiords. But how could he give up now, when Kryssa was still out there? How could he rest, so long as the Knights had her?

Yet he did not know where they had taken her. There was just one main road out of Townirwin, but the Knights could have taken any of a dozen smaller trails, or even set sail again on the southern seas. There was no telling where they would go now. It would take precious time to discover their path, and every moment Devon wasted, Kryssa drew further away.

And the solstice drew closer.

One by one, he watched as the villagers filed out of the inn. They all stopped to thank him, for risking his life to see them safely home, but not one offered to continue. In the end, when the last had disappeared through the double doors, Devon slumped in his stool and fought to keep himself from crumbling.

"Good morning," Pela announced cheerfully, appearing from the corridor leading to the rooms upstairs. Wandering across the tavern, she frowned. "You look awful."

Devon scowled, but before he could reply, the innkeeper reappeared with his plate of sausages and eggs. He replaced Devon's empty mug of ale with coffee, then took Pela's order and returned to the kitchen. Contemplating the plate, Devon breathed in the scent of fresh herbs in the sausages and pepper on the eggs, and fought the urge to throw up. Instead, he picked up his knife and fork and began to eat.

"So what's the plan?" Pela asked, drumming her fingers on the wooden bench.

Her eyes were alight. Devon could understand her excitement—last night they'd thought her mother was dead. Discovering she was still alive had restored Pela's hope. If only Devon could find the same strength of spirit.

"I don't know," he grunted, not wanting to have the conversation but knowing Pela would persist until he answered. "They could have taken Kryssa anywhere."

"Caledan already left for the marketplace, to ask around," Pela replied easily. "He says we should be gone by noon, before the Order changes its mind."

There was an expectation in her eyes as she watched him. Devon knew that look. She believed he could do anything, defeat anyone that stood in their way. His aches redoubled as he closed his eyes.

"What does it matter, girl?" he snapped. "Look around! The others are all gone. They've abandoned us. We're all alone now. How do you hope to get your mother away from the Knights, with just the three of us?"

"Four," Genevieve said quietly, emerging from the corridor and joining them at the bar. "And we don't need the others."

"Yes!" Pela added. "We just need courage! Like Enala and Eric when they stood against Archon."

Devon snorted. "Don't believe everything you hear, girl," he roared. "I met them both; they had far more than just courage on their side. They were the most powerful Magickers of a generation."

"It doesn't matter!" Pela insisted. "You saw what those people were doing in the Castle. They're monsters, someone has to stop them!"

Ay, Devon thought wearily, *but why does it have to be me?*

Out loud, he only grunted: "Maybe."

"Please, Devon," Pela whispered, and for a second he saw a flash of terror behind her eyes. "I can't do this without you. You're a hero."

Devon smiled despite himself. "I've never been a hero, little one," he murmured. "And last night, you were the hero. You saved us all."

His niece looked away. "I...I froze though—I could barely move. I don't even know how I...killed him." She swallowed at the final words.

"You did more than anyone could have expected," Devon said gently, placing a hand on her shoulder.

"Please, Devon," Pela murmured, "We need you."

He sighed. "I know," he said. "I just hope…that I don't let you down."

Pela grinned. "You could never let me down, Uncle."

At that moment the innkeeper emerged with a plate of beans in sauce and eggs, along with several pieces of toasted bread. Pela dug into the food without another word. Devon made a half-hearted effort to finish his own plate. In his mind, he sent up a silent prayer to the long-dead Gods that she was right.

CHAPTER 23

B raidon groaned as sunlight filtered in through the windows of the cabin, dragging him from the depths of sleep. Squeezing his eyes tightly shut he rolled over and reached for Marianne, only to discover the sheets empty. He groaned again; it must be later than he thought if his wife had already risen.

The ship rocked gently back and forth as he sat up. The cabin was empty but he could hear the sounds of the crew overhead as they moved about the deck, readying the oars to continue their passage upriver. Idly, Braidon wondered if it wouldn't be better to turn back—after all, there was a reason ships rarely sailed through the lower reaches of the Lane.

But a storm had come over them in the night, and the river delta had been the only safe birth they could reach before it broke. With the summer upon them, rain was scarce but for the great storms that came rolling in from the southern ocean, and it hadn't been long before Braidon had been thanking the dead Gods for the safety of the Lane.

Of course, he hadn't been so foolish as to thank them out loud. In their eight years of marriage, he had rarely had cause to argue with his wife, but the Three Gods and the Order of Alana had often been points of dispute. It was a strange thing, to be arguing about his sister and her relationship with the Gods, thirty years after her death.

In the end, Braidon had granted the Knights some influence in far-flung settlements of Plorsea on Marianne's urging. It had been a canny solution to the nation's struggles. The Knights had brought peace and order to many towns, without costing the crown a copper austral. Though he was loathe to admit it to his wife.

Chuckling, he threw off the duvet and dressed himself. What would his sister think if she could see him now? As a youth, he could never have imagined the title of king would entail so much tedious administration. Anything that broke the monotony was a welcome distraction.

He was not excited about returning to Ardath, and if the captain successfully negotiated the delta, they would arrive several days ahead of schedule. The thought filled Braidon with a longing to abandon his crown and flee. In his worst moments, he found himself dreaming of the old days, when he had travelled with Devon and Alana and Kellian—though they had been dangerous times, with his father hunting them.

Perhaps his life would seem less monotonous, if anything he did actually made a difference. Yet no matter how long he spent in negotiations or how hard he worked, Plorsea continued its slow slide into poverty.

Braidon shielded his eyes as he opened the door of their cabin and stepped out into the sunlight. Sailors raced to and fro across the deck of the galley, trimming sails and slotting oars into place in preparation to set off. With the shallow sandbars dotting the delta, the going would be slow the first few leagues, and a watch would need to be kept, ensuring they did not run aground.

The King's Guards standing outside the cabin saluted as Braidon emerged, but he gestured them to stand down. They grinned. Rylle and Salver were old hands and had served with him in the civil war; they were practically family, and knew well such formalities annoyed him.

"Where is my wife?" he asked a little sharply.

His head ached and he wondered what time he'd gotten to sleep the night before. The storm had raged long through the night, and while the river had sheltered them from much of its wrath, it had not stopped the ship from rocking wildly with each gust.

"At the stern, sir," Rylle replied.

They followed him as he crossed to the stairs and climbed to the upper deck. There the captain stood at the tiller, his eyes on the bow where a man stood with rope and anchor. As they drifted, the man tossed the anchor overboard, letting the rope run between his fingers, before quickly dragging it back up. Beside him, a second man waved a red flag, and the captain adjusted their heading, presumably to avoid a shallow patch.

Braidon found his wife at the stern staring back the way they'd come. She had a distant look about her, but as he approached she turned and smiled.

"My husband," she said, stepping forward and embracing him. "Finally awake, I see."

She lifted her face and he bent to kiss her. "You should have woken me," he replied as they broke apart. A grin touched his lips as he held her close. "I would have enjoyed your company."

Marianne smiled but did not reply. Turning, she leaned

against the railings again. "The storm has broken," she said. "The captain says we'll reach Lane by nightfall."

"That's...excellent," Braidon replied with a sigh.

His wife laughed. "You almost sound sincere."

"I tried." A smile broke across Braidon's face. "Though it will be good to see Calybe again."

Calybe was their son. He was only five, too young for such a journey. Marianne had wanted to bring him, to show him the city she'd grown up in, but with the uneasy tensions with Lonia and the growing presence of Baronians, Braidon had refused.

A distant look came over his wife's face again. Frowning, he stepped up and placed an arm around her waist. "Are you okay?"

Marianne nodded. "I'm okay, only...I will miss him." Her voice cracked, and Braidon was surprised to see tears in her eyes. "I would have liked to have been there, at the end."

"I know," Braidon murmured, squeezing her shoulder. "And I'm sorry we didn't bring Calybe. Things will be better soon. Next year, we'll take him down the Jurrien. The last of the dark forest should have been burnt from Sitton by then. It'll be safe."

"Will it?" There was an edge to his wife's voice now. "Or will a new threat conspire to keep us at home?"

Braidon raised his eyebrows, but a shout from the helm drew his attention back to the captain. The man was gesturing wildly at them—no, *behind them*. Spinning, Braidon looked out over the waters of the Lane. They were a murky brown here, impenetrable but for the strange pink dolphins that were sometimes seen in the deeper channels. Islands of mud and mangroves split the river into a multitude of channels; a ship could get lost under the command of a lesser skipper.

But it was not their course that upset the captain. He was pointing behind them, directly off the stern, and Braidon felt a tingle of fear as he saw the sails of a ship emerge from a nearby channel. Trumpets sounded from the lower deck as it turned to follow them. A black flag flew from its mast.

Baronians.

Braidon cursed. What was a pirate ship doing in these waters? They must have taken refuge during the storm as well, and thought they'd stumbled upon easy pickings. His hand dropped to the sword on his belt, but after a second he released it again. There were civilians onboard, accountants and negotiators who had joined him to speak with the Lonian council. Not to mention Marianne.

No, best they outrun the Baronian scum. The barbarians had no oars, not even a sail out; they couldn't hope to catch the king's galley. He would send a squadron to hunt them down once they reached Lane.

"Outrun them, Captain!" he shouted, joining the man at the tiller.

"At the oars!" the man bellowed. "Count of three!"

"Marianne, get below." Braidon said urgently, then: "Where are your guards?"

"I'll find them." She darted down the stairs to the main deck.

Braidon was relieved to see several of the Queen's Guard waiting for her at the bottom. He followed them as they made a beeline through the chaos below and disappeared into their quarters. Only then did he turn his attention back to the Baronian ship. A frown touched his forehead.

AARON HODGES

"Captain, they're gaining. What are you doing?"

The captain glanced back at the chasing ship, a panicked look on his face. "I've no idea, Your Highness," he gasped. He bellowed down to the oarsmen below. "Double count!"

Striding to the stern railing, Braidon watched the oncoming vessel. Now he noticed the smoke hanging about the vessel, heard the distant clanging of steel. It surged upstream—despite the currents—as though propelled by some unseen source. He shivered. What magic was this?

"Sir?"

The King's Guard were forming up behind him. He had twenty of his own men aboard, plus ten of the queen's, but he trusted them not to leave her side. Against them, a horde of men and woman stood atop the decks of the enemy ship. They were armed with axes and short swords for the most part, though many were spotted with rust.

Braidon's heart quickened as he realised it would come to a fight. They were badly outnumbered, but he had seen Baronians fight before—they were brave warriors, yet undisciplined and poorly trained. He was confident the King's Guard would see them off.

"Captain, bring us around!" he shouted. There was no point risking running aground when they could not hope to escape. "Let's show these scum some Plorsean steel!"

Braidon was touched by a sense of deja vu as the ship swung out into the current. Decades had passed since he'd fought alongside Devon. Yet as they raced down the river, Braidon found himself recalling the day a Baronian tribe had hailed the hammerman their leader. That had been before the Gods had died with his...sister, when magic still flowed through Braidon's veins. He'd used that power to create an illusion, to make Devon seem some giant sent by the Gods themselves.

It was strange, how illusion became truth in the eyes of men. The hammerman was spoken of with reverence now, Devon himself almost a myth to those who had come later. Standing at the rails, Braidon's mind wandered to the old warrior. He hoped Devon had finally found peace in Skystead. The man had never been the same after Alana's death. Braidon guessed they had that much in common.

The shouts and taunting of the Baronians carried to Braidon's ears as the gap between the vessels narrowed. Then a sharp *crack* came from the other ship, and a line arched across the waters and slammed down into the galley. Another followed before the first could be cut loose. The ship lurched beneath Braidon's feet as the lines snapped tight.

Then the ships were side by side and the Baronians were leaping to the railings of the galley. Bellowing a war cry, Braidon met them with steel in hand. The King's Guard raced after him, and the screams of the dying engulfed the royal ship. Braidon's sword rose and fell, striking down the poorly-armed warriors left and right, but there were more than enough to replace them, and the black tide continued unabated.

A giant of a man leapt forward, his axe sweeping down. Braidon spun to the side and the axe buried itself in the wooden railing. Driving his sword up, Braidon sought to impale the Baronian, but the black-garbed warrior released his axe and threw himself back, and the king's blow went wide. Before Braidon could swing again, his foe snatched up the axe and dragged it free.

Across the ship, the Baronians attacked with a berserker rage that surprised even Braidon. His men met them with tightly controlled fury, enraged that these savages dared challenge their strength. The red and gold of the King's Guard was an honour reserved for only the bravest soldiers, and not one of them gave an inch. But the black-garbed warriors were taking their toll, and bit by bit the Guard was forced back by the greater weight of numbers.

Braidon cursed as the axeman came at him again. This time his foe slipped in the blood that ran thick beneath their feet, and the king dispatched him with a thrust to the groin. The axeman staggered back, his eyes showing fear, and collapsed against the railing. A great *crack* came from the wood as it gave way beneath his weight and the damage dealt by the axe. He disappeared over the side, followed by a great splash as he struck the water.

Steel rang out behind Braidon, and he spun in time to see a massive Baronian almost decapitate one of his guards with a swing of a broadsword. Ice spread through Braidon's veins as the man turned and saw him standing there. The Baronian had cut a path of blood through Braidon's men and now he stood alone, the rest of his Guard pushed back by the tide of black-garbed warriors.

He glanced to the right, where his men still held strong. Beyond, the Queen's Guard stood in a ring around their cabin, and he breathed a sigh of relief that at least his wife was safe. Spinning to face the giant, he retreated slowly towards his Guard, aware that to turn his back on such a man would mean certain death.

Roaring, the giant swung his blade in an arc that would have cut Braidon in two—had he not thrown himself to the floor. A great *thud* rang out as the blade struck the railing, sending another piece tumbling into the river. Braidon staggered to his feet and stabbed out clumsily with his blade, but the Baronian swatted the blow aside.

Off-balance, Braidon drove his shoulder into the giant's midriff. A groan came from the giant and they toppled backwards. Braidon threw out an arm to catch the railing…

…but the railing was not there. He cried out as he found himself falling. His arms windmilled, searching for anything that might break his fall, but there was only empty air. He twisted in time to see the river come racing up to meet him, and with a great splash, he vanished beneath the swirling currents of the Lane.

On the banks, alerted by the screams of the dying and the scent of blood on the air, the crocodiles went sliding into the water…

CHAPTER 24

Pela and her companions reached Lane late in the afternoon, two days after setting out from Townirwin. By then the city was alive with the news, and even with sunset approaching, the streets were clogged with people and wagons.

King Braidon was dead and no one knew what that meant. What would become of Plorsea now? With the king's son not even passed his fifth birthday, who would lead their armies, who would keep them safe? And what of Lonia? Would their war-faring neighbour turn its sights south?

Tens of thousands inhabited Lane, for it sat on one of the main trading routes through Plorsea. But if war came, the city would be one of the first to fall, for its walls were in disrepair and most of its buildings constructed of wood. Many stood five or six stories tall; a fire within the city would be terrible to behold.

Struggling through the crowds, Pela and the others tried to make sense of the news. Some claimed the king had been slain by rogue Lonians, others that it had been the Baronians, and still more that a great storm had swept his ship to the bottom of the ocean, that his sister had reclaimed his soul, or he had somehow suffered the wrath of the Three Gods.

The only thing for certain was that Braidon was gone, and the world had forever changed.

Devon led the way through the twisting streets. He had denied the news at first, but as it was repeated by each passing stranger, his face had darkened and he'd picked up his pace. It was even worse for Caledan. Pela knew of his agreement with Devon—that her uncle was to give him an audience with the king—but no one knew what he'd wanted from the man. Now he walked with shoulders slumped and eyes fixed straight ahead, as though he no longer had a purpose in the world.

Pela didn't know where Devon was taking them, but within a few blocks she was lost. The buildings here were far larger than in Skystead or even Townirwin, and the streets were unpaved. Rainwater pooled in the grooves left by the passage of wagons through the mud, and the stench of sewage wafted from nearby alleyways.

Pela could not have imagined a fouler place. Townirwin had been chaotic, but at least the canals had flushed away the occupants' waste with each outgoing tide. Turning to Caledan, she tried to draw him out of his stupor, to bring life back to the sellsword.

"Why would they create such massive buildings from wood?" she asked.

The sellsword did not so much as glance in her direction, though she was sure he'd heard her. She swallowed, preparing to try again, but Genevieve answered in his stead.

"Lane was never meant to grow so large," she said.

"Once, Sitton was the main hub for trade between Lonia and Plorsea. But it was destroyed during Archon's second coming, and eventually turned back to forest. Even then, the Jurrien River was still used to ferry goods. Then the Gods fell, and the dark creatures within Sitton Forest revealed themselves. Now none pass that way. The Lane River became the new trade route, turning Lane from quiet back-water to bustling city."

"But why didn't they at least build in stone?"

Genevieve shrugged, gesturing into the darkness ahead. "Beyond the banks of the Lane lies the Forest of Plorsea. Though much diminished now, the forest supplied the orig-inal timber for the city. Those who came after have only added to them, building upon what the founders left. And so they rise, up and up, until their weight grows too great for the foundations."

A shiver ran down Pela's spine as she looked at the wooden structures. Many were lopsided, leaning against their neighbours as though the merest breeze might knock them down. She swallowed as the wind went howling down the street. She could have sworn some of the buildings began to sway.

"How can he be dead?" Caledan snarled so suddenly that Pela jumped. The sellsword's face was like thunder and he looked ready to lay into the first person that crossed him. "*How?*"

"We're about to find out," Devon muttered.

The hammerman had come to a stop in front of one of the few stone buildings in the city. Built of worn red sand-stone, it rose only two storeys from the muddy street, and was separated from its neighbours by an alley on either side. Bars protected the windows facing the road and two men

stood guard outside its door, watching them with undis-
guised suspicion.

"Hey!" one shouted as Devon approached. He hefted a
spear and pointed it at Devon's chest. "Stay back!"

Coming to an abrupt halt, Devon lifted his hands in a
gesture of peace. "Easy," he said, "we're friends, boys."

"We're rather short of those tonight," the second man
growled. He stepped towards them and gestured with his
spear. "Why don't you get out of here, ruffians?"

Devon's face darkened. "I've come a long way, sonny,"
he rumbled. "And I'm in no mood for a fight."

"Then you'd better piss off, hadn't you?" the guard
snapped.

Lowering his hands, Devon fixed the guard with a glare.
Almost unwittingly, the man retreated a step. Devon
advanced on him, and he fumbled with the spear, trying to
bring it around.

"Easy, sonny," Devon murmured. "I do not lie, I
am...*was* a friend of the King." He placed a hand on the
guard's shoulder and nodded to the door. "Whoever's left of
the King's Guard, tell them Devon is at the door."

The guard hesitated, glancing at his comrade in askance.
Then, his courage seemed to snap, and almost dropping his
spear, he darted to the door and disappeared inside.

Devon grinned at the second guard. "New recruit?"

The man glared back at him, spear still held at the
ready. "Your story better check out, old man."

Devon lifted one grey-streaked eyebrow. "There's no
need for compliments, sonny. Don't see me calling you a
piss-riddled biscuit, now do ya?"

"What did you say to me?" the guard grated, his face
turning a mottled-red. "I'll—"

"Devon!" A voice shouted as the door opened with a crash. The guard swung around at the interruption, but the speaker was already advancing through the mud, a weary grin on his face. He wore the familiar uniform of the King's Guard. "Didn't think we'd ever see you again in these parts!"

Pela breathed a sigh of relief as the men embraced. The second guard retreated to his post without a word. His face still showed rage, but it was impotent now. Laughing, the King's Guard took a step back and appraised Devon, before turning his eyes to Pela and the others.

"You've brought quite the company, old friend," he said, his voice losing some of its shine. He looked back at Devon. "You've arrived at a bad time."

"So I hear, Rylle," he replied, grimly.

Rylle nodded. "You'd better come inside."

They bundled inside and a third guard slammed and bolted the door behind them. Though it was still light outside, it was dark within. Rylle ushered the group down the corridor. Silence permeated the house as they filed through the building, though Pela sensed there were unseen eyes watching them.

Rylle led them down several corridors, before they suddenly found themselves back outside. Several lanterns had already been lit, casting light over a courtyard stacked with crates and sacks of cloth. Taking one from its bracket, Rylle continued until the lanternlight caught on water.

Pela blinked as she came to a stop beside Devon. It took several seconds for her to understand what she was seeing. Amidst the tall buildings, she hadn't noticed how close their journey through the city had brought them to the river, but the villa had been built right on the banks of the Lane. The courtyard led right out onto its own private jetty.

There was only one ship at the docks, though it was larger than any Pela had ever seen. With a raised fore and aft deck and twin masks, it was four times the size of the little fishing vessel that had brought them from Skystead. A dozen men stood watch onboard and spaced along the jetty.

"So it did not sink," Devon murmured, looking from the ship to Rylle. "What happened?"

"Baronians," Rylle replied. "They came upon us in the delta of the Lane. At first we thought to outrun them, but they had some magic that propelled them through the current without need of sails or oars. We fought them off, eventually, but the king was dragged overboard by one of the thugs."

"Then he could have survived?"

"The water was infested with crocs," Rylle replied, his voice thick. "Nobody that went in came out alive, though we looked for him."

Pela's stomach tightened as she remembered the Baronians that had attacked the *Seadragon*. Surely it couldn't have been the same crew, and yet…

"Devon…" she started, but her uncle waved a hand.

"I know," he said, slumping onto one of the barrels strewn around the courtyard. He pressed a hand to his forehead. "I know."

"Devon?" Rylle said, his voice raising an octave. "What do you know?"

"The Baronians were led by a man called Julian," her uncle whispered. "They set upon us a week ago, but I knew him from my days serving beneath the Tsar. He spared us. I…I should have put an end to him then and there…"

Rylle sat down hard beside him. "You could not have known," he croaked. "It was we who failed him, myself and the rest of the Guard. Braidon relied on us to protect him. In all these years…"

"What of the queen, and his son?" Devon croaked. "Did the boy…?"

"They're safe," Rylle replied quickly. "The queen was aboard, but her guard kept the Baronians from her. Once we fought them off and freed the ship, we made for Lane with all haste."

"Thank the Gods."

Rylle flinched. "Don't let the queen hear you speaking of such things," he murmured. "She's in no mood for blasphemy."

"Since when did it become blasphemy to speak of the Three Gods?" Devon replied, his voice hardening. He rose from his seat. "Though that is what brought us here."

"What has happened?" Rylle did not move. His face suggested he could guess what was coming.

"The Knights of Alana sacked the old temple above Skystead," Devon began.

"That's not so bad—" Rylle tried to say, but Devon cut him off.

"They killed several of the villagers they found there and took the rest hostage. We followed them to Townirwin and freed most of them, though Aldyn lost his life in the effort. But…they brought Kryssa here, for some Great Sacrifice they have planned for the solstice."

"Oh…" Rylle whispered, his face losing its colour. "Devon, I'm…" he trailed off, and sat staring up at Devon, as though waiting to hear it was all some joke. Finally his eyes slid closed and he wavered in place.

"*Gods!*" He said the word like a curse. "I warned Braidon not to trust them."

"We must act quickly," Devon continued, "before they realise I'm here. If they find out, Kryssa—"

"They're already gone," Rylle said.

Pela's heart lurched in her chest. "*What?*" she croaked.

The King's Guard frowned at Pela, before his eyes darted back to her uncle. "I'm sorry, Devon. I know how much Kryssa meant to you. But you're too late, the Order and their Knights are already gone."

"What do you mean, 'gone'?" Devon growled.

"Whatever this ceremony of theirs is, they're not holding it in Lane. The entire Castle is empty—the Knights and their followers all set off into the Forest this morning. From what I've heard, it's the same all over Plorsea."

No, no, no. Pela shook her head.

This couldn't be happening, not again. Every time they got close, her mother slipped through their fingers. The solstice was less than a week away now. Heart in her throat, she looked at Devon.

"We need to go after them," Devon said quickly. "How many of the King's Guard can you spare?"

"None," Rylle replied. He looked up at Devon, his eyes hollow. "The King's Guard leave at first light."

"*Leave?*" Devon yelled.

"The rest of the Guard is already on its way from Ardath," Rylle continued. "Birds were sent as soon as we made port. We're going to track down the Baronian who killed the king, and make them pay."

Fists clenched, Devon stood towering over Rylle. For a moment, it seemed he would grab the man and shake him, but in the end he only shook his head. "Rylle, I loved him as much as you," he whispered, "but he's gone, and killing a few Baronians won't bring him back. But there's a chance we can still save Kryssa."

"That's not my decision to make, Devon."

"Then whose is it?" Devon bellowed.

"It's mine, Devon," a woman spoke from behind them.

Pela spun towards the voice. Her sapphire eyes alive with grief, a woman threaded her way through the courtyard towards them. A rapier hung from her belt, though she was even shorter than Pela and of a lighter build. She wore a silken dress, all black, its edges seeming to merge with the growing dark, and her auburn hair was tied back at the nape.

A sinking feeling weighed on Pela's stomach as she realised who the woman was, though Devon asked the question all the same:

"And who might you be, missy?"

"The queen," Marianne replied. "It is so good to finally meet you, Devon."

CHAPTER 25

D evon sat in the dark, staring into the flickering light of a single candle. Pain was his constant companion now, an ache that started in his shoulder and radiated through his entire body. He still had not recovered from the battle in the Castle, and he found himself yearning for the old days, when he could fight all day and drink all night, then get up and do it all again the next day.

A smile touched his lips. Maybe it had never been that easy. But he was damned sure he'd never ached for three days straight after a fight.

A *bang* came from the door of the quarters the queen had offered them. He looked up as Caledan staggered inside. Crossing the room, the sellsword smiled down at him —then stumbled sideways into the table. His hands slammed onto the tabletop as he tried to steady himself, almost knocking the candle from its stand. Finally he managed to slump into the chair across from Devon.

Devon smelt spirits on the sellsword's breath as he laid his head on the table.

185

"All this time," Caledan muttered into the wood, slurring his words. "All these years, for nothin'!"

"I'm sorry, sonny," Devon grunted. "Don't know what you wanted from the king, but…" He trailed off as the warrior looked up suddenly.

Squinting, Caledan narrowed his eyes. "It's typical, life." His head bobbed up and down. "Should have known better. Learnt nothing all these years. Typical!"

Devon watched as the man put his head back on the table. He'd seen Caledan drink a time or two, but had never seen him even tipsy—let alone drunk to the point of falling down. Caledan was normally so controlled, calm even in the heat of battle. Whatever he'd needed from the king, it must have been important.

"What did you want from him?" Devon asked softly. "I swear, if it is within my power…"

"I don't think so!" Caledan chuckled.

Sitting up suddenly, he jerked back in the chair, his head lolling. He leered at Devon, then reached into his coat and drew out a flask. Devon cursed and tried to snatch it from his hands, but the warrior still managed to take a swig before he could take it.

Devon returned to his chair as the sellsword cackled again. "Good stuff, that."

A sniff of the flask confirmed his words. Devon's eyes watered as he found himself staring at the candle again. Silently, he wondered what Selina would think of him now. It seemed everything in his life had fallen apart after her death. He'd fought with Kryssa not long after the funeral; though he couldn't remember over what now. It hadn't been important—Kryssa had never forgiven Devon for his part in her husband's death. She'd only been looking for an excuse to cut him from her life.

That had stung, but Devon could accept it, so long as Kryssa and her daughter were safe. But then Pela had come running into his courtyard, upheaving his world yet again. And now Braidon was dead, and it seemed no matter what Devon did, things would never be right again.

The queen had listened in silence to their story, but not even Pela's pleas could move the woman from her course. She would sail south with the king's fleet in the morning, five ships to scour the River Lane and the southern coast until they found Julian and his Baronians. They were welcome to join the hunt, but Marianne would not spare any soldiers until the king's killers were brought to justice.

So Devon would be left to search the Forest of Plorsea alone. A forest teeming with Knights who wanted him dead. The task would be the death of him, and yet he had to try. But he would not bring Pela with him, not this time, when death was almost certain. He would send her back with the queen in the morning. She might hate him forever, but at least Pela would be safe with the King's Guard.

Remembering his friend brought Devon full circle, and he raised the flask. "To the king," he said, and drank.

The liquor burned its way down his throat and he had to choke back a cough.

"To the king!" Caledan bellowed, raising an invisible glass. "May the miserable bastard rot at the bottom of the river!"

Devon frowned at the sellsword. "You never did say what you wanted from Braidon," he said quietly.

"I wanted to watch the light fade from his eyes," Caledan hiccupped. "For him to die by my sword. But the bastard Baronians beat me to it."

For a full ten seconds, Devon sat staring at the man.

Blood throbbed in his temples as he rose to his feet, fists clenched hard against the table.

"Ruined my life, you see," Caledan continued, unaware of Devon's rage in his drunken state. "Destroyed our family. Or at least, his sister did. Just had to die, and take the Gods with her, didn't she? The Gods and their bastard magic."

Now it was the sellsword who sat staring into the candlelight. Devon slumped back into his chair, the anger falling from him like water over stone.

"My father borrowed every shilling he could to pay for the healer, but when the man's magic failed, he fled," Caledan continued. "I can barely remember her face now. I *wish* I couldn't remember my father's. Bastard drank himself into a stupor for most of my childhood." His eyes flickered up, though he didn't seem to see Devon. "That's why I wanted it to be *me*. I wanted him to suffer like I suffered. I wanted the *witch* to know."

Sitting there in silence, Devon wondered how he could have been so blind. Madness shone from the sellsword's eyes, borne of the pain he had suffered as a youth, of the hatred that had driven him for all his adult life. It made little sense, the blame he placed at Braidon's feet, but who else could a child blame but the king?

"It wasn't Braidon's fault, you know," Devon murmured, though he sensed it was hopeless to argue.

Caledan cackled. "Oh I know." Now his voice took on a steely tone. "But an eye for an eye, as the Knights say, and nothing cuts quite so close as family."

A chill raised the hackles on Devon's neck.

"I wanted *her* family to suffer, as mine suffered," Caledan spat bitterly. "To die, knowing it was justice."

"Braidon was a good man," Devon said. "What would murdering him have achieved?"

"*Why should her family get to live,*" Caledan roared, coming to his feet, "when mine is all gone?" He finished, his words a misery.

"And what about Plorsea?" Devon asked, mustering all the calm he could manage. "You've seen what his death has brought, the chaos. Is this what you wanted, for the sake of revenge?"

"What do I care for Plorsea?" Caledan retorted. Anger seemed to have sobered him somewhat. "What has *Plorsea* ever done for me? The only person you can rely on in this life is yourself, hammerman. Or haven't you figured that out yet?"

Devon laughed. "Quite the opposite, sonny. I wouldn't be here if I'd stood alone all these years." Faces flickered through his mind—Kellian and Merydith and Alana, and so many more now lost to him—and he continued in a softer voice. "I learned long ago that no matter how long I trained, or how hard I fought, there will always be someone better. Magic or no."

"There is *no one* better than me," Caledan hissed, drawing his sword and holding it aloft.

"Is that so?" Devon asked quietly. He rose and advanced on Caledan, until the sword pressed against his chest. His hammer lay at the foot of the table, but Devon had no need for it.

"What are you doing?" Caledan growled.

"I owe you a debt, don't I?" Devon murmured. "You helped me rescue the villagers. I could not have done it without you. If you wanted to hurt Alana, to hurt the ones she loved, you never needed to kill Braidon."

"What are you talking about, old man?" the sellsword slurred.

"Alana died to protect me," Devon whispered. "That is a

truth the Knights refuse to heed. She gave her life for mine. If you wish to hurt her, you only need kill me."

Caledan stared at him, his face contorting with agony. The tip of his sword trembled, and the razor-sharp blade sliced through Devon's tunic. Eyes wild, Caledan bared his teeth, an almost inhuman growl rumbling from his chest. Then he stepped back and pointed at Devon's hammer.

"Pick it up!" he shouted.

"No, sonny," Devon said, moving forward until the sword rested on his chest again. "I'll not fight you."

"Do it!" Caledan screamed. "Let us see who's the better fighter!"

"No," Devon rumbled, his voice echoing through the room. "If you want your revenge, *take it*!"

Caledan pressed down with his sword until blood began to flow. Devon said nothing, only stared at the sellsword, waiting to see what he would do. The strong spirits burned in his stomach and he had no idea why he'd challenged the young warrior. It was madness, and any second now he expected Caledan to skewer him.

What then for Kryssa? There would be no one left to rescue her from the Knights, no one to free her from their clutches. He could not afford to die here, so why had he handed his life over to a madman? Fists clenched, he waited for Caledan to strike the killing blow.

But with an awful scream, Caledan spun and hurled his sword away. Sparks flashed as it struck the bricks of the fireplace. He stumbled away from Devon and crumpled onto the sofa lying in the corner.

Standing by the table, Devon watched him for a long time, until the soft whisper of his snores filled the room and he was sure the swordsman was asleep. Then he retrieved Caledan's sword and returned it to its scabbard.

After a moment's hesitation, he leaned the sword against the sofa.

He hesitated again before departing for his own bed, staring down at the sellsword. The man had had his chance for revenge. Devon could not understand why he'd refused to take it, but he was relieved. Despite his aging body, he'd realised in that moment he was still needed. He could not allow despair to conquer him now, not so long as he still breathed. Only when he lay cold in his grave would he finally rest.

THE NEXT MORNING, Devon was woken by a groan and a curse. He looked up to see Caledan stagger into the room. For half a second his heart began to race…and then he recalled he was sharing the room with the sellsword. The man's eyes were red and his face pale; it looked like he was suffering. Stumbling past Devon, he made for his bed before apparently deciding better of it.

He reached the window just in time to hurl the contents of his stomach out into the street. Somewhere outside a voice shouted out, but Caledan was already sinking onto his bed.

"Don't think that'll help our relationship with the door guards," Devon remarked. "Better?"

Caledan shook his head. "I'm never drinking again."

"I've rarely seen a man in such a state."

Caledan shrugged. "The king is dead."

Devon eyed him closely, but the sellsword did not seem to recall the conversation from the night before.

"I suppose you'll be leaving us then?" he asked.

Caledan looked up. "Why?"

"The king is dead," Devon said, repeating the obvious.

"Yes…" the warrior trailed off, his face taking on a pained look. "But…the Knights still have Pela's mother."

"Ay, but I can't afford you, sonny," Devon said softly.

Caledan shrugged, his eyes distant. "It can't all have been for nothing," he murmured, almost to himself. Then he shook himself. "You can't rescue the woman without me."

"I'm not sure we can rescue her *with* you."

"Even so." Caledan gave a pained grin. "I have a reputation to uphold. I cannot go abandoning a quest half-done."

Devon eyed the man, remembering his rage the night before. Finally he sighed. "Very well, sonny." He glanced out the window. The first hint of light now lit the world. "We'll take the first ferry across the Lane. But first I need to talk with Pela. She won't be continuing with us."

"Good luck with that," Caledan remarked.

"I wish I'd never let her come this far," Devon murmured. "But it can't go on, not now, when so much is at stake."

"Did you have a plan for how to rescue the woman from a hundred of the bastards?" Caledan grunted.

"Ay," Devon replied. "I have a few ideas."

CHAPTER 26

Caledan's head pounded with each step as he descended the stairwell and stepped out into the backyard of the villa. His stomach swirled and he wanted more than anything to return to his bed and sleep. Silently, he cursed his weakness of the night before, for letting grief sweep away his self-control. After watching his father drink himself to death, he rarely tasted anything stronger than ale.

But the king's death had shocked him, cutting him adrift. He had no purpose now, no dreams, nothing to aspire to. For so long, he'd dreamt of slaying the king. But always Braidon had been protected, surrounded by his Guard. Only the most loyal soldiers could join the King's Guard, and Caledan had never been the soldier type. He fought for himself—or whoever could pay the most.

So why had he agreed to continue with Devon's foolish quest? After all, his skills would be in high demand in the coming days, as vultures circled the flailing country. Nobles and merchants alike would offer good gold for his sword. Instead, he'd agreed to help a man who could pay nothing.

Yet his time as a sellsword had only ever been a means to an end. Now that that end no longer existed…what was the point? But neither could he simply retire. Sure, he had coin enough to buy a farm, but what joy would he find eking out an existence on the land? He was a warrior, and he would sooner lie down in a ditch by the Gods Road than surrender to such an existence.

So he would ride with Devon for now—at least until a better opportunity presented itself. Whatever he'd told Devon, he didn't intend to see out his quest until the end. Storming a Castle was one thing; only a madman with a death wish would go up against the full might of the Order.

Caledan grimaced as the clouds parted overhead and the sunlight lit the courtyard. Spotting Devon standing at the docks, he started towards him. The hammerman wore a grim smile, but it fell from his face when he turned and saw Caledan approaching. Their eyes met, and Caledan hesitated.

If you want your revenge, take it!

A frown touched Caledan's forehead. The words were spoken in Devon's voice, but he could not recall the old warrior saying them. Dismissing them, he crossed the courtyard to where the rest of the King's Guard were gathering.

Two dozen remained of the garrison in Lane, along with those men and women who'd survived the Baronian attack. All were garbed for war, their red and gold armour gleaming in the morning sun.

"Caledan!" Pela shouted behind him before he could join the Guard.

The young woman came storming across the courtyard, her face twisted in a fiery rage, and drew to a stop in front of him.

"You can't let him do this!"

Caledan sighed, the pain in his forehead redoubling. The crunch of footsteps saved him from answering as Devon appeared alongside him.

"This discussion is over, missy," Devon rumbled. "You're going back."

"No." Pela's sword flashed into her hand. She pointed it at Devon, her eyes shining. "You can't!"

Devon lifted a finger and moved the point of the sword away.

"I can," he said quietly, crouching beside her. "I told you at the start; I should never have brought you. In that forest, I can't protect you—"

"And who will protect *you*?" Pela snapped. "Or did you forget I saved you in Townirwin?"

"I did not forget," Devon murmured, crouching beside her, "and you have my thanks. But…"

"You don't think we can win, do you?" Pela croaked.

The hammerman closed his eyes and his head bowed. "I…I won't give up, Pela."

"You need me."

"Maybe we do," Devon whispered, and for a moment hope showed on Pela's face. "But Kryssa would not want you to trade your life for hers."

"I won't go," Pela grated. "I'll follow you."

"I know," Devon replied, coming to his feet. "That's why I told Rylle to look out for you. You'll be on the queen's ship, nowhere near the battle, should they find the Baronians. They'll take you home."

"You're passing me off to the King's Guard," Pela hissed.

"Yes," Devon sighed, and Rylle stepped up beside him.

"You can't—"

"I can," Devon cut her off. "You're going, Pela—if I have to chain you to the mast myself, you're going."

Pela's eyes darkened. "I'll never forgive you for this," she hissed, then turned on her heel and stomped down the pier to the queen's ship.

Genevieve appeared from the shadows at the edge of the courtyard. She raised an eyebrow at Devon, but the old warrior only shook his head. "It's for the best," he murmured, then looked at Rylle. "You'll look after her?"

"She's the daughter of Derryn and Kryssa," Rylle replied, as though that was all that needed to be said.

"Thank you," Devon said. His eyes flickered to Genevieve. "Are you sure you're up for this? Going against the whole Order is more than any of us bargained for back in Skystead."

Smiling, Genevieve stepped around the hammerman and crossed the courtyard to where a line of horses waited for them. She swung herself into the saddle of a white gelding and took up the reins of the pack horse.

"Let's get moving," she said shortly, "before we miss the ferry."

A smile flickered on Devon's face and he followed suit. Struggling to keep the last remnants of his supper in his stomach, Caledan hauled himself onto the last horse and followed his companions out the side gate of the villa. Glancing back, he caught a glimpse of Pela on the deck of the queen's ship. She stood with sword in hand, hacking and slashing at invisible enemies—or perhaps at Devon—and Caledan felt a touch of sadness at their departure.

Despite his initial reservations, he'd liked the girl. Terrified as she might have been, Pela had shown more courage over the last few weeks than many adults Caledan had known throughout his thirty-three years. But he supposed the old warrior was right—chances were, none of them would survive an encounter with the entire Order of Alana.

Which raised the question again: why was he following Devon on this suicide mission?

CHAPTER 27

P ela shrieked as she lashed out with her sword, skewering an imaginary enemy and then spinning in time to deflect a second. A sharp hiss followed each swipe of the blade, her breath coming in short gasps. The deck of the ship rocked gently beneath her as the oars rose and fell, propelling them ever downriver.

She barely noticed. The queen's ship was crowded, but she had managed to find some space at the bow where she could practice the drills Caledan had taught her. Not that they mattered now. She cursed and speared an imaginary heart.

After everything they'd been through, how could Devon have done this? He needed her! Pela had not forgotten the despair in his eyes back in Townirwin, how close he had come to giving up on her mother. Now he had lost faith in himself; he was defeated before he'd even begun.

Shouting again, Pela brought her blade down in an overhead slash that would have beheaded anyone standing in her path, then stepped back and sucked in a breath.

What was she going to do? The queen was taking her back to Skystead, to the sleepy little town she had always called home. But what was left for her there now, without her mother or grandmother or Devon? How would she support herself?

Her eyes dropped to the sword in her hand and a shiver ran down her spine. He'd hid it well, but Caledan was no pauper. He had spent his life fighting other men's wars and grown rich doing it. Remembering the rush as her blade sliced through the Elder's back, Pela felt a tremor of excitement, but it was quickly doused by the icy hand of reality.

Most of her life had been spent in fear of one thing or another; how could she think that would change now? She could never be a sellsword, nor a soldier like her father. Her courage would fail. Maybe that was why Devon had sent her away. Had he seen her terror, and given her an escape?

I am not a coward.

Swallowing, Pela brushed a tear from her eye and clung to the thought. She had killed a man, had helped save her fellow villagers against all odds. And still Devon had packed her up and shipped her off as though she were a child in need of protection.

Angrily she sheathed her sword and moved to the railing. Four other ships carved their way downriver alongside them: the King's Guard that had come from Ardath. Men and women packed their decks, red and gold armour shining in the morning sun as they scanned the way ahead for a sign of the Baronians. The survivors of the attack had warned how the black ship had suddenly come upon them, as if out of nowhere. There would be no surprise attacks this time.

Only a few King's Guard remained onboard with Pela,

including Rylle. The rest wore the silver and red of the Queen's Guard, her personal order.

Pela had spent the first few hours exploring the vessel. But while it was the largest ship she'd ever seen, there was little of interest to discover. Only the catapult bolted to the aft deck had perked her interest, though it was covered by a canvas and did not look to have seen any use for a long while. Otherwise, there were the usual sacks of cloth and rope and barrels of whatever supplies the queen had seen fit to stock for the journey, and Pela had soon returned to her sword practice.

Sailing downriver with the oars pounding to the count of five, they were already nearing the delta of the Lane. Pela was glad she would at least be able to see the end of the vicious Baronians. Once the fleet reached open ocean, they would split in two and scour the coast. No matter what magic propelled the Baronian ship, they could not simply vanish.

"What are you doing up here, little one?"

Pela started and spun around, her eyes widening to find the queen standing behind her. Her mouth dropped open, before she remembered her manners and snapped it closed again, biting her tongue. She swore, then slapped a hand to her mouth in horror.

The queen only smiled and joined her at the railings. "I have never been to Skystead, though I hear it is beautiful," she commented. "Do you have those…beasts there?" She nodded to one of the great crocodiles basking on the banks of the Lane.

A shudder ran down Pela's spine. "Sometimes," she murmured, "but mostly the water is deep and too cold in the fiord. They only appear after a storm, when they've been washed from the marshes or the delta."

"They killed my husband," the queen murmured. "I was in my cabin when it happened. I did not see, but they say when he fell overboard…" She shook her head, and for a second the mask of royalty cracked. Her eyes shone in the morning sun. "They say the water was red with blood."

"I'm sorry," Pela whispered. Tentatively, she placed a hand on the woman's shoulder, unsure how to comfort a queen.

Marianne shrugged and looked away. "We'll have the bastards who did it soon," she said, a smile touching her lips. "We'll make them pay for taking him from me."

"I hope so," Pela replied. Sadness tinged her voice as she thought of her mother, all alone with an entirely different set of monsters.

"Devon will find your mother," the queen said, as though reading her mind. "My husband always spoke highly of him, though the hammerman retired his commission long before we were married."

"And what about the people who took her?" Pela asked, a little too sharply.

The queen's eyes flickered closed. "I am so sorry," she whispered. "In Lonia, there have been those who claim to follow the path of Alana, who have committed such acts. I did not think they had reached my adopted nation. Trust me, whatever radicals have taken her will face the queen's justice."

"Thank you," Pela whispered, though she wished the queen had cared enough to send some of the King's Guard with Devon.

The fleet had close to four hundred soldiers between them; against no more than fifty Baronian warriors, it would be a slaughter when they tracked them down. Though when the fleet divided, Pela supposed those odds would narrow.

"You are most welcome, young Pela," the queen replied, embracing her. Then she smiled and gestured at the sword on Pela's belt. "Do you wish to become a warrior yourself someday, like Devon and your father?"

Pela's jaw tightened and she looked away. "I don't know," she murmured. "Maybe I will when we reach Skystead, but then...if my mother never returns, there is nothing for me there."

"Perhaps you should consider returning to the capital with my people?" Marianne offered. "I'm going to need brave women and men around me if we're to keep Plorsea from tearing itself apart."

"You would really want me?" Pela stammered, her vision blurring as she fought back sudden tears.

The queen smiled, but just then a shout carried across the water from the leading ship. They swung around as a dark vessel emerged from the mangroves ahead. Pela's heart clenched as she recognised the black flag atop the strange masts. It raced upriver towards them, hugging the starboard bank.

"What are they doing here?" Pela gasped.

"Trying to get past us," the queen replied.

Pela saw that it was true. The fleet had been negotiating the deeper waters to port and been caught unawares. If they did not act quickly, the Baronians would shoot past and escape upriver. But the first of the Plorsean ships was already turning to cut them off. The King's Guard were bulkier and slower to respond than the Baronians', and Pela held her breath.

At the last moment it became clear the Baronians would not make it. Julian must have realised it too, for the ship turned sharply, abandoning any attempt to escape and angling towards their pursuers. Unable to manoeuvre as quickly, the King's Guard turned to meet them and found themselves floundering in the surging currents. The captain bellowed orders and the men struggled to withdraw their oars…

The Baronian prow slammed into the wallowing ship with a crash of breaking timber. Oars shattered and men were hurled overboard by the power of the collision, disappearing beneath the murky currents. Pela gasped as screams drifted across the open water, followed by the cheering of Baronian voices.

The black ship surged on, struggling to escape the tangles of the King's Guard.

"*No,*" Pela whispered. They were going to escape.

She looked around for the queen, but her guard was already shepherding her below deck to her cabin. Pela cursed and returned her gaze to the entangled ships. A line rose from the Plorsean vessel, clanking down onto the enemy ship. A second followed, then a third, and suddenly the Baronians were no longer pulling away, but being dragged back towards the floundering King's Guard.

"Yes!" Pela punched the air as the ships crashed together.

A roar came from the King's Guard as they surged over the railings onto the pirate ship. The Baronians met them with bellows of their own, and the forces came together in a clash of steel on steel.

With the two ships locked together, the remaining vessels of the King's Guard powered closer and hurled lines of their own. Wood splinted as the ships converged, surrounding the Baronians on all sides. Only the queen's ship hung back.

Outnumbered and outmatched, the Baronian black slowly gave way to the red and gold. Though they fought like demons, there was no hope for them now. One by one they fell, until only a small ring of armoured fighters remained in the centre of the ship.

Movement came from within the circle as one of the Baronians leapt onto a barrel. Pela recognised Julian, his fists and mouth open as he shouted his defiance. Then one of the King's Guard hurled an axe. The heavy blade embedded itself in Julian's chest and he toppled backwards without a sound.

After that, the remaining Baronians fell quickly, and a heavy silence returned to the river. The five ships bobbed gently together, the four vessels of the King's Guard locked to the black one. Their oars unmanned, they drifted slowly downstream, their progress mirrored by the queen's galley.

"Long live the king!" As one, the King's Guard lifted their swords to the sky.

Pela smiled and was about to answer their cry, when shouting broke out behind her.

"*No, what are you doing?!*"

CHAPTER 28

D evon, Caledan, and Genevieve took the river road for the first day, following the directions of strangers who had seen the Knights depart. No one recalled seeing a woman of Kryssa's description though, and Devon was beginning to doubt that Kryssa had ever reached Lane. It mattered little now though—his path had been chosen; he would not retreat from it now.

Older and more disused than the Gods Road, the track they followed was overgrown and washed out in places, and they had to take care with their horses not to slip from the banks into the river. They were far above the delta here and the currents were quick, still muddy from the storm of several days past.

Not long after they'd started out, the fleet had drifted past, oars beating the water in their haste to catch the Baronians. Devon had waved and looked for Pela, but if she was watching she had not made herself known.

Now he wondered if he'd done the right thing, sending her away, but it was too late to change his mind now. At least if they did somehow rescue Kryssa, she was less likely to kill him offhand for endangering her daughter.

Devon was surprised though to find himself with companions on this final quest. Glancing sidelong at Caledan and Genevieve, he wondered again at their motivations. Caledan still had not said anything of the night before, and Devon hadn't pressed the matter. The king was dead and there was no need to revisit that pain—for either of them.

Watching Caledan ride, Devon felt conflicted. He respected Caledan's skill—and was grateful for his aid—but there was a darkness to him as well. To be willing to kill the king and plunge Plorsea into chaos…

Devon shook his head, turning his attention to the huntress. If anything, Genevieve's continued devotion was even more perplexing. When they'd first set off from Skystead, he'd thought her motivations the same as Tobias's and his own. Yet there had been no one for Genevieve amongst the villagers they'd rescued, no loved one to embrace.

With a start, Devon realised what he'd missed. In the rush of discovering Kryssa was alive, he'd forgotten the dead women on the floor of the pantheon. Touched by guilt, he looked sidelong at Genevieve. He'd been too consumed by his own grief in Townirwin to notice her state of mind, and he wondered who that unknown woman had been to the huntswoman. Devon wasn't game to ask now.

They continued downriver for several hours. The passage so many men and horses had churned the track to mud, but as they struggled to free their horses for the third time, Genevieve reassured them it was a good sign. Such a large group travelling on these backroads could only be the Knights. They would not go unnoticed; tracking them might yet prove easier than Devon had expected. And where the Knights went, surely they would find Kryssa.

"Have you thought of a better plan yet?" Caledan asked as the sun passed noon and began its descent towards the west.

"No," Devon sighed. "It's the only way."

"We don't even know they'll have her," Caledan put in.

"That's a gamble I'm going to have to take," Devon replied.

Caledan nodded and dropped the subject, but on the other horse Genevieve shook her head. "It's suicide."

Devon chuckled. "I'll admit, I'm open to other ideas."

They rode on in silence for a while, until the path veered suddenly inland. At the bend, a smaller track led down to where a wharf stuck out into the river. Water raced past beneath the wooden struts, but there was no sign of the crocodiles below. Bootprints led up from the wharf to join the churned-up mess the Knights had left.

"Looks like more joined them here," Genevieve commented.

"If things go to plan, numbers aren't going to matter," Devon answered.

"Easy for you to say," Caledan said. "You're not going to have them on your trail."

Devon grunted but did not reply. They plodded inland, the great trees of the Plorsean Forest rising up to swallow them. They were lucky the main body of Knights was ahead; the track was badly overgrown, and their passage had crushed many of the young saplings that had taken root in the open earth.

Even so, by the time night fell Devon was puffing hard and cursing the Knights for leading them so far off the Gods Roads. The sun had dropped early beneath the canopy, but they'd pressed on at pace, eager to close the gap before the last shadows faded beneath the trees. Finally, they made camp in a small glade not far from the track.

Against Caledan's warnings, Devon lit a fire before sitting back on a tree stump to enjoy the warmth.

"What makes you do it, Devon?" Caledan asked after they'd finished a sparse dinner of dried beef and onions.

"Do what?" Devon asked as Genevieve leaned in.

"All this." Caledan gestured around the clearing, as though that explained his question. When Devon only raised an eyebrow, he sighed and elaborated. "Play the hero. What do you get out of it? You know you're more than likely going to fail, so why put yourself at risk?"

Devon stared into the flames. "Because Kryssa needs me," he whispered.

Caledan snorted. "You're not even related."

"No," Devon answered quietly. "I never let her call me 'Father', when she was young. I never understood why Selina brought her into our house. Life was hard enough as it was."

He looked up at them then, taking them in. Genevieve still sat slightly apart, her eyes distant, as though she were lost in some other time. The sellsword stared back at him though.

"Then why didn't you leave?" he asked. "That was, what, twenty years ago? You had your youth, your strength…you could have done anything, gone anywhere."

"I still have my strength, sonny," Devon replied, then shook his head. "And I'm glad I didn't leave. What Selina and Kryssa gave me, no amount of strength or coin can buy. They were—*are*—my family."

Caledan looked away sharply, and Devon knew he was thinking of his own family, torn apart by the death of magic. He swallowed, wondering what words of comfort he could offer the man. Yet Caledan did not know that Devon knew about his past—nor of his secret quest to kill the king. After a moment's hesitation, Devon decided to remain silent.

"I never had a family," Caledan replied finally. "When I was young, I learned to rely on myself. I need no one else," he finished, his voice taking on a sharp tone.

"I won't argue with you, sonny," Devon murmured.

"Do you think the others made it safely to Skystead?" Genevieve interrupted.

Devon smiled and nodded his thanks for the change of subject. "I hope so. Tallow is a fine captain."

Caledan laughed. "Poor Tobias, returning to that farm in the mountains. How will he cope after having a taste of the good life?"

"I don't know that he thought of this as the good life," Devon commented mildly.

"Ha!" Caledan straightened. "Don't tell me you weren't bored in that village, Devon. A man like you, you used to be a hero! People worshiped you. I don't know how you turned your back on that life."

Devon shrugged. "I've never been a hero," he replied. "I am merely a man who was better than average with a warhammer. It saddens me now, knowing that is the legacy I leave: as a man that excelled at violence. There is nothing heroic about that."

"The villagers we freed would disagree."

"Ay, I suppose that's true," Devon replied. "They look at us and see warriors, men to walk the mountains with, who guard the nation against evil. But that's not really the truth, is it? We are only men, just like them, only we're afraid to live an ordinary life, to earn an honest living toiling in the earth, to build something rather than tear down the works of our betters. The life they live in Skystead, that takes real courage, sonny."

"What rubbish are you talking, old man?" Caledan snapped, quick to anger now. "Have your advanced years finally addled your mind?"

Devon chuckled. "Maybe," he said, "or maybe I'm just the wiser for them. Tell me, Caledan, which is more noble? The man who spends his life growing crops to feed his family and others—or the man who comes with a sword and takes those crops for himself?"

"The farmer, of course," Caledan retorted. "There is no honour in theft."

"Devon said nothing of theft," Genevieve said with a smile. Caledan glared at her, but Devon gestured for her to go on. "Is that not what a conquering army does? Takes from those they have defeated?"

"That's different."

"How?" Genevieve pressed.

"A soldier takes no coin from those they fight. The crown pays their wage."

"Ay, but where does the crown's coin come from, when they go to war?" Genevieve laughed.

Caledan swore and exploded to his feet. "That still does not explain how the farmer is braver than the warrior!"

"Do you not fear such a life then?" Devon asked quietly, though he knew the answer. He'd seen it in the man's eyes the night before, with his talk of having nothing left to live for.

A stillness came over the sellsword. When he said nothing, Devon continued:

"I know I did, once. There was a time when I feared just the thought of such a life. The idea of rising each morning, to etch out an existence in the same menial job, day after day…it filled me with dread."

"And now?" Caledan croaked, his eyes wide, like a deer caught in an open field.

Devon made to reply, but at that moment there came a *crack* from outside the circle of firelight. He was on his feet in an instant, hammer in hand, searching the darkness for signs of movement.

"I'd stop talking with him now, if I were you," a voice spoke from the shadows, raising the hairs on the back of Devon's neck. "Devon's spent far too much time drinking with Selina."

A figure stepped into the firelight. Braidon's clothes were torn and mud-stained, and his beard was matted with grime, but the king wore a ragged grin on his lips as he staggered across to the fire and slumped onto a log beside them.

"Lovely evening," he said conversationally, holding his hands out to the flames. "What brings you to this part of the woods, Devon? Last I heard, you were happily retired in Skystead."

CHAPTER 29

F or Braidon, the seconds after his fall were a blur, as he had first tried to fend off the berserker who'd gone over the side with him—and then escape the croc that had torn the man in two. Blood had stained the river red, the waters churning with the ravenous creatures. Desperate, Braidon had swum faster than he ever had before, making for the shallows.

Miraculously, he had made it. Perhaps the crocodiles had been occupied by easier prey, or perhaps he'd just been lucky. But his luck had run out once he'd hauled himself ashore and looked around. Locked together in battle, the two ships had been caught in the currents and were already drifting out of sight. By the time he'd called out, they'd been far away, already disappearing into one of a myriad of channels.

He had waited for long minutes, knowing his ship would return—if his King's Guards managed to see off the Baronians. But as the waters grew still, Braidon had sensed unseen eyes watching him. Marshland bordered the lower reaches of the Lane and he'd still stood in knee-deep water. With the thick mud beneath his feet, there would be no opportunity to manoeuvre should the crocs seek fresh prey.

Remembering the ferocity of the Baronians, Braidon had sent up a prayer to the Gods that Marianne was safe. After a moment's hesitation, he'd added Alana to the prayer, though even in his desperation had failed to keep a grim smile from his face. Not in a million years would his ten-year-old self have guessed his sister would become a deity worshiped by thousands.

Fear of the crocodiles and the return of the Baronians had eventually forced Braidon away from the river. He had trekked inland until coming to solid ground, then followed the first trail he could find leading north. Lane was the nearest settlement of any size, though on foot and on poor roads the journey could take as long as three days.

That had been two days ago. By now the world must think him dead, and Braidon feared for what might have transpired in his absence. Had Marianne survived? Was his son safe? And what of the Lonians? They would take advantage of any Plorsean weakness they could exploit.

Then there was the matter of the Baronian ship. Its design remined him of the strange vessels he'd seen at the docks in Lon. He wondered if the Lonians had had a hand in the attack, and what this new power was they possessed. In a world without magic, it posed a threat he did not know how to counter. And if the Lonians were bold enough to act against him, even under the guise of Baronians…he feared what that meant for Plorsea, and for his family.

But finding Devon here, in his darkest hour, gave Braidon hope that all might not be lost. Surely it was a sign. He didn't care if it came from the Three Gods or his sister, only that he could return to Ardath with the hero beside him. It might even give Lonia second thoughts about attacking Plorsea, with their faith in the Knights of Alana and Devon's place in those tales.

Holding his hands out to the fire, Braidon couldn't help but grin at the shock written across his friend's face.

"You look like you've seen a ghost, old friend," Braidon announced finally, after Devon had not said anything for a long moment.

Stepping quickly across the clearing, Devon hauled him up and engulfed him in a bear hug. "Good to see you, sonny," he bellowed, then in a softer voice that only Braidon could hear: "*Say nothing of your name.*"

Frowning, Braidon stepped back as Devon gestured to his companions. "This is Caledan and Genevieve," he said, indicating each in turn before pointing at Braidon. "This is Brenden. He fought with me in the Plorsean army, for a time."

Braidon shook each of their hands. "Nice to meet you," he said, then sank back onto the log. "Don't suppose you've got any food? I'm starving."

"What happened to your gear?" Caledan asked, his tone unwelcoming. Braidon had lost everything but his sword in the fall.

"You heard the news?" Devon asked before Braidon could respond. "The king is dead."

"Here," Genevieve added, holding out a strip of dried beef.

Braidon took it with a grin. "Cheers," he said, then looked at Devon. "This morning. I heard Baronians were involved."

"Baronians? In Plorsea? Now how would such bandits have crept into our great nation?" Devon asked, his voice heavy with sarcasm.

"If I remember correctly, you led a band of them once, didn't you?" Braidon replied, trying not to respond to the man's baiting. "Regardless, do you know what's to be done about them?"

"The queen is leading an expedition to hunt them down," Devon answered.

"*The queen!*" Braidon gasped, before swallowing back his shock and continuing in a more measured tone. "Surely that would be the job of the King's Guard."

"They're going with her. Five ships in all. We saw them sail past us."

"Well, I hope they catch the bastards," Braidon muttered.

"I doubt they'll have much trouble, once they track 'em down," Devon said, "but the Baronians are not our biggest problem just now."

"Oh?" Braidon asked. "So it was not the king's death that brought you out of retirement?"

Devon smiled grimly. "No," he replied. "It was the Knights of Alana."

Braidon snorted. "What have those fanatics done now?"

"They came to Skystead and attacked the temple, took Kryssa. I believe they plan to sacrifice her at the midsummer solstice."

"Wha...what?" Braidon gaped. "This...you're joking, right? Who's Kryssa?"

It was the wrong thing to say.

Devon's face darkened. "Kryssa is the child Selina adopted, when we still lived in Ardath. You have met her in fact, many times. But then I would not expect—" He cut himself off, and Braidon realised he could not finish the sentence without giving his identity away.

"I'm so sorry," he whispered, knowing it was not

215

enough. Still reeling from the last few days, he had forgotten the name for half a moment, though he did not expect Devon to take his word for it. "When did this happen?"

"We have been hunting the Knights who took her for weeks," Genevieve said when Devon did not answer.

"Been a while since the two of you saw each other," Caledan murmured. "How did you say you met again?"

Braidon's heart quickened beneath the man's hawkish gaze. Sweat trickled down his neck as the moment drew out. He didn't know why Devon wanted to keep his identity secret, but Caledan had the look of a killer about him. Braidon knew a man he did not want to cross when he saw one.

"Brenden fought with me in some border skirmishes," Devon answered finally.

"I'm sorry, Devon," Braidon repeated. "Do you know where these Knights are heading?"

"Somewhere in the forest," Genevieve answered.

"The Forest of Plorsea? It spans for leagues in all directions from here. And the deeper you go, the more dangerous it becomes."

"We'll find them," Genevieve replied with feeling. "I've been following their tracks, from one group at least. More have joined them since we left Lane. There must be hundreds in the forest."

"*Hundreds?*" Braidon exclaimed, looking from her to Devon. "You can't be serious? With the king…dead, the queen needs people she can trust to keep the peace. We cannot afford for you to throw your life away on some hopeless quest!"

"The queen can take care of herself," Devon replied, his eyes shining. "My…Kryssa needs me."

"You're just one man, Devon," Braidon whispered. "Not even you can defeat so many."

"It doesn't matter."

Braidon knuckled his forehead and turned to the others. "What about the two of you? Surely you can't be going along with this?"

Caledan shrugged and Genevieve gave a quiet grin. "The old man has a plan."

"A plan!" Braidon burst out, swinging on Devon. "*Now* you have a plan?"

Devon shrugged and looked away. Braidon swallowed. Devon had always had a presence about him, an unyielding strength that made people believe he could move mountains. But in the flickering firelight, Braidon could see the lines on his face, the bags under his eyes, and for a second he wondered how long his friend had for this world.

Then the hammerman blinked, and the image vanished, his familiar confidence returning.

"Please, Devon," Braidon said. He needed to get back to Ardath and his son, to take command of the situation. But even more, he needed his old friend at his side, to stand against this new darkness. "Plorsea needs you."

"Kryssa has a daughter," Devon rumbled. "Her name is Pela. I promised I would not return without her mother. She needs me more, sonny."

"What is one woman, one girl, to the fate of a nation?"

"What is a nation, if it cannot protect the innocent?" Devon countered.

"*Everything!*" Braidon snapped, leaping to his feet. Breath hissed between his teeth as he inhaled, then he realised Caledan was watching. Slowly he sank back to his seat. "If the king is dead, the Lonians will come. It's only a matter of time," he explained. "We're not ready. We need a hero like you, or Plorsea will be lost."

"And what of it?" Caledan growled. "What is Plorsea but a name? What does it matter if we are ruled from Lon? They can't be any worse than the fool we had until two days ago."

Braidon glanced at Devon, expecting his friend to disagree, but the hammerman only raised an eyebrow. It was left to the huntress to come to his defence.

"Thousands will die," she murmured.

"And others will find their fortune," Caledan replied. "It's how I made mine."

Braidon looked at Devon. "You truly believe this woman is worth sacrificing a nation for, Devon?"

"What's the point of saving Plorsea, if I can't save my family?" Devon replied.

The breath caught in Braidon's throat and he had to look away. His mind raced back to the day they'd lost Alana. The Tsar had been defeated, his armies sundered, but for Devon and Braidon there had been no joy, no celebration. The price had been too high. Braidon had lost his sister, Devon his love.

"We could use an extra sword, sonny," Devon murmured.

Braidon's head whipped around, his eyes catching in Devon's amber gaze. He remembered another time then, long ago, when Devon had stood aboard the *Songbird* and defied a demon to protect Braidon and Alana. And again in Fort Fall, against the Tsar's Stalkers, and in the throne room against their father himself. Again and again, down through the decades, this man had been there for Braidon, had laid his life on the line for the Three Nations.

Now he was asking Braidon to do the same for him.

Looking into his eyes, Braidon glimpsed again Devon's pain, the exhaustion he tried so hard to disguise. Age had caught up with him, diminished his once-great strength. He had no right to be wandering these country roads on a quest to rescue a kidnapped woman, no right to stand against the Knights of Alana. Yet he would, because he was Devon.

And Braidon could not deny him.

"Okay, Devon," he said. The decision was surprisingly easy to make. "What's the plan?"

CHAPTER 30

"We'll reach the Cove tomorrow," Putar declared as they dismounted.

"If we survive the night," Ikar grunted.

They had recovered their horses not long after Putar's appearance, and from there had veered from the Gods Road onto the backtrails of the Forest of Plorsea. A ferryman had helped them across the Lane the same day, and they'd spent another two days within the forest before moving out onto Chole's volcanic plateau.

It had not been until this morning though that they had left Plorsea behind, and ventured into the uncharted jungles of Dragon Country. Ikar had pushed them hard, eager to leave the forest behind. Putar had assured him the Red Dragons would not touch them, but Ikar was far from convinced. The beasts were vicious, hateful creatures and would attack at the slightest provocation. He would be glad to reach the end of their journey.

Even more so to bid farewell to the Elder. The last few days on the road had diminished Putar. The man needed

Ikar's aid just to climb into the saddle each morning, and spent most of his time complaining of one discomfort or another. He seemed to blame Kryssa for his situation, and as his mood grew fouler each day, Ikar was forced to place himself between the Elder and their captive.

He untied her from the saddle now, though he left her hands bound, and helped her to dismount. She staggered as her feet touched the ground, cramped from the long hours in the saddle, but she recovered without Ikar's aid. He quickly withdrew the hand he'd extended to help her, but not before Kryssa noticed.

"Thank you, oh Knight," she said, a smile twisting her lips, "but I am quite alright. Perhaps the fat man has need of your assistance?"

"Blasphemous witch!" Putar cursed. He swung from the saddle with a little too much violence and his foot caught in the stirrup, toppling him face-first into the mud.

Ikar snorted as the Elder thrashed in the mud. By the time Putar finally sat up, he was covered from head to toe, and Ikar was glad for the helmet concealing his face. He did not think the Elder would appreciate his amusement. Kryssa's mirth had enraged him enough.

Dragging himself to his feet, he tore the riding crop from his saddle and advanced on Kryssa. Ikar stepped between them and raised a hand.

"We cannot touch her," he said quietly, though there was steel in his voice. "Were those not your orders?"

Putar's face went a mottled purple. "Ay, they were *my* orders. And now I command you to step aside, Knight. The witch must pay for her disrespect."

Ikar remained in place for several seconds longer than was proper, but finally he stepped aside. Whatever his personal thoughts, he had no right to defy an Elder, though in truth he had come to enjoy the woman's company far more than Putar's on this journey. Despite her predicament, Kryssa remained surprisingly light-hearted throughout the long days, although that was perhaps only to deflect their suspicions from her own schemes.

She had made another two escape attempts since the first, frustrating Ikar to the point of violence. He had been forced to knock her from the saddle at almost full gallop the last time. The hard mountain earth had been unforgiving, and a dozen scratches and bruises now marked her arms and legs.

"Is it disrespectful to point out the obvious, fat man?" Kryssa laughed, her head tilted to one side.

"Witch!" Putar bellowed, his teeth bared. "You dare to laugh at an Elder of the Order!"

Kryssa snorted. "Only when they fall on their—"

She broke off as Putar whipped her across the face with his cane. Her hands still bound, Kryssa toppled backwards into the mud, a cry on her lips. Ikar gasped and took half a step forward, but Putar flashed him a warning glare, and he stilled once more.

The cane still in hand, he advanced on the woman. Still on her back, Kryssa glared up at him, her sapphire eyes defiant. Snorting, she spat a bloody glob of saliva at his feet.

"Is that the best you can do?"

Snarling, Putar lashed out with his boot, catching her in the stomach. The blow lifted her from the ground and sent her rolling across the clearing. Nearby, the horses snickered, made nervous by the woman's cries. Ikar swallowed and looked away, disgusted by this new level of cruelty from Putar.

Air whistled between Kryssa's teeth as she struggled to her knees. "Coward."

The cane descended again. Ikar winced and closed his eyes to the *crack* of wood on flesh. Again and again it came, punctuated each time by a scream from Putar. Clenching his fists, Ikar struggled to control his rage. Putar's malice had revealed him for what he was: a cruel, vile man, obsessed with his own power. His prior virtue had only ever been a deception.

A scream rent the clearing and finally Ikar could take it no more. Spinning, he reached for his sword…

…and froze when he saw Kryssa half crouched in the mud, Putar now lying motionless at her feet. Eyes wide, she stared back at him, as though waiting to see how he would react.

"What have you done?" Steel hissed on leather he drew his blade and advanced on the woman.

She did not move, not even when he stretched out his sword and rested the point against her throat. A fresh bruise was already beginning to darken on her cheek where Putar had struck her.

Ikar's eyes darted to the Elder, but it took only a glance to confirm he was dead. Putar's neck was bent at an unnatural angle, and his open eyes stared back at Ikar, unblinking. He swallowed. Kryssa's hands were still bound before her— how had she killed him? A shudder raced down his spine as he tensed, readying himself to strike her down.

"Do it," she hissed, eyes aflame. "Go on!"

Shocked by the venom in her voice, Ikar took a step back. Unperturbed, Kryssa rose and advanced until his blade touched her throat once more.

"Please," she whispered. "Or let me go. I refuse to be your sacrifice, to feed whatever hatred burns in your Order."

For a moment, Ikar was prepared to do it, such was her

desperation. All it would take was one thrust, and her suffering would end. Then he looked into her eyes...

"I can't," he croaked.

"You must!" she snapped. "I murdered your precious Elder."

He glanced again at the body lying by his feet. Even in death, Putar's face had a hateful look about it. Slowly Ikar shook his head.

"He was no Elder," he murmured. "He defiled the title with his malice. You are chosen by the Saviour, if he died by your hand, it must be her will."

Kryssa stood unmoving for a long time, her eyes transfixed on Ikar, as though somehow her gaze could pierce the steel confines of his helmet.

"So be it," she said suddenly, her words as sharp as razors. "But know this, from now on you are my enemy, and I will not hesitate to kill you."

Ikar opened his mouth to laugh, then he saw again Putar's body, and the laughter died on his lips. A shudder raced up his spine, lifting the hackles on his neck.

"So be it," he agreed.

That night, Ikar did not rest, only sat watching the woman in her sleeping sack, and when the first light of the morning found them, they were already well on their way.

CHAPTER 31

Pela sat crouched amongst a cluster of barrels, arms wrapped tightly around her chest. In her mind, she could still hear the screams of the dying men, rising like banshees above the crackling of flames. She could still see the burning ships, still smell the stench of roasting flesh.

A shudder rippled through her body and she struggled to keep from crying. She couldn't afford so much as whimper, lest they hear and find her. Closing her eyes, she prayed to the Three Gods for deliverance, for rescue, to be anywhere but the queen's ship.

She still could not process what had happened. One second, the King's Guard had been celebrating their victory, their cheers rising up from the defeated Baronian vessel. The next, someone had been screaming, and Pela had spun in time to see a melee break out on the queen's ship, to glimpse the catapult crouched like a spider on the stern deck.

Then with an awful *crack*, the weapon had released,

225

hurling a burning barrel high overhead. Up and up it had risen, until it reached the peak of its arc, and went tumbling back down. Down into the cluster of ships it had fallen, and with an awful *boom*, exploded.

Almost in slow motion, the Baronian vessel had lifted from the water, as though propelled upwards by the hand of the Gods. Men had been hurled screaming into the air as flames blossomed, then suddenly the five ships were gone, vanished amidst the flaming tempest now burning upon the waters of the Lane.

Pela had hurled herself to the deck as pieces of wood and debris rained down. A wave had swept across the queen's ship and for a moment she'd thought they would all burn. Clenching her eyes closed, she had waited for death to find her.

But somehow, Pela had been spared, and the heat had gone racing away, to be replaced by plumes of smoke that went billowing across the river. The clashing of steel had rung out across the deck of the queen's ship, but amidst the putrid fumes Pela could not see who was fighting.

Stumbling through the chaos, she'd searched for the queen, but the woman had vanished, and Pela had searched for a hiding place of her own. With the screams of the dying and the roaring of flames all around, she'd stumbled into the pile of barrels at the stern—and had crawled between them.

Only when she was deep in the depths of the pile, did Pela realise the barrels were the same kind the catapult had hurled at the Baronian ship. Crouching low, she cracked the top off one, revealing a strange black powder within. An acrid stench touched her nostrils and she quickly replaced the lid, the hackles lifting on her neck.

If one barrel could do so much damage, what would a dozen do? But silence had fallen across the queen's ship now and there was no time left to search for a new hiding place. She held her breath, waiting to find out who had won.

"There's men in the water!" a voice called out.

A soft *thud* followed, then another, before a second voice replied, "Not for long."

Pela choked back a sob as she realised the men were firing on any of the King's Guard who had survived. Stuffing her fist into her mouth, Pela scrunched her eyes closed and waited for the nightmare to end.

Except it never did. As the hours crept by, Pela found herself dozing, made drowsy by the heat beneath the canvas covering the barrels. Eventually someone spoke nearby her hiding place, snapping her awake.

"Anyone seen the girl?" a man's voice carried on the breeze.

"Not since the attack," another replied. "Probably jumped ship.

Someone cursed. "Then she's croc food. I wonder who the third sacrifice will be now."

"The Elders will find one. Maybe the Consort, or one of his companions. I hear they're riding straight for the Cove."

The first speaker laughed. "More fool on them," he said, then after a moment had passed: "Have you ever seen such a sight?"

"The flames?" came the reply, the speaker's voice touched by awe. "Never."

"That black powder…"

"Not even the cursed Magickers could have done so well," another added. "Truly, the engineers have outdone themselves. When all of Lonia's ships possess the black powder and steam engines, no force in the Three Nations will be able to stand against us."

"Praise be Alana!" the other exclaimed. "Her sacrifice finally bears fruit for our people."

"Her sacrifice, and all those who have followed," another chuckled. "The solstice approaches. How long until we reach the Cove?"

An icy chill spread through Pela's stomach as she listened. Their words revealed them as members of the Order, but how had the infiltrated the queen's ship? And where was the queen? Pela had not seen or even heard her since the explosion. Had she been caught in the melee?

The men had spoken of the Elders finding a third sacrifice. A cold breeze touched her neck as she realised the first must be her mother, the second the queen.

She was to have been the third.

Suddenly Pela was unable to catch her breath.

They planned to murder me!

Pela gripped the top of a nearby barrel, struggling to keep quiet, and only the tiniest of squeaks slipped from her lips. She felt as though she were suffocating. Then another thought struck her:

They know about Devon!

They knew her uncle was coming. She shuddered, the blood pounding in her ears as true panic took hold. What was she going to do? She was trapped aboard this ship, going who-knew-where! The rowers had taken to the oars not long after the battle; they could be anywhere by now.

I must warn Devon!

But she couldn't even help herself.

No, she hissed in the silence of her mind. *You are a fighter*.

Her hand dropped to the hilt of her father's sword. Derryn had fought for the king himself, had saved the man's life. How could she do anything less? If she could get the queen away from wherever they were keeping her and over the side, Pela thought they could make it to the riverbank before anyone noticed. It was already growing dark, and it did not sound as though there were many men left onboard. And those that remained were relaxed, thinking the day won.

"Tomorrow night, I expect. I'll not be sad to see this ship burn. Tired of rowing."

The other laughed. "Can't stand a little hard work?"

"Not when a bit of coal will do it for me."

"Soon enough," came the reply. "Come on then, the girl's gone. Let's put our backs into it. The harder we row, the faster we're there. Then we can finally burn this archaic heap of timber."

"Ain't that the truth."

The voices retreated, and Pela crawled to the edge of the stack of barrels. She poked her head out from the canvas and saw the red light staining the horizon. The yellow orb of the sun was just visible through the wiry branches of the mangroves. The speakers were just disappearing beneath the deck to the oar banks. Pela had only been down there once and was in no hurry to return. It stank of rotting fish and sweating bodies, the air stifling in the summer heat.

Silently, she crept from her hiding place. The aft was raised, with a single flight of stairs leading down to the rest of the ship. Beside the stairs, a railing prevented anyone from accidentally falling from the upper to lower deck. Pela crept forward until she was positioned behind the railings and peeked over the edge.

Directly below her, two men stood with their arms folded, guarding the door to the main cabin positioned beneath the aft deck. She cursed silently to herself. That had to be where they were keeping the queen.

Pela loosened her sword in its scabbard, then thought better of it. Both guards wore plate mail armour and carried heavy broadswords on their belts. She wouldn't stand a chance if it came to a fight.

I should never have brought you.

She shrank as Devon's words whispered in her mind. Retreating to her hiding place, Pela crouched in the shadows and hugged her knees to her chest. Her uncle had been right. She should never have come. What chance did she stand against full-grown men, when they'd already cut down the best of the King's Guard? She should just do as the men thought she had and jump overboard. She could swim to shore and head for Lane, and report the attack to…

Who?

There was no one left. The King's Guard were all gone, slaughtered to a man. The queen was held hostage and Devon was walking into a trap. If she fled, she would be giving up her one chance to do something, to fight back against the Order and their Knights.

Pela sucked in a breath, thinking again about the guards outside the queen's door. They were well-armed, but relaxed, confident of their victory. Their barrels of magic powder had won the day with them hardly having to lift a hand.

Remembering the awful explosion, Pela shuddered. Then an idea came to her. How much did the Order truly know about this magic powder of theirs? It was obviously dangerous. What would they do if anything happened to their supply?

She couldn't risk a fire. Pela had seen the damage done by a single barrel; there wouldn't be much left of the queen's ship if a dozen took light. But if she made them *think* something had happened …

Studying the barrels, she tried to estimate their weight, but dismissed the idea. They must weigh eighty pounds each; there was no way she could lift them. But she might be able to knock one over. Putting her shoulder to the closest, she heaved with all her strength.

The barrel rocked on its base and started to tip, but she let go before it could fall. She sucked in a breath, wondering if she was truly game. Angrily, she shook her head. If she hesitated, she was lost. She shoved the barrel again until it tipped, teetered on the edge of its base, and then toppled to the deck with a *crash*.

"What was that?" a voice shouted from below.

Pela retreated as the barrel rolled across the tilting deck. Clearing her throat, she shouted in her deepest voice: "Fire!"

Panicked shouts followed, then the *thump* of boots on the stairwell. Pela reached the railing just before the guards reached the aft deck, and vaulted over the top. Lowering herself down, she landed softly on the main deck. There was a slight overhang and she quickly stepped beneath it so she could not be seen from above.

The cabin door was closed and Pela cursed under her breath. She hadn't thought about a lock…but it was too late to turn back now. Casting aside the last of her caution, she gripped the handle and turned.

Her heart skipped a beat as it opened with a click. She quickly stepped inside, swinging the door gently shut behind her. Within, the cabin was dark and warmer than outside, but at her entrance she sensed movement. A glow appeared in the corner.

The queen blinked, holding out the lantern and sitting

up in bed. A frown crossed her delicate features as she saw Pela standing in the doorway.

"Pela?" she murmured, and Pela could tell she was struggling to wake.

"Dim the light!" Pela hissed, glancing at the glass windows. "Before they see!"

CHAPTER 32

Crouched on the hard earth, Caledan's muscles were beginning to cramp by the time the Knights had finally ridden into view.

Devon had spotted the group the day before, while they'd been riding up into the foothills of Mount Chole and its two unnamed shadow peaks. They'd been a long way off amongst the mountain tussock, but there was no mistaking the shining armour and long white capes.

The Knights might have only been late to the gathering, but Caledan thought it more likely the men were hunting them. If that was the case, they had not sent enough men. He'd counted half a dozen—against Devon and Caledan alone they would have struggled. With Genevieve and the man Brenden adding their swords, the Knights might still have the numbers, but not the advantage.

Caledan glanced across the track, trying to spot where Genevieve and Brenden had hidden themselves amongst the trees. The forest was sparse here in the foothills, little more than a few wiry mountain beeches. Even so, his companions were well concealed, but Caledan was patient, and eventually their movement gave them away.

The huntress was crouched in the shadows of a jagged boulder, sword in one hand, hatchet in the other, while Brenden hid behind a narrow tree trunk with sword in hand. Caledan eyed the man, then shook his head. Their new companion might have fought beside Devon, but he was obviously out of practice—no veteran would have wasted energy drawing his sword so soon.

Devon himself stood in the centre of the trail, hammer in hand. The pounding of horse's hooves slowed as the party galloped around the bend below and spotted him barring their passage. A voice carried up the mountain, ringing from the cliffs that rose at their back.

"Who goes there?"

"You know who!" Devon bellowed, raising his hammer. "Who are you, Knight, to follow me?"

The Knights drew up a few yards from Devon. "The queen asks you return to Lane," their leader answered. "The culprits of the attack on Skystead have been found, and the woman Kryssa freed."

For a moment, Caledan thought the hammerman would believe them. Their words seemed to stagger him, his hammer lowering half an inch. But finally he shook his head.

"I wish I could believe you, sonny," he croaked. "But you are Knights of Alana, not the Queen's Guard. Why would she send you?"

"My heart grieves for the hurt these radicals amongst my Order have dealt you, Devon," the Knight answered. "We come to make amends."

Devon shook his head. "You came for blood, sonny," he

murmured. "Is that not why your Order has come to these lands?"

"My brothers come on pilgrimage, to witness a ritual to the Saviour, to commemorate her sacrifice," came the Knight's response. "None of us wish for more bloodshed."

"Then throw down your swords and remove your helms."

"We cannot," the Knight answered, his voice taking on a harder edge.

Devon hefted his hammer. "Then blood it shall be."

The Knights exchanged glances, then as though suddenly realising they were wasting their time, they drew their blades. Caledan tensed as the hiss of steel whispered up the trail.

"You will not grant me the honour of a duel?" Devon asked.

The leader chuckled. "No, Consort. I'm going to ride you into the ground like the animal you are." He lifted his sword and his horse reared. With a scream, he charged towards Devon.

Caledan braced himself, but the old warrior's words rang in his ears—*wait for my signal*—and he forced himself to still. The Knights closed in rapidly, the steel-shod hooves of their horses tearing up the trail and filling the air with dust. The damp of the river lands was far behind them now and in the shadow of the mountains, the earth was hard.

Bellowing in the face of his attackers, Devon drew back his arm and hurled his hammer. His aim was true, and the heavy weapon struck the leading horse in the chest with a sickening *thud*. The beast screamed and crashed to the ground, hurling its rider from the saddle. Behind, the other horses reared, toppling several of their riders, while others furiously tried to regain control.

"*Now!*" Devon shouted. Charging forward, he swept up his hammer and launched himself at the nearest Knight.

Shouting a war cry, Caledan leapt from the trees. A Knight was just coming to his feet and died without ever drawing his sword. Leaping past the dead man, Caledan glimpsed Brenden engaged with a second, and Genevieve burying her hatchet in the helmet of a third.

Another man came at Caledan, sword raised and shield in hand. Cursing, Caledan parried the blow and riposted, but the man blocked the attack with his shield and then thrust forward. The shield caught Caledan in the wrist, almost jarring the blade from his hand. He retreated, and his feet became entangled in the dead man.

Glimpsing an opportunity, the Knight attacked again, and only a desperate flick of Caledan's blade saved him from being impaled. Even then, he felt a slash of pain from his arm as the broadsword nicked him.

He leapt back, clearing the dead man, and blocked another flurry of blows from the Knight. Then he grinned. The man was good, but Caledan had his number now. Every time the Knight attacked, his shoulder dropped, exposed the joint in his armour at the throat. As the man lunged again, Caledan's blade speared through his gorget, hard enough to sever his spine.

Blood spurted from the wound and the man fell. Caledan twisted his sword to free it, but the jagged tear in the man's armour caught the blade, dragging the weapon from his hand.

Caledan leapt for the man's fallen sword as a horse screamed behind him. Lifting the unfamiliar blade, he turned to see a horseman barrelling down on him. The broadsword was heavy in Caledan's hands, sluggish as he tried to raise it. The Knight's sword swept down...

…A shriek erupted from overhead as Brenden appeared in front of Caledan, his long sword leaping to deflect the Knight's attack, then spearing up through the Knight's armpit, where the joints in his armour were weakest. The horse's momentum carried the Knight past, tearing the blade from Brenden's grip, but after a few paces the Knight topped from the saddle with a *crash*.

Caledan looked around for the other foes, but Devon had already toppled the final man. The Knight's steel plate armour had been caved in and blood now stained Devon's warhammer.

Caledan shuddered at the sight. With the sword, one had to seek the weak points in an opponent's armour—the throat or groin or armpits. Devon had no such concerns. It didn't matter where he struck: one blow from his hammer and a man would be crushed within his own armour.

A groan came from the road beyond Devon, where the first Knight had fallen. His horse had landed on him in its death throes, but protected by his armour, he had survived mostly intact. The little good it had done him—he was still trapped beneath the beast.

Devon strolled over and crouched beside him.

"Help me," the Knight croaked.

"Oh I will, sonny," Devon replied. "Right after we've had a little talk."

CHAPTER 33

Devon groaned as he lowered himself onto a tree stump. The Knight of Alana lay on the road beside him, arms bound tightly behind his back. They had stripped him of his weapons and armour; without them he was a Knight no longer, only a man, and there was little sign of the defiance he'd shown earlier.

The Knight flinched as Devon tossed his hammer down beside the man's head. They were alone on the road now— Devon had sent the others for firewood and to check their backtrail for signs of further pursuit. He hadn't wanted to risk their hostage giving away the king's identity to Caledan.

Not for the first time in the last few days, Devon sent up thanks to the Three Gods that Caledan had only ever glimpsed Braidon from afar before their meeting in the forest. But then, few would have recognised Braidon without his crown or armour.

"So…" Devon said softly. "You came to kill me."

"Capture." The Knight spat on the dusty ground. "Our Elders have plans for you, Consort."

Devon chuckled. "Do they? What do those fools want from me?"

"Blasphemy!" the Knight snarled. "The Saviour would—"

He broke off as Devon leapt to his feet and planted his boot on the man's chest. "Do not seek to lecture me on the woman I loved, Knight," he grated.

"Loved?" The man sneered. "Hollow words, when you spit in the face of her sacrifice."

Devon could only shake his head at the fervour in the man's eyes, the absolute belief in his own truth. He was young, not even in his twenties. He had never lived with magic, yet the Order had taught him to fear it, to hate the Gods that had died with Alana. They said nothing of the miracles the Gods and their magic had performed, the peace and prosperity they had once brought to the Three Nations.

Letting out a long sigh, Devon sank back onto his stump. "I honour her memory by doing as she once did for me— giving my life to protect the ones I love. How do *you* honour her?"

The man's eyes shone. "By following the preaching of the Elders, by renewing her Great Sacrifice, by burning the scourge of the False Gods from our land wherever I find it."

"The Three Gods are dead, sonny," Devon sighed. "They're not coming back, however much some may pray for it."

"Blasphemy!"

Devon waved a hand. He wasn't getting anywhere with this line of questioning. "And what is this Great Sacrifice of yours, sonny? Where have they taken Kryssa?"

The man blanked. "Knowledge of the Great Sacrifice is not for non-believers."

"How about we make an exception, given my prior relationship with your Saviour?"

The man opened his mouth, but before he could refuse, Devon picked up his hammer and twirled it in his hand. "Keep in mind, I'm only asking nicely this once."

The Knight swallowed. "I believe in the power of the Saviour."

"Alana's not going to help you now."

"The Saviour does not protect, only grants us the free will to live our lives."

Devon chuckled. "Then you'd better get talking."

The Knight swallowed, his eyes flicking from Devon's face to the hammer. "You wouldn't kill an unarmed man."

"You're right," Devon rumbled. He drew a knife from his bag and moved behind the knight, cutting his bindings loose. The Knight sat up, looking confused. Devon tossed him his sword. "Get up. Let's see how you fare against an old man."

The man paled as he looked at the sword, but he made no move to pick it up.

Devon smiled. "I thought as much," he said, crouching alongside the man. "Listen up, sonny. I'm not going to kill you, not unless you piss me off." He nodded at the trees. "Now Caledan, he's not so forgiving. I sent him out to look for firewood, to give us some time to talk. But when he returns, he plans to string you up by your neck."

Colour fled the Knight's face. He began to shake, his hands clenching into fists, though his lips remained tight shut.

"How old are you, sonny?" Devon asked.

The man swallowed. "Sev...seventeen."

"A young age to die, whoever your Gods," Devon

commented. "You seem like a good kid. Misguided maybe, but you still have time to learn."

The young Knight swallowed. "What do you want to know?"

Devon gave a cold smile. "What is the Great Sacrifice?"

"It's…a renewal of Alana's sacrifice. We…it has been performed every decade since her death, to keep the powers of the False Gods apart from this world."

"And where will this sacrifice be performed?"

"This year…the Elders wanted a demonstration of our strength. They…the sacrifice will be held in Malevolent Cove," he whispered. "Where the Goddess Antonia was struck down, where the False Gods first revealed their mortality."

A cold breeze slid down Devon's spine. Malevolent Cove was only a day's march from where they sat, assuming they survived the journey. Once they crossed the plateau, they would be entering Dragon Country. A party of armoured Knights would be troubled by even one of the beasts—the four of them wouldn't stand a chance. Even the greatest of Magickers had feared the creatures, in the times before magic was lost.

And then there was Malevolent Cove itself.

Legends told that the Old King Thomas had lost himself to darkness there, succumbing to the call of his magic and unleashing a demon upon the Three Nations.

And Devon's ancestor, his great, great Grandfather Alastair, had been slain on its black sands.

A shudder swept through Devon at the thought, but summoning his courage, he continued with his questions. "How many Knights will there be?"

"It is the thirtieth anniversary," the Knight replied as though that answered Devon's question. When Devon only glared at him, he went on: "They will come from all over Plorsea *and* Lonia. Hundreds of Knights, and more still of our followers."

A lead weight settled in Devon's stomach. It was too many. Even with a distraction, how could they possibly hope to free Kryssa and escape?

To say nothing of the beasts that would hunt them in the wilderness of Dragon Country.

For half a moment, Devon wondered if Braidon had been right. The threat of the Order could not be ignored any longer; if hundreds were willing to gather for this sacrifice, what else might be at risk? How many more innocents would be persecuted, if the Knights were not stopped? Only the king could gather an army great enough to crush this insurrection once and for all.

But what then of Kryssa?

Silently, Devon imagined telling Pela he had failed, that he had turned his back on her mother. He could almost see the judgement in her eyes, the accusation, a mirror of the day he had returned to Skystead with Derryn's body. Kryssa had met him on the pier, the light in her eyes turning from joy to despair, and finally to rage.

You were meant to keep him safe!

Devon shuddered. No, whatever the odds, he could not go back now. Kryssa and Pela were family, and he could not let them down, not again.

Standing, he held out his hand to the Knight. "Give me the sword."

"You're...you're not going to kill me, are you?"

"I gave you my word, sonny," he replied.

"Even so..."

Devon's eyes flashed. "My word is iron," he snapped. "Now give me the blade, before I change my mind."

The Knight flinched and tossed the sword on the ground. He scrambled backwards as Devon retrieved the weapon.

"Go!" Devon snarled, pointing the blade at the man's chest. "Return to Lane and tell your masters of your failure. Or go home, I do not care. But do not come this way again, for if I see you, I'll not hesitate to strike you down, armed or no."

The Knight swallowed. "My armour, it's sacred—"

"*Go!*" Devon bellowed.

He went.

Genevieve appeared from the nearby bushes a few minutes later. From the pointed look she flashed him, she'd been listening, but she said nothing when the others returned carrying an armful of firewood each.

"You let the bastard go?" Caledan asked.

Devon shrugged. "He told me what I needed to know."

"Oh?" Braidon questioned. "So where are we going?"

Devon drew in a deep breath. "Malevolent Cove."

CHAPTER 34

Ikar breathed a sigh of relief as they cleared the last of the trees and emerged into the open. Ahead, campfires lit the night and the stench of smoke was heavy in the air. They had ridden hard all through the day and into the night to reach the safety of the Cove. Shouts carried through the darkness as figures moved in the shadows, and Ikar raised an empty hand.

"Hello, brothers," he hailed them, "well met."

"Who goes there?" came the response.

"Ikar." He grinned as the shadows slowed. "The Elders are expecting me."

A torch was lit and several Knights strode forward, the flames reflecting from their metallic helmets. Ikar shuddered —in the dark, his fellow Knights no longer seemed human. There was no expression to read in their steel faces, no warning as to their attentions, and for a moment Ikar saw what others must see when they looked upon him.

His hand was halfway to his helmet before he caught himself. Swallowing, he gestured at Kryssa. She sat on the packhorse, her eyes on the ground. Despite her threats, she had made no further attempt to escape since killing Putar. It seemed as though she'd finally come to accept her fate. Sadness touched him.

"Ay, you are just in time. We'll send for them," one of the Knights replied.

A brief discussion was held and then they ran off, clambering down a ditch laden with spikes before disappearing through the gates of a wooden palisade. Ikar was surprised at the span of the fortifications—the Elders must have been planning this for some time.

"Come," one of the Knights said, gesturing them forward. "We have made the dragons fear us, but there are other creatures in these woods. It's not safe to stand here in the dark."

Ikar nodded. Taking up the reins to Kryssa's horse, he followed the Knights inside. The gate groaned as it closed behind them, sealing them within. Dismounting, Ikar moved to Kryssa and freed her hands from the saddle. With his help she stepped down. After a moment's hesitation, he untied her hands as well.

She rubbed her wrists and frowned at him, a puzzled look in her eyes, but Ikar only shrugged. A young boy appeared, bowed to Ikar and the other Knights, and then took the reins of their horses and disappeared into the darkness.

Ikar watched him go, and then turned to survey the rest of the camp. The smell of smoke was stronger here, and he saw that the ground was covered in soot. Fire must have been used to clear the trees. The Red Dragons would not be pleased, and he glanced over his shoulder nervously.

It was then he noticed the great catapults lining the interior of the palisade. Barrels lay stacked alongside them and men stood nearby, their eyes on the starry sky. Ikar swallowed, recognising what they were. He wondered how the Order had gotten hold of the black powder. But it gave him at least a small measure of confidence that the Red Dragons could be handled.

The rest of the site was similar to the military encampments of the Lonian army. Rows of canvas tents stretched away from the gates, with a single avenue leading deeper into the camp. At this late hour there were few members of the Order awake, but those he saw wore the armour of Knights. He noticed with distaste that most carried large crossbows on their belts. They were the weapons of cowards, though he supposed they were needed to keep the beasts at bay.

A distant banging could be heard, as of hammers striking wood, along with the faint crashing of waves on a sandy shore. Ikar found himself wondering about the Cove, and what waited for him on the infamous shore. It was said his ancestor Alastair had died there, though few knew of the association. The man was despised by the Order for his magic and his service to the Gods.

The association shamed Ikar as must as his family's secret—that they had inherited the man's magic, at least until the Gods had fallen. He prayed to the Saviour that tonight he would finally help put that past behind him. It was the reason he had joined the Order in the first place, to purge the darkness from the world, to make amends for his family's past evils.

Now, remembering his Elders sick joy at Kryssa's pain, and his own treatment of her on the ship from Skystead, Ikar found himself wondering…

No, he thought, clenching his fists tight. *The False Gods must be kept from this world.*

He looked up caught Kryssa staring at him. Warmth touched his cheeks, though she could not see beneath his helmet. The whisper of a sigh from her, and she turned away, casting her eyes over the camp.

The thud of hooves announced the approach of a new group of men. Ikar edged closer to Kryssa as Servo rode up, surrounded by a large party of Knights. He was surprised to see the Elder here. The man had been intending to remain in Lane, when Ikar had departed. How had he come here so quickly?

"Ikar," the Elder announced, "well met." His eyes flickered to Kryssa and his voice took on a hard edge. "Where is Putar?"

"He caught up with us on the road to Lane. But...we were set upon by a Raptor," he lied. "The Elder...died well."

Servo stared at him for a long while. Ikar held his gaze, and finally the Elder nodded. "His wisdom will be missed," he said, then smiled, and Ikar sensed the fabrication had not gone unnoticed. "You did well to defeat such a beast, without even a scratch to your armour, Knight. I thank you for delivering the woman safely."

Inclining his head, Ikar spoke without thinking: "What is to become of Kryssa now?"

A stillness came over Servo. Without speaking, he dismounted and strode to where Ikar stood. "As you know, Knight, the *woman* is to be one of the three for our Great Sacrifice," he said dangerously. "Is that a problem?"

"No," Ikar replied, though his heart was racing now. "And what of the others?"

"We already have the first," Servo said, his voice growing light once more. "Fate has conspired to deny us a third. But fear not, the Saviour plays to her own tune. The third comes."

"Who?"

"Our scouts report the Consort and his companions are within a day's ride from our camp. They have evaded our forces until now, but they cannot remain free forever. If our people do not find them, the dragons will."

"Devon is close?" Ikar asked, a weight lifting from his shoulders. Surely this was a sign from the Saviour. "Good. I will put an end to him."

"*No*," Servo shot back. "He must be taken with the others. If the Saviour wills it, her Consort will join her in the heavens."

Ikar clenched his fists, though his armour revealed no other sign of his anger. For a long moment he stood staring at the Elder, struggling to push down his rage, to gather the will to agree. Finally he bowed his head in acquiescence.

"Very well," he rumbled, his voice betraying him despite his best efforts. "If it pleases you, my Elder, I will wait here. I would ensure my cousin receives an appropriate greeting." He glanced at Kryssa, feeling the need to say something, to bid the woman farewell, but the words died on his tongue. "I trust you will see the woman safely to her cage."

With that he turned away, but not before he caught a last glimpse of Kryssa. She wore a look of disappointment on her face, as though she had expected more from him. Shame burned his throat, though he knew...knew in his heart he was doing the right thing.

Head bowed, Ikar marched slowly back to the gates to wait for his rival.

CHAPTER 35

The humid air clung to Braidon's skin as he hacked at the dense forest, moisture dripping down his back and making him long for the icy air of the mountains. The heavy armour they had taken from the Knights only made it worse, and he wondered how the men stood to wear the plate mail all day long.

They had left the volcanic plateau last night, dropping down into the jungles of Dragon Country, where the air was stifling, so thick it felt like he was breathing sludge. Even with his horse doing most of the work, Braidon had been sweating, and they had left their mounts in a clearing half an hour before. The creatures could not go quietly through the forest, and as they neared the Cove, they could not risk detection. Only Devon had kept his mount, riding on ahead down the broad trail left by the Knights.

Braidon just hoped the horses would still be there when they returned. They would be needed once Kryssa was freed. But even given free rein to roam, the horses would stand little chance if they were discovered by a Red Dragon.

But then, nor did they, whatever their accumulated skills with the blade.

Thinking of the great creatures, Braidon felt a pang of longing, as he recalled the powers he'd once commanded as a child. Though it had developed late, he'd feared and appreciated his magic in equal measures. Since the day Alana had died and magic was sponged from the world, it had been as though a part of him was missing, stolen away along with his sister.

Ahead of him, Caledan released a branch, which whipped back and struck Braidon in the face. The blow snapped him from memories of the past, and he cursed. Caledan glanced back and grinned.

"Better pay more attention," he whispered.

"Ay," Braidon snapped. "And I don't need you reminding me of it." He shouldered past Caledan and settled himself in behind Genevieve. "What's a sellsword like you doing here anyway?" he asked over his shoulder. "Gold's not much good if you're dead."

"I'm still trying to work that one out myself," Caledan replied.

Braidon raised an eyebrow. "Better figure it out quickly."

In the front, Genevieve gave a throaty chuckle. "Caledan's just embarrassed to admit he has a conscience."

"You wound me, woman," Caledan replied, then chuckled. "I thought I'd have figured it out by now, but…" He shrugged. "Maybe you're right. Or maybe I'm just curious to see if the old man can pull it off."

Braidon grunted. "I've seen Devon win when he had no right to—but I think even he might have bitten off too much this time."

He raised his sword and was about to slice through a

vine Genevieve had missed, when a hand gripped him by the shoulder.

"*Wait,*" Caledan hissed.

"What?" Braidon asked, shrugging him off. "I don't see—"

"Listen," Genevieve said.

Braidon lowered his sword and frowned. Turning on the spot, he scanned the forest, listening for what Caledan had heard, but: "There's nothing."

"Ay," Caledan replied. "Not a sound."

Braidon's heart lurched, then began to race. They were right. A moment earlier the forest had been alive, a cacophony of hissing cicadas and squawking parrots, but now there was…nothing.

The Knights? Braidon mouthed, but Genevieve shook her head.

Scanning the undergrowth again, Braidon sought signs of pursuit. Raptors were known to lurk here; the monstrous creatures could stalk through the undergrowth with hardly a whisper, and tear a man's head from his shoulders before he knew what had struck him. He swallowed, the hackles raising on his neck as he imagined some dark monster watching them from the shadows.

"*Down!*" Genevieve shouted suddenly.

They threw themselves into the mud a second before the canopy exploded inwards with the shriek of breaking wood. Something red and massive crashed down through the branches, knocking a giant ficus tree sideways and ripping its great buttressed roots from the soft earth. The ground shook as the creature landed not twenty feet from where they crouched. Silence fell as it exhaled, the heat of its breath washing over them. The only sound was the slow creaking of the ficus as it continued to topple, followed by a muffled *thud* as it slammed into the earth.

Humans…

The dragon's voice sounded in his mind like iron on a chalkboard. Braidon wanted to slap his hands over his ears in a desperate attempt to block it out, but he remained frozen to the spot. Scarlet scales rippled in the sunlight streaming through the newly created hole in the canopy. The dragon took a step towards them. Horns twisted up above its massive head, tearing through vines as though they were made of paper. Claws the size of swords flashed out, ripping apart the trunk of another tree. It crumpled before the beast's power.

Filthy wretches, trespassing in our land.

There was no doubt it had seen them, and cursing, Braidon hurled himself to his feet and drew his sword. Almost instinctively, he reached for the power that had once been his, before remembering once again it had died with his sister.

Laughter roared in his mind, so loud he had to clench his teeth to keep from crying out.

You think to defy me, human?

Caledan and Genevieve joined Braidon, swords and daggers in hand. There was open fear on the woman's face, but she showed no hint of panic. In contrast, Caledan remained his usual impassive self. Braidon was impressed with the man's calm in the face of almost certain death. For himself, he had to grip his blade in two hands to keep the tip from shaking.

There was nothing they could do against this creature. Only blades that had been enchanted in the days of magic could pierce a dragon's thick hide. Its great black eyes were vulnerable, but the creature stood twenty feet high and they had no bow to even attempt such a shot.

Once, Magickers had hunted down any dragon that crossed the boundaries of Dragon Country, but now the creatures were almost unstoppable, only ever defeated by sheer numbers.

And there were just the three of them.

Braidon let out a long breath and sheathed his sword. He faced the beast with empty hands.

"No," he said, trying to keep the tremor from his voice. "We come to make an alliance."

"*What?*" Caledan exclaimed, while in their minds the dragon's laughter sounded again.

You have mistaken me for my long-extinct cousins, human.

"You need us," Braidon replied, ignoring its taunts.

We need for no one, the dragon snarled.

It stepped forward, nostrils flaring, and another wave of heat washed over them. Braidon shuddered as its jaws opened a fraction, revealing the red-hot glow deep in its throat.

"Then why do the Knights of Alana trespass in your lands?" Braidon asked.

A rumble sounded in the dragon's chest and a tendril of flame escaped its jaws, incinerating a nearby sapling.

The Knights shall pay for their impudence.

"No," Braidon replied. "There are too many, even for your great powers."

The dragon bared its teeth. Braidon gagged at the putrid stench of its breath, but this time it did not reply.

"The Knights are our enemies as well," Caledan added, finally understanding Braidon's plan. "We seek to drive them from our lands, and yours."

The giant eyes of the dragon studied them. *Then why do you wear their armour?*

"To deceive them," Braidon answered. "To sneak into their camp and take back what they stole from us."

And how does this aid my peoples?

Braidon swallowed and glanced at his companions. It all came down to this. Whatever resentment Caledan carried for the Plorsean King, Braidon would have to take his chances. The dragon would kill them all if he did not act. H pulled the helmet from his head and tossed it aside.

"Do you not know me, dragon?" he asked.

Caledan stared at him in confusion, but the Red Dragon's eyes narrowed to slits. It stepped closer, the long neck bending down to inspect him, the slits of its nostrils widening to breathe in his scent.

*King…*its voice sounded in their minds. It bared its teeth. *Or is it Tsar? Yes I know you, pup. Your father enslaved us! Tell me, why should I not roast you where you stand?*

Braidon flicked a glance at Caledan. The man stood beside him, eyes hard and jaw clenched, sword trembling at his side, but Braidon could not be distracted now.

"Because it was my sister and I who freed you!" he called. "And because I am your only chance. Help me, and I will bring my armies against the Knights. I will drive them from your lands."

The Knights have great weapons, King, the Red Dragon replied. *Perhaps yours is the wrong side to choose.*

"And if you choose the Knights, what then?" Braidon shot back. "At least my people have always respected the boundaries of your lands."

The Red Dragon bared its teeth. *We would have new boundaries.*

Braidon's heart palpitated. He sensed the eyes of his

companions on him, but there was no going back now. "So be it," Braidon whispered, knowing it was a betrayal of his people, "but the Red Dragons must pledge a new oath, to honour my rule and all my line that comes after."

Our Golden cousins once made such an oath, the Red Dragon snarled. *To their doom.*

"And how long will your people survive against these new weapons?" Braidon asked, taking a gamble. He shuddered to think what type of weapon the Knights had, that even the Red Dragons feared them.

The Red Dragon growled and clawed at the ground, tearing up roots and great chunks of earth. Lifting its head, it howled. The sound tore at their ears, echoing up through the canopies and the skies beyond. From the distance, there came an answering cry, then another and another. Braidon shuddered, looking again at the Red Dragon, but its eyes were opaque now, its mind elsewhere. Then it blinked, the awful intelligence returning.

Very well, King, it rumbled in his mind. *We swear, though know this, our price is the land from here to the Lane.*

Braidon's stomach tied itself into knots, but he inclined his head. "So be it."

I am Ingytus. Call when you have need, and I shall answer.

With a roar, the dragon bounded into the air, a single beat of its wings carrying it free of the canopy. An icy sweat dripped down Braidon's back as he watched it disappear into the sky beyond. Then he sucked in a breath and turned to face his companions, aware he had only traded one enemy for another.

Caledan stared back at him with ice in his eyes.

"Draw your sword, *Braidon.*"

CHAPTER 36

"Draw your sword, Braidon," Caledan repeated, thrusting his blade at the man's chest.

Brenden—Braidon—leapt back and raised his empty hands. "I'm not going to fight you, Caledan."

"Then die!" Caledan screamed, and made a wild swipe at the king's head. Braidon ducked and his blade took a branch from a tree.

Caledan's heart was pounding in his chest and he wanted nothing more than to see the king's blood soaking the leaf-strewn earth. Devon had betrayed him—though how the man had known what Caledan intended, he could not guess—and now he would die, too. But not before Caledan finally had his revenge.

"Caledan, stop!" Genevieve tried to get his attention, but when she darted towards him, he spun, his boot flashing out to catch her in the stomach. She crumpled to the ground clutching her midriff, and turning, he advanced once more on Braidon.

Crying out, the king tripped and crashed to the ground. Caledan leapt after him, his sword aiming for the man's back, but Braidon rolled and Caledan's blade sank deep into the dirt. Tearing it free, Caledan stalked after his foe.

Now Braidon scrambled to his feet and drew his sword. "Let's not do this," he hissed. "You'll draw the Knights down on all of us."

"Let them come!" Caledan roared, directing an attack at Braidon's head. The king blocked it smoothly and retreated. Caledan followed with a roar: "*Fight me!*"

"Why?" Braidon gasped as Caledan's blade slid beneath his guard and slashed his plate mail.

A shrill scraping sound rent the air, then Braidon's mailed fist swept around, catching Caledan in the helmet and sending him staggering back. His ears rang, but snarling, he recovered his feet and started towards the king once more.

"You destroyed my life!" he shrieked, emphasising each word with a wild swing of his blade. He made no effort to defend himself, only attacked with relentless fury. "You took *everything* from me!"

"What are you talking about?" Braidon snapped, parrying each blow.

"*You will pay for what your sister did!*" Caledan bellowed. "For leaving my mother to die!"

Braidon's eyes still showed his confusion. Steel rang out as their blades met again, then he spun on his heel and struck Caledan with his elbow. Caledan stumbled back, and the king held out his hands for peace.

"I'm sorry!" he gasped. "Whatever Alana did to your mother, I'm sorry! But I cannot change it."

"No, but you can pay for it with your life!"

Braidon leapt away. "And the rest of Plorsea with it?"

"Plorsea be damned!" Caledan cursed.

The king parried another blow, but Caledan lashed out with a boot, catching him in the chest and toppling him with a crash of metal. He swung his sword again, but Braidon raised an arm and the blade went shrieking off his heavy wrist guards. Rolling clumsily, the king came to his feet.

"And what about Devon?" Genevieve interrupted. She was up again, a massive dagger in hand. "You swore you'd help him."

Caledan glanced at her. "He lied to me," he gasped. "I'll kill him next." He raised his sword to strike at the king again.

"And what about Kryssa?" Braidon shouted. "What about Pela? You might not care for me or Devon, but they have done nothing to harm you!"

An image of Pela flashed into Caledan's mind, back on the *Seadragon*, when she'd first asked for his help. She'd dropped her sword, made a fool of herself, almost run in the face of his laughter, but in the end she had picked it up and tried again.

Angrily, he bared his teeth. "We're all alone in this world," Caledan hissed. "Best the girl learn that now."

"No, Caledan," Braidon replied. "We're not. We have friends, family. You said Alana left your mother to die—will you do the same now to Pela?"

"It's not the same!"

"It is!" Braidon bellowed. "Can you not see it? If you kill me, if you murder Devon, Kryssa dies! *Pela's mother dies!* And what will you achieve? It won't bring your mother back, only destroy more innocent lives."

"I…"

"Caledan," Genevieve whispered, edging forward. "Please, don't do this. We need you, Kryssa needs you. Please help us bring her home."

Caledan glanced from the woman to the king and sucked in a breath. His entire life he had waited for this moment, to have the king standing before him with nothing but blades between them. He had trained and saved and brokered deals, all to this one end. Now fate had finally brought them together…

"I swore on my mother's life," he croaked. "I have waited so long…"

"Then wait a little longer," Braidon hissed. "Until we've rescued Kryssa. Then, if you still wish to fight, I'll happily oblige you."

Caledan looked up. "Why should I believe you?" he whispered. "You have lied to me for days."

"Because it's the right thing to do," Braidon snapped. "Because you have no other choice."

"Fine," Caledan hissed, sheathing his sword in a rush. "But the second we're free…"

"We fight to the death," Braidon replied wearily.

Caledan let out a long breath. In the distance, shouts whispered through the trees. Together the three of them turned towards the sound.

"Better put your helmets back on, boys," Genevieve said lightly. "We're Knights of Alana now, nothing more. Think you can do that?"

"Sure," Caledan muttered.

Braidon had just settled the helmet back on his head when the cracking of forest litter announced the arrival of mounted Knights. They rode into the clearing with swords drawn, all wearing the familiar armour of their Order. Now though, heavy crossbows also dangled from their saddles.

Caledan narrowed his eyes at the sight. The Knights usually scorned such weapons, preferring the test of hand-to-hand combat. As they neared, he realised these bows were different from any he had ever seen. The wooden bow arm was gone, replaced by smooth steel and a winch to reset the wire string. Caledan couldn't help but remember the dragon's words.

The Knights have great weapons.

Were these what it had spoken of? Caledan shuddered to think of the damage the bolt from such a crossbow might do. It didn't bear thinking about, and raising a hand, Caledan hailed the Knights.

"Hoy, lads!" Caledan shouted. "Well met."

"Well met indeed," the Knight in the lead said. They had slowed upon seeing their armour, though the group still eyed the broken trees cautiously, as though expecting a dragon to appear at any moment. "You're well off the regular path. What are you doing out here?"

"Dragon spooked the horses," Caledan replied. "Lost the path, and the stupid beasts."

"Lucky you didn't lose your lives," the Knight replied. "We saw it fly off, big bugger. Still, a few of shots from these and they turn tail quick enough." He patted the crossbow in emphasis.

"Where are you from?" another asked, kicking his horse forward. His eyes bored into Caledan, and he sensed the man's suspicion.

"New recruits from Goldtown," Caledan answered, naming a Lonian town far up in the Sandstone Peaks.

"Long ride," the Knight grunted.

"Ay, we'll be glad to reach the Cove."

The first Knight snorted. "I'll bet." He turned his horse on the spot. "Well, I don't think your horses are coming back. You can walk with us though. We'll see you safely to camp. Wouldn't want any brothers eaten by those red buggers."

"Thank you," Caledan said, with feeling this time. "One encounter was more than enough."

CHAPTER 37

Devon walked slowly down the beaten path, savouring
the tranquillity of the forest, the quiet chirping of birds
and the whisper of wind in the branches overhead. Unfortunately, the breeze did not reach the undergrowth, and taking a
rag from his pocket, Devon wiped the sweat from his forehead. The warhammer hung heavy on his back, and he found
himself doubting whether he still had the strength to wield it.

His misgivings grew with each twist and turn of the
path. Once it might have been only a deer trail, but the
passage of Knights had carved a broad passage through the
jungle. He scanned the undergrowth as he walked, though
alone he would stand little chance against even a Raptor, let
alone a dragon. He wondered how the Knights had grown
so bold, to venture into a place like this.

Because if the Knights of Alana no longer feared the
Red Dragons…

Devon squared his shoulders and pushed away the
defeatist thoughts. He could not afford them now, not when

he was about to walk into an enemy stronghold and demand Kryssa's release.

A shudder ran down Devon's spine as he imagined Kryssa bound and chained, readied for the slaughter on the solstice—tomorrow.

What foul minds had created such a ritual: this *Great Sacrifice*? The Order claimed it was in honour of Alana's own sacrifice, but Devon had been there, had witnessed her final moments.

And it had not been for the Gods, or magic, or even the Tsar that she had sacrificed herself.

It had been to save Devon's own life, to shield him from her former lover, his rival Quinn.

Even thirty years later, the memory scorched him. He felt an awful sadness that her final moments had been so twisted by the Order, that deceitful men now ruled in her name, manipulating thousands into believing such an awful lie.

There was a bitter taste in Devon's mouth as he continued through the jungle. He could have prevented this long ago, had he paid attention, spoken out against the rising Order. But after Alana's death he had been tired of the world, of leading, of fighting other men's wars. So he had retreated, and the Order had taken full advantage of his absence.

Now their vile beliefs were ingrained in the Order's followers, its Knights so fanatical they could attack inno-cents at worship and believe they were heroes for doing so. It made Devon sick to his stomach and he longed to put an end to them.

But after all this time, he was only one man, well past his prime. His name no longer had the power to turn back armies, to send fear down the spines of his foes. He was just Devon, the roof-layer, the tavern keeper.

It would have to be enough.

Voices carried through the forest as he rounded a bend, drawing him back to the present. He sighed and marched on until the trees gave way to open ground. Ash stained the earth black beneath his boots, crushed into the earth by the passage of men and horses. A wooden palisade and trench barred his path and he drew to a stop.

Shouts came from behind the wall, followed by the squeal of hinges as the wooden gates were dragged open. A Knight strode forward, flanked on either side by others. He came to a stop several feet from where Devon stood and crossed his arms.

"So, you are Devon," he said, his voice echoing within the helmet.

The Knight stood shoulder to shoulder with Devon, and in the steel-plated armour he made an imposing sight. Devon had fought many large men in his life, and had defeated them all, but the sight of the Knight now gave him pause. There was something familiar about the man, something that called to him, though he did not recognise the voice.

Finally Devon grinned. "I am," he replied. "And who might you be, sonny?"

Laughter rumbled from the Knight's helmet. "My name is Ikar," he said. "Well met, cousin."

"Cousin?" Devon frowned. "Can't say I'm aware of any family in these parts."

"Our lines separated after Alan," Ikar replied. "Followed different paths. Yours claimed the hammer of heroes, while mine…"

He trailed off, and recovering from his surprise, Devon

grimaced. "Remained." He took a step closer. "Tell me, cousin. If my family followed the warrior's path, what of yours? Were they Magickers, like our great, great grandfather, Alastair?"

A stillness came over Ikar at his words, while behind him the other Knights shifted nervously and glanced at the giant. Devon laughed, knowing he'd struck a nerve. "That is quite the career change, from Magicker to Knight."

"Silence!" Ikar snarled. He reached for his sword, but something gave him pause, and with an effort of will he released the hilt. "I am here to make amends for my family's past, to reclaim the legacy of Alan the Great."

"You're here to kill me then?"

"No," Ikar said shortly, and Devon sensed what he said next was not his desire. "I'm to take you before the Elders."

"And why would I allow that?" Devon rumbled.

"You don't have much choice." Ikar shrugged, gesturing to the men behind him. "But, for the sake of avoiding further bloodshed, I'm told you care for the woman, Kryssa."

Devon bared his teeth. "Ay," he growled. "If you've har—"

"The woman is safe," Ikar interrupted, raising his hands in a gesture of peace. "Or she was last night, when I delivered her into the custody of the Elders. But if you wish to see her, you must come with me."

For a long while, Devon stared at the Knight, though he could decipher little of the man's intentions behind the steel visor. Like so many of his brethren, he spoke with the fervour of the devout, and yet...he seemed different, as though touched by the slightest of doubts, and finally Devon nodded.

"Very well," he murmured. "Take me to my...to

Kryssa."

Ikar inclined his head, and turning, he marched through the gates without a backwards glance. The other Knights fell in around Devon as he followed the man into the camp. Beyond the palisade, they marched down a great avenue of canvas tents. Men and women raced amongst the tents, most dressed in ordinary clothing rather than the armour of Knights, and Devon wondered where so many worshipers of the Order had come from. Surely there weren't so many in all of Plorsea?

Devon walked with his fists clenched tight at his side, aware he was truly in the dragon's den now. He could sense the Knights watching him from beyond the dark slits of their visors, but kept his eyes fixed straight ahead, determined not to show his fear. Focusing his mind, he breathed deeply, concentrating on the action rather than his surroundings, and his heartbeat slowed.

The meditation helped to calm him, and by the time they reached the cliffs, his mind was focused, fixed on the task ahead. He prayed the others had managed to infiltrate the camp and were even now seeking out Kryssa's prison. If all went to plan, Devon's distraction would allow them the opportunity to free her, and they would escape unnoticed before the Knights noticed her absence.

"Our ancestor died here, you know," Devon said, making conversation as they started down the narrow trail that had been carved into the granite cliffs. Unlike the path in the forest, the steps appeared to have been there for centuries.

"Alan the Great died at Fort Fall."

"Ay, and his father-in-law, Alastair, died on this beach, betrayed by one of Archon's minions."

"An evil man betrayed by an evil man," Ikar replied

shortly.

But Devon was hardly paying attention to the man's words now. His eyes had been drawn down into the Cove, across the black sands and jagged fingers of rock, to where a great project was underway.

Men and women bustled to and fro across the beach, disappearing into a massive wooden structure that stretched almost to the tops of the cliffs. From his vantage point, Devon could just see over the top of the outer wall, where row upon row of benches spiralled down to a wooden platform in the centre. It was almost an amphitheatre, stretching from the cliffs all the way down to the ocean, where in place of a fourth wall, a makeshift dock extended out beyond the waves.

Devon could only shake his head at the undertaking. The Knights had built a great stadium in which to conduct their cruel ritual, to make an exhibition of Kryssa's sacrifice —or perhaps a threat to those that opposed them.

As they neared the beach, Devon finally turned his attention to the warships floating in the bay. Most were anchored far out beyond the barrier reefs, their passengers using the rowboats now lining the shore to make landfall. The green flag of Lonia flew from most, outnumbering the red of Plorsea three to one.

Only one ship had sailed close, almost to the docks of the amphitheatre itself.

Sand crunched beneath Devon's boots as he stepped down onto the black sands of Malevolent Cove. How different it must be now, from when his ancestor had died here. A powerful Magicker, Alastair had sacrificed everything to protect the Three Nations, abandoning even his wife and his daughter to answer the call of the Gods. His very existence spat in the face of everything the Knights of

Alana believed in. No wonder Ikar wanted to sponge his lineage from history.

Looking out over the murky waters of the bay, Devon wondered if he too had come there to die, if this dark shore would be his doom. He could almost accept it, if it meant Kryssa would live.

Ikar led him along the sand and through a tunnel into the amphitheatre. Within, the structure groaned and creaked, and Devon wondered how long such a creation could last. The Knights were well-armed, but surely the Red Dragons would not stand this interference. If the stadium caught light, everyone within would be consumed in minutes.

He shuddered, but after a few minutes they passed safely back into the open, onto the wooden stage at the centre. Attendants raced past hauling sand and spreading it over the platform. Whispers came from overhead and Devon was surprised to see the stands above were already beginning to fill. The sun was dropping fast towards the horizon, lighting the sky aflame, and Devon realised with a start midnight was only a few hours away.

The solstice was approaching.

The Knights led him out onto the docks. At the end, steps led down to the water, where a rowboat bobbed. Devon's heart dropped into his stomach. If they were holding Kryssa on the ship, how would Braidon and the others reach her in time?

But there was no going back now. He closed his eyes, and prayed his old friend would find a way.

They boarded the boat and the tiny vessel surged forward as several Knights took up the oars. The ship itself was not far, just a hundred yards off the pier. Its open deck was easily visible from the amphitheatre, and Devon was touched by a premonition: that this ship would somehow form part of the spectacle.

He swallowed, his gaze turning to the men standing at the railings of the ship. He recognised the face of one of the Elders from Townirwin, but the rest of the men were unknown to him, though all wore the red, green and blue robes of Elders.

A rope ladder was tossed down to them. Ikar went up first, then gestured for Devon to follow. Oars splashed below as the remaining Knights turned the boat back to shore, robbing Devon of his only escape route. He might be able to swim the distance to shore, but he would make an easy target for the heavy crossbows of the Knights.

Reaching the deck, Devon swung over the railings and found himself surrounded. Ikar stood closest, his armour shining in the noon sun, along with a dozen other Knights. Beyond, the Elders stood watching him in a half-circle. The one from Townirwin stepped up beside Ikar, his eyes aglow.

"Welcome, Consort of Alana," he whispered.

Devon couldn't help but chuckle. "You did not welcome me the last time I stepped foot in one of your Castles."

A frown touched the Elder's forehead, but he continued unperturbed. "I am called Servo, and we did not know you then," he replied. "Now we know you come before us by the Saviour's will."

"I've come to free…Kryssa," Devon snapped, his good humour evaporating. "Alana has nothing to do with it."

"The Saviour has proclaimed that Kryssa must join her in the struggle against the Gods," the Elder replied.

Devon's heart beat faster. "If you've hurt her…" His hammer leapt into his hands and he took a step towards the Elders.

Ikar moved to intercept him, his silent helmet vacant of

emotion, while the Elders took a collective step back.

"The woman lives," Servo replied. Of all of them, only he had not retreated. "The Great Sacrifice is to be completed on the birth of the solstice."

Devon lowered his hammer half an inch. "I wish to see her."

"She's otherwise occupied," another of the Elders said with a laugh. Devon fixed him with a glare and he fell suddenly silent.

"You will not take her," Devon growled, his voice rumbling across the broken waters, carrying even to the distant shore. Then he bowed his head. "Free her, and I will take her place."

Whispers spread across the deck of the ship as the men exchanged glances, building until finally Servo's voice rose above the others. "Silence!"

Devon looked up as the Elder approached. Their eyes locked and a shudder slid down Devon's spine at the passion in the man's eyes.

"You would sacrifice your life for the Saviour?" he murmured, coming close.

For a moment, Devon considered striking him down. The man's insanity was a plague that would sweep across his nation. But then there would be no bargaining, no saving Kryssa, no walking away. His shoulders slumped. "I would."

Abruptly, Servo turned away, re-joining the Elders. "We have our third!" he proclaimed, turning back to Devon. "The three will join the Saviour at midnight!"

"What?" Devon hissed, his hammer coming up. "That is not the deal I offered!"

"The Saviour's will is clear," Servo continued, ignoring him now.

Snarling, Devon advanced until Ikar blocked his path

again. He glared into the metal mask. "Out of the way, cousin," he snarled. "Or you'll be the first to die."

Quick as lightning, Ikar drew his sword. Devon leapt back, readying his hammer to attack.

"No!" Servo screamed as the two warriors faced off against one another. "It cannot be this way!"

His words gave Ikar pause, but Devon roared his anger and charged. The Knight's sword leapt to meet him and sparks burst from their weapons as they clashed. They sprang apart once more as the Elder continued to scream.

"I'll kill you all before you harm my daughter!" Devon bellowed.

A woman's laughter carried down from the upper deck before he could launch another attack. He paused, a frown creasing his forehead as he searched for the source. Then he staggered, almost losing his grip on his hammer, as he saw the woman standing atop the stairwell.

An amused smile on her lips, the Queen of Plorsea slowly descended to the main deck. The rattle of armour came from Ikar as he dropped to his knees before the woman.

"My queen!" he cried, clearly as stunned as Devon to see her there.

"Marianne," Devon whispered, a pit opening in his stomach. "What are you doing here?"

Ignoring him, she turned to Servo. "My dear Elders," she murmured. "Would you deny us all the battle of the ages? Let the men fight, let all of our people see it."

"But my Queen, what of the Great Sacrifice?" Servo howled.

Marianne only laughed. Her eyes flashed as she set them on Devon once more. "My dear Elder, there will be blood enough for all by the time these two have finished."

CHAPTER 38

Standing at the edge of the cliff looking down into Malevolent Cove, Braidon wondered how he could have been so foolish. It had all been there for him to see, but he had walked blindly into a catastrophe of his own making.

Maybe it was the memory of his sister that had misled him, a desire to see her memory live on. Yet now, looking down upon the packed amphitheatre and knowing what was to come, he felt ashamed that he had allowed her name to become so sullied.

"I have failed my people," he whispered.

"You did that a long time ago," Caledan snapped.

Genevieve placed a hand on his shoulder. "You haven't failed yet, Braidon."

Braidon gestured at the bay. Only one warship had entered, but a dozen others bobbed at anchor out beyond the dangerous reefs. Most flew green flags, only a few the red of Plorsea. "Those are Lonian warships. And they're using the same devices as the Baronian ship that attacked us. They've been working together all along. If our army isn't roused, they could sail right up to Lake Ardath and take the capital."

Caledan snorted. "Ardath won't fall so easily."

"Just now, I think we need to worry about how we're going to find Kryssa in all this," Genevieve murmured.

"They'll have her somewhere down there, I'm guessing." Braidon nodded at the amphitheatre. "If this is for the Great Sacrifice they've all been talking about, they'll…make a spectacle of it."

Genevieve's jaw tightened. "It'll be dark soon. We'd better get down the cliffs before we lose the light." She set off without looking back.

Braidon followed after a moment's hesitation, Caledan a step behind.

"You don't think it's time to call the dragons?" the sellsword asked as they picked their way down towards the beach.

"No," Braidon replied shortly, "we wait until we find Kryssa. All hell's going to break loose once the Red Dragons become involved."

"Fair enough," Caledan chuckled.

"Keep it down," Genevieve hissed. "There's men on the beach."

They descended the last dozen feet in silence. The whisper of voices inside the amphitheatre rose in pitch as they stepped onto the sand, then became a roar. They swung around in time to see a line of fire leap along the rim of the stadium. Braidon held his breath as the flames raced outwards, waiting for the whole structure to catch alight, but they did not spread beyond the rim. Finally he caught the dim glint of steel amidst the flames, and realised a line of torches had been placed around the top of the stadium.

"I don't think light is going to be a problem," Caledan muttered. "Though how we're going to escape…"

"Let's figure that out once we've found her," Genevieve snapped, taking the lead.

In their armour they had passed unnoticed, but Braidon was more than aware how flimsy their disguise would become under questioning. They knew little about the particulars of the Knights and their Order. The beach was crowded with worshipers and other Knights, but Genevieve cut across the cliff before they reached the bottom, leading them through the faint shadows towards the rear of the amphitheatre.

As they neared, Braidon saw that the structure had been built right into the granite cliffs. The wooden outer walls blocked their path. They stood there for a moment trying to find a door or some other entranceway, but the shadows revealed nothing. Below, men and women were beginning to file through the tunnel into the amphitheatre. It appeared to be the only entrance.

"What now?" Caledan hissed.

"Maybe we should try the front door," Braidon suggested, nodding to the tunnel.

The *crack* of splintering wood came from behind them, and they spun in time to see Genevieve lining up a second blow. Her boot slammed into the wall of the amphitheatre, and the wood gave way, revealing the pitch-black beyond.

"What are you doing?" Braidon gasped.

"Those people down there are spectators," she replied. "I'm not going to sit around and watch while they hang Kryssa. Come on, help me with this."

"That's—"

Before Braidon could finish his objection, Caledan joined the huntress and they managed to tear another plank from the wall. Braidon swore and checked on the crowd below, but between their hushed whispers and the roar of the ocean, the commotion had gone unnoticed.

Joining the others, Braidon saw the wooden boards that made up the amphitheatre's walls had been cut haphazardly and hammered together to fill in the gaps. He'd rarely seen such poor construction outside the slums of Lane, though he supposed the Knights did not need the place to last. The thought of all the worshipers now perched above them gave Braidon pause, but Genevieve and Caledan had already disappeared into the darkness, and taking a deep breath, he followed them through the jagged hole, into the hollows of the out wall.

Within, not even the great torches above the stadium could penetrate, and they found themselves in the pitch black. Braidon fumbled around for his flint, but Genevieve beat him to it. Sparks flashed and then a tongue of flame cast back the darkness. Half-a-hundred support beams packed the open space like the trees of a forest, while above the roof zigzagged downwards. They were directly beneath the stands of the amphitheatre.

They spread out, searching for an exit that would lead into the main areas of the amphitheatre. This section appeared completely unused, its floor littered with discarded pieces of wood and construction materials. Threading his way through the support beams, Braidon was beginning to think they would have to return to the beach and attempt the tunnel after all, when a call came from Caledan across the space.

Braidon and Genevieve stumbled to join him. A tiny crack, no wider than a fingertip, allowed a sliver of light to pierce the darkness. It was a door, though the shadows crisscrossing the light indicated it had been boarded up from the other side.

Caledan put his eye to the crack, then withdrew once more. He looked at them, his jaw clenched. "There's a guard."

Braidon loosed his sword in its scabbard. The time for caution had run out; if they didn't find Kryssa soon, they would be too late. Devon could only distract the Elders for so long.

"Are you ready?" he asked, glancing at Genevieve and Caledan. Once they went through, there would be no turning back.

They both nodded and Caledan stepped aside, clearing the way for Braidon. He launched himself forward, aiming a kick at the thread of light. The door gave way with a *crash*, and they rushed through with swords drawn.

CHAPTER 39

"Hurry up," the guard growled, shoving Pela in the back.

She cried and almost tripped over the final step before the door above was yanked open. Her eyes watered as the light struck her and she blinked, unable to shield her face with her arms bound behind her. Before she could continue up, rough hands grasped her arms and hauled her up the rest of the way.

The breath hissed between Pela's teeth as the guard tossed her to the deck. Gasping, she struggled to sit up. The flickering of firelight in the distance lit the deck of the queen's ship, blinding her until her eyes adjusted.

"*Pela!*" a woman shrieked. "No!"

Pela gasped and swung around, recognising Kryssa's voice. After all this time, she'd begun to think she would never see her mother again. Hope swelled in her heart, only to wither and die as she found Kryssa edged by two guards, her arms similarly bound. Tears stung Pela's eyes as she took in her mother's dishevelled hair and bruised face. Gritting her teeth, she tried to fight back, but the guard only grabbed her and dragged her across the deck to join her mother.

"What are you doing here?" Kryssa croaked, her face a mask of grief.

"I invited her."

The two of them looked around as the queen stepped from her cabin out into the twilight. She strode across to join them, a smile on her perfect lips.

"You witch!" Pela screamed, struggling in the grasp of the guard. "I trusted you!"

Marianne sighed. "I am sorry, young Pela," she replied. "Truly I am. Had the Baronians not failed so spectacularly, we would not have needed you. My dear husband was meant to be our sacrifice against the Light, but alas, the fool had to go and die too soon. We had to make...last minute adjustments."

"*No!*" Kryssa shouted. Tearing free of the guards, she charged at the queen, but a fist caught her in the stomach, doubling her over. She crumpled to the deck, her breath coming in half-shrieked gasps.

Teeth bared, Pela threw herself at the man that had attacked her mother, but he was twice her size and her hands were still bound. His iron fist caught Pela in the face and sent her crashing down alongside Kryssa.

"If we're quite done?" Marianne murmured, wandering closer. "Mother and daughter—has there ever been a bond so strong?"

"May the Three Gods curse you," Kryssa snarled.

The queen chuckled and leaned in close. "My dear, you and I both know those sorry creatures are dead," she whispered, before saying in a louder voice, "Even now, at the end, you cling to your cursed deities. Get them up."

Men raced forward and hauled them to their feet. Kryssa seemed to shrink into her captive's arms as she stared at the queen. "Please," she whispered. "Do what you want with me, but leave my daughter——"

"Your daughter is twice the heathen you are, witch," an Elder snapped, stepping forward. Pela started as she realised she recognised him from Townirwin. "She killed an Elder in cold blood. She'll burn at your side for her crimes against the Order, as our sacrifice against the Light God. As you will burn against the God of the Sky."

"Please…" Kryssa tried again, but the Elder back-handed her across the cheek.

"Speak no more, witch!"

Kryssa's face hardened, her eyes taking a dangerous glint. "By the Three Gods, I'll see the both of you dead," she hissed.

The Elder raised his hand again, but something about Kryssa seemed to give him pause, and after a second he smirked and stepped back, though now Pela thought she glimpsed fear on his face.

The queen stepped between them. "Enough of this," she announced gaily. "We're about to find out who our sacrifice against the Earth is to be!" She pointed off the bow of the ship.

Pela followed her arm and finally saw the source of the firelight. A thousand torches burned around the rim of a massive structure stretching out from the cliffs of a cove. She had never heard of its like anywhere in Plorsea. Where in the Three Nations had the queen brought them?

Then her gaze was drawn to the two figures standing on the great stage of the theatre. A lump lodged in her throat as she saw the massive man with warhammer in hand. It had to be Devon. Blood pounded in her ears and she barely heard her mother's scream.

"What is he doing here?"

"Devon?" Marianne chuckled. Arms folded, she stepped between them. "Why, he's here to save you, of course. I told him if he could defeat Ikar, he could take your place in the flames."

"*No...*" Kryssa whispered, her silver eyes wide.

"He *must* know we intend to betray him, but the man refuses to give up. Of course, we didn't leave him much choice."

"You witch," Pela gasped. "*Devon!*" She screamed his name until one of her captors thumped her in the head, but it made no difference. He could not hear her over the waves crashing on the black shore.

Pela sagged in her captor's arms. Looking from her mother to Devon, she struggled to find the strength that had carried her this far, but it had abandoned her. Across the narrow waters, Devon stood out stark against the burning torches, his aged face cast in shadows. Against him stood a mammoth of a man, larger even than Devon in his plate mail armour. As she watched, he drew a broadsword from his back and saluted.

"May your legend end with courage, cousin!" his voice boomed out across the waters.

"And may yours end in flame," the queen said to the two of them.

She gestured to the guards, who dragged them to the mast and bound them there, back to back. The Elder and his guards departed, followed by the rest of the Knights, until only Marianne remained with them on the deck of her ship.

The clash of weapons echoed from the cliffs as the battle in the stadium began. Wood creaked as the ship rocked at anchor. Pela strained against her bonds, glaring at the queen, but it made no difference.

Smiling sadly, Marianne wandered across to them. "I am sorry, you know," she murmured. "But you really are the best sacrifices I could have asked for."

"You don't even believe!" Kryssa shrieked, her jaw snapping closed as though to tear out the queen's throat.

"No," Marianne shook her head, "but the Elders, they discovered long ago there was a power in death. They just lack the…creativity to use it efficiently."

"You're insane," Pela said.

"We'll soon find out, I suppose," the queen responded. She reached into her pocket, and withdrew two necklaces of polished metal, though not of any kind Pela had ever seen. Runes had been carved into the dark steel. "I'm afraid you will not live to find out though. Here, would you be so good as to wear these?"

She fastened the steel to their necks, despite their protestations. Bound tightly to the mast, there was nothing either of them could do to resist. An icy cold slid down Pela's spine as the clasp clicked shut, though the metal was warm from the queen's pocket.

"There!" Marianne said, stepping back. "Now we match." She held up her arm, revealing a similar band around her wrist.

"What are they?" Kryssa grated.

"Oh don't worry, they can't harm you," Marianne replied easily. "They're just a prototype, based on a little something we took from the Tsar's records."

"So what do they do?" Pela snapped.

But the queen was already turning away, one hand raised in farewell. "Farewell!" she laughed. "I do hope you enjoy the show."

Then she was gone, disappearing over the side into the rowboat, leaving the two women alone aboard the ship.

CHAPTER 40

D*efeat my Knight, and I will set your family free.*
Devon's heart thumped in time with the pounding waves as he watched Ikar. All around the stadium, the stands were packed with the followers of the Order. Their jeers and taunts rained down upon him, but Devon hardly heard. There was an ache in his chest as though he'd been impaled, as though the queen had already struck him a mortal blow and he was simply living out the last motions of his life.

And perhaps that was the truth. Somehow, he had convinced himself that this plan could work, that he could march into the centre of the Knights of Alana and cause a commotion, a distraction of some sort that would give his friends the opportunity to free Kryssa.

How foolish he'd been.

Marianne, the queen who had stood beside Braidon all these years, was behind everything.

And he had delivered Pela right into her hands.

Roaring, Devon threw himself suddenly forward,

swinging his hammer with all his might. In his heart, he knew this battle had no meaning, that ultimately Marianne would betray him as she had everyone else. But in that moment, he did not care. So great was his rage and desperation that his exhaustion, his age, all were forgotten in the face of this foe that dared stand against him.

But for all that, Ikar was faster still. He twisted from the path of Devon's hammer and lashed out with his fist. Devon's ears rang as the blow struck him in the side of the head and he staggered back, holding up his hammer to deflect a riposte.

But Ikar did not follow, and cursing, Devon began to circle the swordsman. The slits in Ikar's visor followed him, and Devon found himself wondering at the man hidden within. This was no green recruit like the Knights they had defeated on the plateau; Ikar was a man grown, as skilled as any opponent Devon had faced in his long years.

The stage had been covered in sand from the cove and raked clean, clearing it of obstacles that might trip an unsuspecting boot. The crowd had fallen silent now, but each time their weapons clashed, it seemed as though the very earth shook with their screams. They knew this battle could not last long, that with warhammer and broadsword, a single blow could end the fight. No one wanted to miss that final blow.

Devon adjusted his grip on his hammer and stilled. Ikar mimicked the movement, the tip of his sword lifting half an inch, and Devon attacked. The broadsword leapt to meet him, and steel rang out as the weapons smashed together. But using his prodigious strength, Devon dragged on the haft of his hammer, redirecting his attack for Ikar's helm.

Ikar cried out, his head whipping back, but he could not completely avoid the blow. There came a great shriek of metal as Devon's hammer ricocheted from Ikar's helmet. Then his foe's sword lashed out, slashing Devon across the chest, and he was forced to retreat before it impaled him.

Cursing, Ikar staggered on the black sands. Devon's blow had warped his helmet and visor, making it difficult for the Knight to see. Devon started forward and then hesitated, his eyes flicking out to where the queen's ship still bobbed at anchor. His stomach twisted as he finally saw Kryssa and Pela, bound now to the masts of the ship. Movement came from the end of the docks as the queen climbed from her rowboat and turned to watch him, a smile on her lips. Her eyes were mocking, as though begging him to strike Ikar down, so that she might betray him one final time.

Turning back to his opponent, he lowered his hammer. "You'd best remove it, sonny."

"I can't!" Ikar snapped. "I am a Knight of Alana. We are forbidden from revealing ourselves to those outside our Order."

"So be it," Devon chuckled, "if you're that eager to die…"

"Wait!" Ikar snarled, then cursed. He tore the helmet loose and hurled it away.

The breath caught in Devon's throat as he saw the Knight's face for the first time. He could have been looking into a mirror of his younger self. Anger and confusion reflected from the man's amber eyes as he lifted his sword once more, preparing himself for the battle to come. Devon swallowed, reminded of his own fervour as a youth, when he had marched against Trola beneath the flag of the Tsar.

He lowered his hammer. "I don't want this," Devon murmured. "There's no need for us to fight."

"Ah, but there is," Ikar said. He unclipped the straps of his breastplate, and it toppled to the ground with a *thump*.

He continued to remove the rest of his armour. Stepping clear, he grimaced and gestured at the pile. "It's no use against a warhammer, is it?"

"No..." Devon replied, his voice sad. He lifted his hammer as Ikar started towards him.

"No," Ikar agreed, his sword coming up.

Unencumbered now, he moved with the speed of a scorpion, his blade flashing out to catch Devon on the arm. A curse tore from Devon's lips as he tried to counter, but the Knight danced clear and the warhammer struck the sand with a dull crash. He jumped back as Ikar attacked again, and this time managed to deflect the blade on the head of his hammer.

Ikar twisted and lashed out with his boot, striking Devon a blow to the calf. He staggered and lashed out wildly, coming within an inch of crushing his cousin's arm. Ikar leapt clear and Devon made to follow, but there was a burning in his chest and he almost staggered. Breath ragged, he recovered and forced a grin, but the disdain in Ikar's eyes told Devon the man had seen.

"It is a shame we could not have met sooner, cousin," Ikar puffed. Rolling his shoulder, he gave a practice swing. "I would have liked to fight you in your prime. It is sad to see you now, your stamina spent, your strength worn away by the passage of time."

Devon's heart palpitated in his chest as he struggled to regain his breath. "You know nothing, sonny," he breathed at last, "or you would not follow the queen's evil. Alan and Alana both would be rolling in their graves to know what you have done."

"And what of your deeds, Devon?" Ikar asked as they circled one another again. "You served the Tsar for years, allowed his avarice to drive Lonia into poverty. What would

Alan have thought of his ancestor wielding *kanker* against his home nation?"

"I never fought against Lonia," Devon snapped. "Not for the Tsar."

"No," Ikar replied, "but you did for Braidon. You served in his guard, fought beside him, protected him from our swords."

"Braidon did not seek war with Lonia," Devon growled. "It was *your* king who started the war…or had you forgotten that?"

"Ashoka only ever took what was rightfully ours!" Ikar thundered.

Devon shook his head. "We could argue over the past all day," Devon said. He pointed his hammer out to the ship bobbing at anchor. "But Braidon never sentenced innocent women to death."

"He may as well have," Ikar snarled, and then he was on the attack, his sword slashing for Devon's face.

Sparks flashed as Devon caught the blow on the head of his hammer. The crowd roared their approval as the fight resumed, a flurry of violence from the Knight driving Devon backwards. But he held on, knowing Ikar could not keep up such a pace, though his arms burned with the weight of his hammer and his mouth was parched.

Finally there was a break in the attack, and digging deep, Devon countered. Unleashing every drop of rage he had left, he forced Ikar backwards across the sands, hammering again and again at his defences. But Ikar avoided each blow with apparent ease, twisting to dodge each whistling swing of the hammer, his sword rising to deflect the occasional attack that came close.

The shriek of steel meeting steel echoed from the cliffs, and the crowd roared again. Their screams drowned out the howling of the wind and the crashing of waves, even the beating of Devon's heart, until all there was in front of Devon was the rush of battle. Adrenalin fed strength back to Devon's limbs and to his surprise, he found his exhaustion falling away. For the first time in years, he felt almost young, his strength renewed, age forgotten.

Ikar cursed and screamed, trying to regain the initiative, but Devon's relentless assault forced him ever back. Sweat appeared on his forehead, and Devon saw the first traces of doubt enter his enemy's eyes. Still he kept on, thoughts of Pela and Kryssa aboard the queen's ship driving him on. He had to keep up the spectacle, distract the Knights from their prisoners long enough for Braidon and the others to reach them. There was no doubt in his mind Marianne would betray him. His life was already forfeit—all he could do now was buy the others time to escape.

But Ikar would not submit and as the battle drew out, Devon felt the familiar pain return. His movements slowed, and with every blow his strength lessened. Slowly Ikar forced himself back into the fight, pressing Devon to defend himself, to duck and weave as Ikar's blade sought his flesh. Blood dripped from the wound on his chest and Devon found himself regretting his earlier mercy.

Slowly Ikar forced Devon to a standstill, then back one step, and another.

Devon gasped as the broadsword sliced at his head. He leapt back, and the tip cut through the collar of his shirt, narrowly missing his throat. Blood thundered in his ears as he sucked in a breath. All the pain of his body came rushing back in an instant, the burning in his arms, the ache in his shoulder, the agony of his knees. He sagged where he stood, almost falling.

His foe saw it and grimaced, but he did not back away.

He had seen Devon's strength now, had learned to respect it. He would not allow the old warrior another chance to recover. Devon raised his hammer just in time to deflect his next attack, though the power in the blow sent him reeling back.

Steel rang out again as he blocked a second blow, then used the weight of his hammer to force Ikar's sword into the sand. The weapon struck the wooden stage beneath with a *thud* and became lodged there.

Seeing his chance, Devon lashed out with a fist, striking Ikar full in the side of the face. The punch shocked the man off-balance and he lost his grip on his sword. He leapt to the side as Devon attacked, seeking to end Ikar's threat.

"Devon!"

Ice slid down Devon's spine as Marianne's voice carried across the stadium. Filled by a sense of premonition, he spun towards her. She still stood on the docks, arms crossed. A smile crossed her lips as their eyes met.

"Time's up," she shouted.

Before Devon could cry out, a flaming arrow rose into the sky. It flashed upwards like a shooting star through the night, higher and higher, before gravity finally took hold and it began its slow descent towards the ocean.

Except it was not the ocean it was aimed at. Down it spiralled, down towards the deck of the queen's ship, where Kryssa and Pela still stood bound to the masts. Pela opened her mouth in a silent scream as it struck, before an audible *whoosh* carried across the waters, and flames leapt from the decks, stealing them both from view.

CHAPTER 41

The breath caught in Caledan's throat as he glimpsed the flaming arrow soaring out over the waters. He followed its path to the ship bobbing in the cove. His gaze took in two figures bound to the masts, silver hair flying in the wild wind.

"Pela!"

Before he could comprehend how she had come to be there, the arrow struck the deck and flames engulfed the ship.

"*No!*" Genevieve staggered past, one hand outstretched towards the flames.

Cursing, Caledan grabbed her and dragged her back. They had searched the entire amphitheatre without success and returned to the shadows of the tunnel—empty now, as the rest of the Order had filled the stands. But just fifty feet away, Devon was down on one knee, his eyes on the flaming ship.

"It's not over yet," he hissed, dragging Genevieve towards the beach. "Come on, there's rowboats on the shore. If we're quick…" He trailed off as Genevieve came alive in his arms.

She threw him off and sprinted towards the beach. He made to follow her, and then noticed Braidon's absence. He swung around and found Braidon still standing frozen at the edge of the arena. A curse left his tongue he stepped towards the king. If the Knight that had defeated Devon noticed him, it would bring the entire weight of the Order down on them. They would never escape, not unless…

"Braidon," he hissed. "It's now or never—call the bloody dragons, or Pela and Kryssa are dead!"

But the king did not respond. Another roar came from the crowd outside, and beyond the king, Devon surged back to his feet and hurled himself at the Knight. But Devon's opponent had the old man's number now, and he deflected the attack almost effortlessly, then smashed Devon with a right cross that hurled him from his feet.

Caledan winced, bracing himself for the end, but instead Ikar turned and addressed someone Caledan could not see. "The sacrifice was meant to wait until the duel was ended."

A woman moved forward, striding across the sand until she stood before the two men, and finally Caledan realised why Braidon had frozen. The queen stood for a moment looking at the towering Knight, then around at the stadium. She raised her arms, and silence fell over the amphitheatre.

"Is this not the Saviour's will?" she called to the fanatics in the stands. "To see her champion crush the defender of the False Gods? To burn the blasphemous believers from our lands?" Her hand flung out to point to the burning ship. A dark band shone on her wrist. "With the Great Sacrifice, our freedom is assured!"

The crowd roared, and after a moment's hesitation, Ikar

dropped to one knee before the queen.

"*Braidon*," Caledan hissed. Heart pounding in his chest, he darted forward and grabbed at him, but the king shrugged him off. "Call the dragons!" he tried one last time.

"Marianne," he croaked, his voice barely a whisper. Caledan shrank into the shadows of the tunnel as the king entered the stadium, his voice roaring up into the stands. "*Traitor!*"

Leaving behind the safety of the entrance tunnel, Braidon advanced on the queen. Her eyes had widened at his shout and her face had lost all of its colour. But she recovered her composure quickly, gesturing her guards forward. They spread out to encircle the king.

"Take him, alive!"

A groan tore from Caledan as the guards surged forward. Braidon swayed on his feet, his face a mask of agony, but his sword leapt to meet the first of his challengers. It speared through the guard's throat and the man collapsed, choking, to the ground. Braidon continued on without slowing, his voice ringing from the stands.

"How could you?" he bellowed, his voice taut with rage. "After everything we shared? After everything I did for you?"

He swayed as a blade flashed at his face, then surged forward, his short sword plunging under the guard's sword arm and deep into his armpit. It sank to the hilt and lodged there, tearing from Braidon's hands.

Drawing his dagger, the king staggered on, but the guards were all around him now. They swarmed him, pinning his arms to his side and bearing him to the ground. In seconds they had Braidon's hands behind his back. They dragged him forward and shoved him to his knees in front of the queen.

"Oh, now my night is complete," her voice whispered across the sands to where Caledan stood.

He couldn't bear to watch any longer. His life's goal had been robbed from him yet again. He might have still run out into the stadium and stolen the king's life himself, but his other mission called to him now. There was still a chance they could save Pela and Kryssa. However small, he had to take it. Turning, he sprinted from the tunnel out onto the beach.

There was no sign of Genevieve and he prayed she was already in the water. Out in the coves, flames leapt across the deck of the ship, but the masts did not seem to be burning yet. Praying the smoke had not already killed them, Caledan hurled himself into the nearest rowboat.

Waves surged around the vessel, almost upending him. He cursed as water flooded over the side, and struck out again, desperate to pass beyond the breakers. The light of the burning ship flickered on the waters, turning them to a living, churning mirror. Just below the surface, he glimpsed the twisted reefs waiting to tear his boat to pieces. He still wore the heavy armour of the Knights. It would drag him straight to the bottom.

Teeth clenched, he heaved again on the oars, and the boat crashed through another wave. He twisted on the bench, saw he was closer, just twenty yards away now. The flames were everywhere and he strained his eyes, searching the heavy smoke for sign of Pela or Kryssa. He redoubled his efforts as the crackling of burning wood rose above the screams from the stadium.

He was still ten yards away when the fire reached the aft of the ship. They crawled up the stairwell, creeping along the railings and catching on a pile of canvas stacked in the centre of the deck. Caledan gritted his teeth, eyes fixed on the rope ladder. The flames still had not reached it. If he could just—

With an almighty *boom*, the rear of the ship suddenly lifted from the water, hurled skyward by a massive column of flames. They spread upwards and outwards in a violent wave of orange, consuming wood and cloth and steel alike. Caledan watched in horror as the entire ship disintegrated before his eyes.

Then the shockwave struck, a roiling, boiling blast of energy that lifted the rowboat beneath him and hurled it shoreward as though it weighed no more than a box of kindling. Caledan tried desperately to turn it, to direct it, but the oars were torn from his hands. He threw himself down and clung to the boat, breath searing in his throat, and prayed to whatever Gods remained to protect him.

The rowboat struck the shore with such force that Caledan was hurled bodily onto the rocky sands. The impact sent an eruption of sand up in every direction and he felt the armour buckle around him, twisting and tearing. Breath hissed between his teeth as his lungs emptied, and he felt the sword torn from his belt and hurled away into the darkness.

Pain swamped him as he lay there on the beach, waiting for death to come, for the swirling flames that had engulfed the queen's ship to reach the shore and consume him, or for the ocean to rise and suck him into its murky depths.

But a minute passed and the roaring of the inferno lessened, and finally he groaned and lifted himself to his hands and knees. The armour creaked and squalled, moving sluggishly, and in a rush of claustrophobia Caledan tore off the helmet and hurled it away. He dragged the dagger from his belt and cut the straps of his breastplate and grieves, until he stood again in pants and tunic, free of the cursed steel.

When Caledan finally took note of his surroundings, he was surprised to find himself at the other end of the beach, two hundred yards from the amphitheatre. A sharp cramp tore through his calf as he stepped towards the stadium. Cursing, he sank to one knee and gripped his leg, and clenched his teeth until the pain ceased.

The crackling of flames drew his gaze offshore. There was nothing left of the queen's ship, and now the waters of Malevolent Cove were aflame with burning debris. Scorched pieces of wreckage lay strewn across the cove. Caledan had never witnessed such a blast, though the great tales told of Magickers who had commanded similar violence.

He closed his eyes, recalling Pela's bravery on their journey. She had faced down Baronians and Knights in her quest to save her mother, but in the end, it had all been for nothing. A wave of grief struck Caledan. He'd failed Pela, had failed them both.

Another cry echoed form the amphitheatre. Caledan wondered whether the queen had struck down Braidon too, if she had robbed him of that last piece of meaning in his retched life. Staggering to his feet again, he found his sword sticking from the sand nearby. He claimed it, and then looked from the amphitheatre to the cliffs.

There was no one watching the path now. He could walk from the Cove without a backwards glance, leave behind Devon and Braidon and Pela and never look back, could go and find a new path, a new purpose.

Then he remembered Devon's words, the night Braidon had joined them.

What's the point of saving Plorsea, if I can't save my family?

Sword tight in one scorched hand, Caledan limped towards the shadow of the amphitheatre.

CHAPTER 42

Braidon stared up at his wife, grief and shock tearing him apart in equal measures. Two members of the Queen's Guard held him tight, but the fight had left him now. He was still struggling to comprehend what he was seeing: that the sweet young woman he'd first met in Lon, that the woman he loved, who had borne his son and slept beside him all these years, had betrayed him.

"Why?" he croaked finally.

Marianne's smile faltered. "Why?" she hissed, stepping closer and raising her fist. "Because I'm not some trophy for you and my father to trade!"

Held tight by her men, Braidon couldn't avoid the blow. It struck him hard across the cheek and he heard something go *crack*. He reeled back, but the guards' grips did not loosen. Tasting blood in his mouth, he spat on the black sands.

Cursing, Marianne retreated a step, holding her wrist. "Damnit," she said, her eyes flickering in the direction of the cove. "They still live."

"I thought you *wanted* to marry!" Braidon snapped.

His wife's lips twisted in a sneer. "Are you really so blind?" she snapped. "I was barely a woman; why would I want an old man like you?"

"You lied…"

"Oh, you poor thing," Marianne snarled. "Yes, I played my part well, obeyed my father's command and brought peace for our nation. But I have *always* loathed you, Braidon. Every second, every time I lay with you, I longed to drive my blade through your heart. How I wept, when I thought my Baronians had robbed me of that chance, how I laughed when they burned."

Braidon shook his head. "We have a *son.*"

"Perhaps there is a Saviour, after all," Marianne continued, her eyes aglow. "For my prayers have been answered: I *finally* have you in my power. Now you will die, dear husband, knowing who it was that killed you. If only I could have done the same with my father, but only poison can slay the snake."

Marianne drew a slender rapier from her belt and held it up to the light. "There is power in death, in our life-force," she murmured, turning her eyes on Braidon. "The greater the sacrifice, the more power spilt. *That* is why I wanted Devon here, why his daughter and granddaughter burn. Only the fiercest, the bravest would do." She glanced again at the bracelet on her wrist, a frown touching her forehead.

"What are you talking about?" Braidon snapped, regaining some of his fight. He strained against the guards, but they pinned his arms behind his back and forced him face-first into the sand. Teeth bared, he spoke into the ground. "If I'd known…"

"You didn't *want* to know, husband," Marianne snapped.

"You only wanted to believe that this beautiful young woman could love you."

Braidon flinched as the cold point of her rapier touched his neck.

"I'm sorry," he croaked, scrunching his eyes closed.

"Oh yes, tell me—"

Boom!

The roaring struck a second before the concussion wave. Braidon cried out as burning air swept through the amphitheatre, hurling sand at his face and staggering grown men. Caught off-balance, the queen and her guard were thrown sideways.

There wouldn't be another chance, and Braidon grasped it with both hands. Leaping up, he slammed his shoulder into the nearest guard, hurling the man from his feet. His sword skittered across the sand and Braidon dove for it. Scrambling back up, he spun in time to slam the blade through a guard's unprotected groin.

The guard went down with a groan and Braidon leapt at the queen—but the giant warrior that Devon had been fighting stepped between them. Unfazed by the explosion out in the cove, he lifted his sword.

"Put it down," he said quietly. "My queen is not done with you."

"But I'm done with her," Braidon snapped.

He launched himself at Ikar, but the big man was faster still, and Braidon's strength was failing. His broadsword swept Braidon's blade aside, then his fist slammed into Braidon's stomach, driving the air from his lungs. Choking, Braidon sank to his knees, the sword slipping from his fingers. A kick from Ikar's boot sent it out of reach.

"No," Braidon gasped.

"Yes," Marianne growled, stepping around the giant.

Looking up at his wife, Braidon saw again that day on the river, how he had done everything he could to protect her from the Baronians. But she had been on their side all along, had even been behind her father's death, if her words were to be believed. Hatred rose in Braidon's chest and he struggled back to his feet.

Ikar held out a hand to bar his approach, but Marianne waved him aside and walked forward until they stood face to face.

"I loved you," he whispered.

"You always were a fool."

Before Braidon could react, Marianne lanced her slender sword out, stabbing him through the chest. He gasped and staggered back, clutching at the blade, but Marianne yanked it back, slicing his fingers. The strength went from Braidon's legs as blood blossomed. He sank to his knees, struggling to slow the bleeding.

Sand crunched as his wife approached. She crouched in front of him, her eyes aglow, drinking in his suffering.

"I'm glad you didn't die in that river," she whispered. Gripping him by the chin, she forced him to look at her. "I want to see you suffer, like I have suffered all these years."

Groaning, Braidon tried to push her hands away, but his bloody hands slipped from her wrist. An icy cold had begun in his fingertips and was already spreading up his arms. His legs were numb, and he knew if he did not stop the bleeding soon…

His vision blurring, he stared past the queen, taking in the flames still leaping from the top of the amphitheatre, the roaring inferno in the cove. There was nothing left of the queen's ship or Kryssa and Pela. Sadness touched him as he realised he had failed even that small task.

Sadness gave way to anger as he looked up at his wife.

"Oh yes, *fight*, it makes this all the sweeter," Marianne mocked, her voice a whisper. "I need no bracelet for this—I know the words. When the life slips from your body, it will flow into mine, as the Elders do it. Who would have thought dark magic could be so joyful."

His entire body numb now, Braidon struggled to understand her, but he could make no sense of her words.

"How it must hurt, to die such a failure," the queen continued. "Knowing you have brought nothing but death and destruction to your people. How you have failed so utterly, that your entire life was meaningless. You could not save your beloved sister, nor Plorsea, not even a single innocent woman.

A groan tore from Braidon as he struggled to break away from her iron grasp, his will to live slipping away with each passing moment.

"Yes, I can feel the life leaving you…" Marianne's eyes were aglow now, lit by some unknown force.

"He hasn't failed yet," a woman's voice spoke from behind the queen.

The darkness was beckoning. Braidon squinted, trying to make out the speaker.

"How?" the queen growled.

She shoved Braidon back and stood. He lay on the sand and clutched weakly at his wound, slowing the bleeding as best he could.

"I said I would kill you," the woman's voice came again, strangely familiar.

"You won't get close!" Marianne screamed. "Kill her, Ikar."

Braidon's head flopped to the side as the giant strode forward.

"Put down that sword," the giant said, his voice strangely muted.

"So, this is you, Ikar," the woman replied, her voice strangely muted. "Step aside," she continued sadly. "Or only one of us will leave this place alive."

"You know that I cannot."

"Then defend yourself!"

CHAPTER 43

Pela watched, horrified, as the flaming arrow struck the deck. She strained against her bonds, tearing the skin from her wrists, but nothing she did seemed to make a difference. The necklace Marianne had placed around her neck seemed to tighten and her flesh crawled, though she still knew nothing of its dark purpose.

"Be brave, my daughter," Kryssa croaked behind her.

Watching the flames crawl across the ship towards them, a sob tore from Pela. Already the smoke was billowing around them, robbing her of breath. Choking, she clutched at her mother's fingers, terror wrapping its icy hands around her chest.

"Please mum," she gasped, "I don't want to die!"

Her mother's hand tightened around her own. "I love you so much, Pela."

Hearing despair in her mother's voice, Pela slumped against her bindings. How had it come to this? She thought back over the past few weeks, everything she had faced, the fears she had overcome. There was so much she wanted to tell her mother: about the fight with the Baronians, the rescue in the Castle, how she had learned to use her father's sword.

The blade lay discarded on the deck now, tossed aside along with the rest of their belongings. If only she could reach it, they might free themselves.

"I love you too, mum," she whispered.

The crackling of the fire crept closer, its heat washing over them. She coughed, the acrid fumes burning her throat, and her vision swum. Each breath was a struggle now.

Then movement came from the railings, and like a messenger from the Gods themselves, Genevieve appeared through the flames. She staggered across the deck, scooping up Pela's sword as she went, and fell to her knees beside the mast. The blade sliced easily through the ropes, and Pela slumped to the deck as she found herself finally free

"Gen!" Kryssa cried, hugging the woman tightly. "What are you doing here?"

"No time," Genevieve coughed. She grasped Pela by the collar and dragged her up, then pulled them towards the railing. "Into the boat, before the fire…"

She trailed off as they reached the railing and saw the rowboat had drifted from the ladder. The flames crackled behind them, spreading quickly across the ship now. Pela's hackles rose as she looked at the aft deck, and saw the inferno had almost reached the store of black powder.

"*Jump, now!*" she screamed, and before either woman could react, she grabbed them by the collars and dragged them over the railing.

They cried out as the waves came rushing up to meet them. The icy water swallowed Pela up and she gasped, kicking back towards the light. She broke the surface and swung around, finding her mother and Genevieve bobbing close by.

"Get awa—"

An awful *boom* drowned out her words as the burning ship turned suddenly to a column of flame. Pela opened her mouth to scream, but a wave of water caught them up before the words could leave her mouth, and then the world had turned to madness…

Sometime later, Pela woke to her mother shaking her. She opened her eyes, and found herself dangling from the side of the makeshift dock. The wave must have deposited her there, for the water was a good four feet below them. She tried to move and groaned—her entire body ached as though she'd just finished training with Caledan. Gritting her teeth, Pela managed to drag herself to her knees.

"Stay here," Kryssa was saying, her eyes on the amphitheatre.

Pela followed her gaze and saw the queen standing on the black sands, flanked by the massive Knight, Ikar. Devon lay nearby, dead or unconscious, while a third unknown man stood before the queen. As they watched, she darted forward, her slender rapier piercing his chest.

Kryssa started down the docks towards the theatre. There was no sign of Genevieve and Pela prayed she'd reached the shore safely. But just now, Kryssa was her greatest concern. She recognised the look in her mother's eyes. Kryssa intended to honour the promise she'd made on the queen's ship. Derryn's blade glinted in her hand—she must have taken it after Genevieve freed them—but as far as Pela knew, she didn't even know how to use it.

Fighting through the pain, Pela came to her feet and started after her mother. The roar of the crowd buffeted her as she approached, almost a physical force in itself, seeking to force her back. She kept on, unable to hear the words that passed between the queen and Kryssa, but determined to intervene.

Then Kryssa dropped into a fighting stance, squaring off against the giant of a man who had defeated Devon. Pela stumbled to a stop, horrified. The giant was twice her mother's size—a single swing of his broadsword would cleave her in two. Pela's eyes caught on a short sword lying discarded on the black sands; she swept it up and raced to join her mother.

Kryssa glanced back, her eyes widening. "Stay back!" she cried. "This is between me and Ikar."

Pela lifted her blade. "Not a chance."

Her mother flashed a look that had once sent terror shooting down Pela's spine. She smiled back—and ignored her. She hadn't come all this way just to run now.

Ikar lifted his broadsword and gestured them forward. "It doesn't matter how many—"

Kryssa attacked before he could finish, her blade lancing for his unprotected head. Ikar's blade barely rose in time to parry her attack; then he was retreating before the force of her fury. He had discarded his armour during the battle with Devon, and now Kryssa's blade found his flesh again and again, opening cuts across his arms and chest.

For a moment, Pela stood frozen, shocked at her mother's sudden violence—and skill. Apparently, she had kept more than just her father's past from Pela. But such revelations would have to wait for later, and gathering herself, Pela edged sideways the way Caledan had taught her, seeking an opening. Kryssa had forced Ikar backwards across the stadium, and she had to rush to catch them.

Above, jeers rained down from the crowd, as though this was all some great show for them. A deep hatred rose in

Pela's throat as she saw the grins on their faces, their open mouths as they shouted for their deaths.

Ikar was slower now than during his fight with Devon. Pela watched him closely, and glimpsing an opening, she darted in, her sword spearing for the giant's face. His eyes flickered in surprise, and a gauntleted arm lifted to deflect her attack. Sparks flashed as the power behind Pela's blow tore open the only armour he still wore, shattering his wrist.

Crying out, Ikar went reeling back. Pela attacked again, but the giant recovered faster than she had expected, and his broadsword swept around in a wild arc aimed at her chest. Too slow, Pela threw up her arm, but there was no way she could deflect the sword...

A dark figure slammed into her before the blow could fall, dragging her from the path of the blade. Breath hissed between Pela's lips as her rescuer's weight slammed down on her back. She groaned, thinking it was the queen and trying to free her blade, before Genevieve's voice hissed in her ear: "Stay down; your mum and I will handle this."

The weight vanished as Genevieve launched herself back into the battle, hatchet in one hand, hunting knife in the other. With Kryssa at her side, they forced the Knight back. The crowd was silent now, and the crackling of flames out in the cove rose above the whisper of the wind. Kryssa ducked as a violent swing of Ikar's blade swept for her head. Genevieve darted in, her hunting knife opening a cut on their foe's face.

Still on the ground, Pela watched as the two battled the giant to a standstill. Her mother's every movement, every swing of her sword, was smooth and practiced, her body telegraphing nothing of her attacks until the blade leapt to do her bidding. Ikar was struggling now, his blood dripping from a dozen wounds.

"Yield!" Kryssa screamed as they forced him back another step. "I have no wish to kill you, Ikar."

Ikar grimaced. Retreating a step, he held up a hand. Pela's heart beat faster, but the Knight was not surrendering. Even so, Kryssa and Genevieve paused, offering him respite.

"Where did you learn such skill?" he asked.

Kryssa smiled. "I was a member of the King's Guard for many years, alongside my husband."

Pela's heart thundered in her ears. She stared at her mother, mouth hanging open. "*What?*"

"I'm sorry, my daughter," Kryssa whispered, and Pela saw that her eyes were shining. "After I lost Derryn, I couldn't..."

"Devon told me..." Pela croaked.

"I should never have kept this part of our lives from you," Kryssa said, swallowing visibly. "But...after Derryn... I couldn't have you following in our footsteps. So I forbade Devon and my mother from speaking of our past, and hung up my sword for good."

"How could you keep this from me?"

"Do not hate me, daughter," Kryssa replied, then turned back to Ikar.

Without warning, she hurled herself forward. Sparks flashed as the two came together again, and all Pela could do was stare, still struggling to comprehend this new revelation. Her father she had never known, but her mother...she had been there for all of Pela's life, had prevented her from even touching a sword, and she had been lying the entire time...

In the centre of the amphitheatre, Genevieve and Kryssa fought on. Ikar had regained his breath and now fought like a man possessed, while beyond the queen stood watching in silence. Most of her guards lay dead on the sand, but Knights still stood in the shadows around the arena.

A roar came from the crowd as Ikar's fist caught Genevieve in the chin, staggering her. The Knight advanced with sword raised, but Kryssa leapt to her defence, forcing him back. Twisting to avoid her blow, Ikar brought his sword around, seeking to cut her in two. Kryssa's sword slammed down, catching his blade near the hilt and deflecting the attack into the ground. But the shock of the impact knocked the weapon from Kryssa's fingers, hurling it across the sand.

Ikar roared and raised his sword, but Kryssa flung herself back and his next blow cut only air. Empty-handed, Kryssa retreated, Ikar chasing after her. Behind them, Genevieve snatched up a sword and tossed it at Kryssa, but the giant swept up his great sword, knocking it aside.

"Damn you!" Genevieve screamed, hurling herself at the Knight's exposed back.

He spun to meet her and grinned, for though brave, Genevieve did not have Kryssa's skill. Wielding the broadsword like it weighed nothing, he knocked aside Genevieve's attack, then kicked out with his boot. The blow caught Genevieve square in the chest and she doubled over. Before she could recover, a second blow from Ikar's fist knocked her out cold.

"*No!*" Pela screamed.

Scrambling for the hilt of her sword, Pela raced in. But her cry had given her away, and Ikar turned to meet her. He batted aside her attack as he had Genevieve's, then lashed out with a meaty fist, sending Pela crashing to the sand alongside her friend.

Gasping, she tried to scramble away, but Ikar grabbed

her by the scruff of the neck. Hauling her up, he spun and found Kryssa several feet away, sword in hand once more.

Her face twisted with fear as she saw Pela in Ikar's grip. "Let her go."

"I cannot," Ikar said, his breath coming in great puffs. "The Saviour calls out for her death. The False Gods must be defeated."

"They were never evil, Ikar," Kryssa whispered, holding out a hand in entreaty. "Your ancestor fought alongside them to banish a great darkness from this world. Alan would never condone what you do here today."

Ikar's face twisted as though in pain. "He lived in a simpler time, but my people cannot return to the yolk of the False Gods. I must preserve our freedom. I cannot allow their evil back into this world."

"And is my daughter evil?" Kryssa asked. "Am I?"

"I don't know!" he cried, swinging away, then back. "But your very belief threatens my world!" His jaw tightened and he raised his broadsword.

"*Wait!*" Kryssa screamed, desperation showing in her eyes. Lines stretched her face as she lowered her blade. "Please, spare my daughter. She is no threat to you. She does not even believe."

"But you do," Ikar said.

"Yes." She tossed aside her sword. "So kill me instead."

"*No!*" Pela screamed, thrashing in Ikar's grip, though it made no difference to the giant.

Ikar stared at Kryssa for a long moment, then with a jerk of his arm, he tossed Pela aside. She flew several feet and slammed into the sand, winding her for the second time in as many moments. Coughing and spluttering, she struggled to pull herself up, to go to her mother's aid. But strength abandoned her, and she collapsed back to the black sand. In despair, she looked at the giant, expecting to see the sword poised above her mother's head.

But Ikar still stood fixed in place, his hulking shoulders looming in the shadows. As she watched, the broadsword slid from his hands and struck the earth with a *thud*. Pela stared, seeing now that a blade protruded from the giant's chest. Sand crunched as a silhouette strode forward, and with a violent yank, plucked the short sword free.

A whisper hissed from Ikar's lips as he swayed, then toppled to the ground. His last, dying breath hissed across the sands, and then he was still.

Caledan strode past him, bloody sword in hand, and pulled Pela to her feet. "I think we'd be going," he said, as a great roar came from the crowd.

Stunned, Pela could only nod her agreement. A second later, Kryssa engulfed them both in a hug. "*Thank the Gods.*"

Then she was gone, darting across the sand to where Genevieve lay. The huntswoman was just sitting up, a confused look on her face, but she smiled when she saw Kryssa.

"Gen!" Kryssa gasped, falling to her knees beside the huntress.

Pela smiled as they embraced, then her mouth dropped as Genevieve pulled her mother into a kiss. Kryssa did not pull away, only pulled the huntswoman closer, kissing her back. They broke apart quickly and looked around with sheepish grins on their lips, but only Pela seemed to have noticed. Kryssa met her eye and mouthed silently:

I'll tell you later.

After everything else her mother had kept from her, this was nothing. Pela would have laughed had they not been surrounded by enemies. Instead, all she could do was smile as her mother helped Genevieve up. Devon was back on his feet and lifting his fallen comrade into his arms. Pela had started towards them, when a wild shriek brought them up short.

"*Stop!*"

Marianne's voice rang with power, and to Pela's shock, her legs suddenly became trapped, as though she were moored in quicksand. Unbalanced, she crashed to the sand. Her head whipped around, finding the others similarly frozen.

The queen herself was crouched beside the fallen Ikar, but now she rose and started towards them.

"Not quite the death I wanted." Her words hissed across the sands. "But it's a start."

CHAPTER 44

Devon ached as though he'd been in a brawl with death itself. The darkness swirled, pulling him back down, but he fought against it—though he no longer knew why. There was a desperate desire in him to lie down, to close his eyes and bid farewell to the world.

But Kryssa's cries and Pela's voice and Braidon's dying groans called to him, and he fought back, if only for a short while longer. He could not fall, not now, not while his family was in danger. Stumbling to his feet, he lifted Braidon into his arms.

All around him, the followers of the Order were on their feet. Many were already streaming from the stands down the stairs towards the arena. The other Knights, silent spectators until now, were moving forward as well. They would be on them in moments, and there were only two ways out of the amphitheatre. He turned towards the tunnel, but several Knights had already reached it and he no longer had the strength to fight them.

The docks then. The queen had left her rowboat there, though it might not have survived the explosion. They would have to risk it. Devon started towards the wooden structure, only for the queen's voice to draw him up short.

"Stop."

His legs shook, drawing him to a stop. He looked back and found himself trapped in the burning rage of the queen's sapphire eyes. A groan tore from his battered body as her will pounded him, commanding him to stay, and despite himself he could not look away. Braidon groaned in his arms, but the king was too weak to stand or even speak by now.

The queen rose from beside Ikar's body. "Not quite the death I wanted, but it's a start."

Blood stained her hands and Devon shuddered, looking at his fallen relative. She had had her sacrifice after all. Power shone from her eyes, commanding them, and somehow Devon knew she had stolen it from Ikar, that the Knight's death had empowered her with something they could not understand.

"Devon," Braidon croaked, his eyes flickering open. "Leave me. It's my life she wants."

"Not happening, sonny," he whispered.

Devon looked at the queen again. She walked slowly towards them, rapier in hand, and Devon knew if he did not act now, they would all be lost. Defeated, broken, he looked around, saw the fear in Pela's eyes, saw Kryssa in Genevieve's embrace, and Caledan standing tall, yet unable to move.

Drawing in a breath, he centred himself, and reached deep within for an extra ounce of strength, for something to fight back with. The passage of years had eaten away at him, corroding his strength, but within he was still the same Devon that had stood against the Tsar, who had fought demons and monsters and Magickers and won. Now, at the end, his will did not fail him. It rose slowly, but unrelenting, an iron core to his soul.

"Caledan!" he boomed, his voice ringing out across the stadium.

The sellsword's head whipped around, dragged away from the queen's call by the steel in Devon's voice. "Guard him with your life," Devon said, and passed the king to the sellsword.

A hint of a grin touched Caledan's cheeks as he accepted the burden.

"Stop!"

The queen's will washed over them again, staggering the others, but Devon had lived sixty years and faced far worse than the likes of Marianne. He staggered, weathering the storm, and found Kryssa next. He placed a hand on her shoulder, and she looked around, her eyes shining with tears.

"Devon," she whispered. "I'm sorry."

"No," he said, embracing her. "I am sorry, my…daughter. I wish I could do it all again, could do it right, but I cannot. I can only say that you are my daughter, now and always, and that I love you."

"No…" Kryssa gasped, her eyes widening as she realised this was farewell.

"Look after the girl," Devon rumbled, before turning to Genevieve. A smile split his bearded cheeks. "And you look after my daughter, huntress."

Genevieve replied with a sad smile and a slight nod of her head, and Devon moved on, drawing Pela to her feet. "I should have never sent you away," he whispered. "Thank you for saving my daughter."

"Devon..." she whispered as he pushed her towards the others. "Thank you."

"Go," he replied, offering one last farewell, then turned to the queen. "Run!"

Her face a mask of rage, Marianne screamed after them. Reclaiming his hammer, Devon stood guard against her, withering the force of her will. The last of his strength was fading now, consumed by the effort of facing the queen as surely as if he had fought the woman herself. He staggered and dropped to one knee, but he only had to hold her a few seconds longer...

A snarl hissed from Marianne's lips, and pointing the rapier, she stalked towards him. "Out of my way, fool!" she spat, the blade trembling in her hand.

The sword slashed out and Devon came to his feet. But his reactions were slowed, his strength spent, and the sword plunged through his thigh. He cried out and fell back. The queen tore her rapier loose and attacked again. Devon brought his hammer up, but the queen's rapier flashed red, and its blade sliced through the head of his weapon, just as Merak's had all that time ago in Skystead.

Devon staggered away, but he knew it was hopeless now, and her next blow took him in the shoulder. Pain lanced down his arm and the broken hammer slipped from his fingers. Still he backed away, still he blocked her path. Clutching his arm, he glanced back and saw the others were at the end of the dock, where to his relief the rowboat still bobbed. Across the floor of the arena, the crowd had now gathered behind their queen. They stood waiting for the final blow to be struck.

"Let's see how a legend dies," Marianne snarled.

"Go ahead," Devon whispered, a smile on his lips. "I'm ready."

"So be it," the queen replied, and rammed her rapier into Devon's chest so hard it sank to the hilt.

EPILOGUE

Pela had just jumped into the rowboat when a roar came from the crowd behind her. She turned back in time to see the queen lunge forward. Devon made no attempt to defend himself as her blade plunged home. Only then did he stagger. He collapsed to the black sands as the queen tore the blade loose.

"*No!*" Pela screamed, scrambling for the docks, but the others grasped her and held her back.

Still on the wharf, Caledan cast off the mooring rope and leapt aboard, just as the queen's voice carried to them: "Stop!"

But whatever power she'd had over them had vanished now, and they turned away. Caledan took up one oar, Genevieve the other, and together they struck out across the cove. Remembering the necklace at her throat, Pela tore it lose and hurled it into the ocean. Her mother did the same and they exchanged a look. Finally they understood their purpose—however the Queen had taken power from Ikar's death…they had been meant to share that same fate.

Burning rubble still lay scattered across the waters, and Pela shuddered at the thought of what might have been.

"Pela, jump in the front and watch for reefs," Caledan gasped. His face was wan and Pela wondered what he'd been through to get there, but she obeyed.

Flames still lit the waters, allowing her to spot the corals and redirect their course, and they passed slowly through the surging waves. The light of the amphitheatre fell further behind, but as Pela glanced back she saw rowboats pushing off the beach in pursuit.

And ahead, the fleet of warships anchored beyond the breakers still awaited. Already torches were being lit on those barring the mouth of the cove, as signals passed from the amphitheatre. Her heart sank. Devon had only bought them a few more moments of life. There was no way they could escape so many. Soon they would follow him on the dark path.

Caledan cursed; he'd seen them as well. "So much for the damn dragons," he muttered.

On the floor of the rowboat, Braidon's eyes flickered open and a word slipped from his lips: *"Ingytus!"*

His eyes closed again before Pela could ask what it meant, but a second later, a voice sounded in all of their heads:

Fool of a King, the voice rumbled, and Pela saw an image in her mind of a great beast lifting off. *If you die, my kin will wage such war against your people, the Gods themselves will tremble in their graves.*

Pela shook her head and the image vanished. A frown touched her forehead as she looked at the others. Her mother looked just as confused, but Caledan and Genevieve had both grown pale.

An almighty roar sounded through the night, and movement flickered across the stars. Pela glimpsed red scales glittering in the firelight. A hushed silence fell suddenly over the cove; even the watchers in the arena did not so much as whisper. All eyes were lifted to the sky, waiting to see what would come next.

A light appeared, a candle before the half-moon in the sky, but in seconds it grew—becoming an inferno that went rushing down to crash upon the waters of the cove. The rowboats giving chase were caught in its light, and then swallowed up by the awful flames. Screamed rent the air as men leapt, burning, into the dark waters.

The shadow passed overhead, rushing out towards the warships in the mouth of the cove. The sailors aboard began to shout at one another, racing about in the torchlight, dragging weapons from their foxholes. Several leapt overboard, in their panic, and a *clanking* noise rattled through the darkness.

The rain of fire fell again, engulfing the first of the warships in its orange glow. In seconds the entire vessel was aflame, its crew incinerated or hurled overboard into the saving waters. An explosion rocked the night as another store of black powder caught light, tearing the ship asunder.

Pela's heart soared as she saw their chance. With the dragon, they might just escape. She clutched a hand to her mouth as the waters around them burned, its light revealing the great beast in the sky.

But the flames had also revealed the beast to the soldiers aboard the other warships, and the *twang* of crossbows followed. An awful scream came from the creature as bolts flashed in the darkness, piercing its great hide.

It twisted again, dark wings beating the air, and another warship was consumed. The shrieks of burning men joined the chorus of terror ringing from the shore.

"There's a gap!" Pela shrieked, pointing to the space left by the sinking ships.

Teeth bared, Caledan and Genevieve rowed on. The light of the flames grew and Pela held her breath, praying the other warships did not see them. But the men aboard were preoccupied with their own survival, their weapons trained on the dragon as it swept down for a third time.

Crack.

Pela saw the catapult on the rear of the warship a second before it fired. She shrieked a warning. The dragon was far too close, almost upon them. The burning barrel rose to meet it, but at the last moment it banked, and Pela breathed a sigh as she realised it would miss.

Boom.

A flash of light burst across the night sky as the barrel exploded, banishing the stars and moon and blinding them but for the dark shadow of the dragon.

Crying out, Pela tripped and fell to the floor of the rowboat. Shadows and light danced across her vision, but through it she saw the fire raining down around them, flickering out as it disappeared beneath the waves. She stared at the sky, straining to see through the chaos, seeking out the dragon.

Then she saw it.

Wings folded in two, it tumbled through the sky towards them. The explosion had torn a great hole in the beast's chest, but still it lived, its screams echoing from the cliffs around them. Pela watched it fall, her hope turning to sudden despair. They had only seconds…

With a great crash, it struck the water alongside the boat. A wave rose from the ocean and rushed towards them, catching their tiny rowboat and hurling it sideways. Pela screamed, clutching desperately to the side of the boat.

But the wave was too great, and suddenly the boat was overturning. Pela's hands were torn free by the violence of the ocean, and then they were all falling, toppling forward into the darkness.

And the waters of Malevolent Cove rose up to greet them all.

HERE ENDS BOOK ONE
OF
THE KNIGHTS OF ALANA
The adventure continues with…
Queen of Vengeance

NOTE FROM THE AUTHOR

Well well well, welcome (back) to the Three Nations. Sorry for the 9 month delay, you could say I've had a little bit of writers block! But I'm back now and you can expect Queen of Vengeance (book two) within the next three months, all going well! I hope you enjoyed this new installment in my world, just be sure to pop back over to Amazon if you did and leave your review - otherwise no one will know! And if you're new here, I hope it inspires you to pick up a few more of my works ;-)

For starters, you might want to **dive into the _Legend of the Gods_, Devon's original story**, or if you'd like to venture even further back in time, there's always my first series - the **_Sword of Light Trilogy_. You can read on below for a free except from each!**

Also, don't forget to **join my VIP list for a free short story** and regular updates on not just my upcoming works, but my adventures around the world! You can also follow me on Facebook and Instagram to be the first to hear the news. I'm always posting photos from my adventures around the world - which also often end up featuring later in my books!

http://www.aaronhodges.co.nz/newsletter-signup/

ALSO BY AARON HODGES

THE THREE NATIONS

The Sword of Light Trilogy
Book 1: Stormwielder

Book 2: Firestorm

Book 3: Soul Blade

Legend of the Gods
Book 1: Oathbreaker

Book 2: Shield of Winter

Book 3: Dawn of War

The Knights of Alana
Book 1: Daughter of Fate

Book 2: Queen of Vengeance

Book 3: Signup for Updates

OTHER WORKS

The Evolution Gene
Book 1: The Genome Project

Book 2: The Pursuit of Truth

Book 3: The Way the World Ends

THE LEGEND OF THE GODS

If you've enjoyed this book, you might want to go back to where Devon's story all began!

Oathbreaker

After two years of war, Devon should have retired a hero. But the gratitude of rulers is short lived, and their anger eternal.

Named a coward for turning his back on the crown, the former warrior has been reduced to a pauper. But when Devon picks a fight with the wrong man, he finds himself drawn back into the world of bloodshed and violence he sought so hard to escape.

THE SWORD OF LIGHT TRILOGY

If you've enjoyed this book, you might want to go back to
where it all began!
The Sword of Light

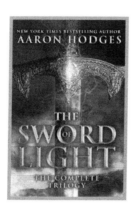

When Eric was young a terrible power woke within him.
Horrified by the devastation he had unleashed, Eric fled his
village, and has spent the last two years wandering the
wilderness alone. Now, desperate to end his isolation, he
seeks a new life in the town of Oaksville. But the power of
the Gods is fading, and in their absence, dark things have
come creeping back to the Three Nations. Civilisation is no
longer the safe haven he once knew, and Eric will soon learn
he is not the only one with power...

Printed in Great Britain
by Amazon